ARKANSAS

TOWARD A NEW BEGINNING

Book One of the *Arkansas Valley* Series

r.William Rogers

LONGWOOD
COMMUNICATIONS

Toward a New Beginning by r. William Rogers
For ordering information or to contact the author:
r. William Rogers
7320 Nugget Court
Widefield, CO 80911
E-MAIL: RWILLIAMR@AOL.COM

Library of Congress Catalog Card Number: 2001092321
ISBN: 1-883928-39-7

1234567   87654321
Printed in the United States of America

Longwood Communications
3037 Clubview Drive, Orlando, FL 32822
407-737-6006

Introduction

 I am thrilled with my friend Bob Rogers' new western novel, *Toward a New Beginning*. It is evident that Bob has done his "homework." He has captured the joys, sorrows and adventures of those brave pioneers who left their homes east of the wide Missouri and journeyed westward in wagon trains to begin their lives all over again.

This captivating story has it all…unique personalities in the wagons, dangerous weather, raging rivers, hostile Indian attacks, hunger, water shortage, vengeance, courage, romance, biblical principals…and a story pivoting on the valor and ingenuity of beautiful Birdsong, a full-blooded Comanche woman.

If you want excitement and page-turning enjoyment… READ ON!

—*Al Lacy*

Born in the Rocky Mountain West and raised on a ranch in the foothills of the Colorado Rockies, Al Lacy has written and sold more than 73 western and historical novels for Bantam-Dell Doubleday and Multnomah Publishers since 1980. Presently an author for Multnomah, he has five series in progress, two of which are co-authored with his wife, Joanna.

Al and Joanna Lacy currently divide their time between Orlando, Florida, and Bozeman, Montana.

Foreword

The Louisiana Purchase of 1803 was the brainchild of then U.S. President Thomas Jefferson. For the price of about three cents an acre, the United States acquired from France territory that more than doubled the land area of the United States at that time. The newly acquired "Louisiana Territory" extended from the Mississippi River in the east to the Rocky Mountains out west, and from British North America down to the Gulf of Mexico. This transaction was and still is referred to as "the greatest bargain in American history."

Not only did this acquisition open up exploration of the Pacific Northwest via the Oregon Trail, but it was also the basis for the establishment of a merchant route between the eastern markets and Santa Fe, New Mexico.

The customary route snaked its way south from the Missouri River to the Arkansas, and then followed the latter nearly to its headwaters. There it turned south again, this time to Taos, New Mexico and finally Santa Fe.

The route was a good one, and its importance to the successful development of the eastward silver and fur trade and the westward transport of manufactured goods was a contributing factor to U.S. seizure of New Mexico during the Mexican War.

Although the Mexican-American War was still being fought in late 1847, the general feeling was that it would soon come to an end. It was mainly a political war stemming from Mexican anger at the United States' annexation of Texas in 1845, as well as a dispute over whether Texas ended at the Nueces River (Mexican claim) or the Rio Grande (U.S. claim).

The war finally did come to an end in February of 1848 with the signing of the Treaty of Guadalupe Hidalgo. As a result of that treaty, huge land grants became readily available to those souls who were hardy enough and who had a strong enough desire and commitment to overcome the hardships involved in settling these vast new lands.

Use of the trail increased under U.S. rule, especially after the introduction of mail delivery service via stagecoach in 1849. But its use ceased altogether shortly after the completion of the Atchison, Topeka & Santa Fe Railroad in 1880.

Independence, Missouri, was the "jumpin' off spot" for folks with a "hankerin' ta head west" as they gathered there by the thousands and formed into wagon trains before beginning their westward trek along the Santa Fe Trail.

Folks who engaged in the fulfillment of their dreams by joining a "train" were usually adventuresome, above-average, spunky kind of folks with a yearning for the wide-openness and unpredictability of a new land.

One such man was a gent by the name of Sam Bartlett.

CHAPTER

One

"Are you sure, Sam? Are you *really* sure that's what you want to do?" Judith asked as she looked across the breakfast table at her husband.

The question remained unanswered while he toyed with a splinter that until then had been minding its own business along the top edge of the table. He appeared engrossed while he picked at it methodically. Finally, hooking it with a fingernail, he tugged and it came loose. He stuck it into the corner of his mouth and raised his gaze to meet hers.

His eyes were normally a hazel color, seeming to change shades as his mood dictated. Right now they were just a mite paler than usual, suggesting maybe a doubt or two with the issue at hand. His rugged features were chiseled to a handsome perfection, punctuated by a square jaw that indicated a man who would stand up for what he believed. There was a genuine good-natured set to his mouth that implied a willingness to smile easily if something pleased him. His hair was thick, wavy and a sandy brown color that did justice to the hazel eyes.

He removed the splinter and tossed it onto the floor. "Why don't you ask me an *easy* question?" he asked while not allowing his mouth to smile. "All I know is that I can't get the thought out of my head. It's like the Lord is telling me what to do." He responded with a subtle gentleness to the concerned look in her eyes by reaching a hand out and resting it on her forearm. "I'm truly sorry if this troubles you, but there's a real opportunity out there," he said tenderly.

"But we'd be doing pretty much what we're already doing right here. I guess I just don't see the sense in us pulling up stakes and traveling all that way to do something that we could continue to do right here where we are. It just doesn't seem to make much sense is all."

He sighed heavily. "You're probably right. I've been trying to sort through that very line of reasoning for the better part of a month now."

"And what reasonable justification did you manage to come up with?"

He lowered his eyes. "None I guess," he said feebly. "It's just that..." The words trailed off as the foolishness of the proposed venture threatened to engulf him. He swallowed his uncertainty and looked into her troubled eyes. "I know it doesn't seem to make much sense at first glance, but it's something I feel a genuine calling to do. I'm not denying that we could do just fine by staying put, but there's folks out there on the frontier that need horses the same as folks right here do. Not to mention the fact that there's army forts and trading posts being built that I'm sure also have a need for good mounts. Just think of the help we would be giving to those folks."

"And just where would you get all these horses? You wouldn't be considering driving them along with the wagon train, would you?"

His eyes lit up as his face broke into an enthusiastic grin. "Now that's the real beauty of the whole thing. The horses are already there."

"What do you mean, already there?"

"The countryside is chock-full of wild mustangs just for the taking. All a fella would need to do is build a few corrals and go out and catch 'em."

"Do you honestly think it would be all that easy?"

The smile faded and his eyes changed to a slightly darker shade as they took on a faraway look. He spoke his answer slowly, "Nooo... but it sure would be an adventure."

"Sam, if you truly feel that the Lord is calling you to pack up your wife and son and head out for wherever—"

Her train of thought was interrupted as she elected to rest her gaze on their son, Tom, seated in his highchair along a third edge of the table. While she watched him playing with his food, she couldn't help but wonder at the hardships they would be faced with if they did indeed join a wagon train.

Her concerns were temporarily pushed aside as the boy scooped up a handful of mush and, while managing to miss his mouth almost completely, deposited most of it on the tray in front of him. "It sure doesn't seem appropriate to place a spoon in front of you, now does it?" she said.

She picked up the utensil and wrapped his tiny fingers around the handle.

"There, you'll no doubt have better luck with this," she then said and guided his hand as they dipped the spoon into the oatmeal. Once she had Tom back on an even keel, she picked up the dishcloth she kept handy and went to work on the mess that had been made.

Sam watched silently as she cleaned. Her tears didn't escape his notice, though, as they slowly worked their way down her cheeks. He fancied himself a pretty good judge of things and figured those tears weren't entirely a result of Tom's antics. With all the

11

tenderness he could scare up, he placed a loving hand on her wrist and said softly, "Sweetheart, look up here and listen to what I've got to say."

She found a clean corner on the dishrag and used it to dab at the tears.

He cupped a hand under her chin and raised her gaze to meet his. "If you're dead set against it, I'll not follow through," he said lovingly. "But if it's just the fear of the unknown, well then, I guess we'll need to pray about it and see if the Lord will give you the needed strength."

She smiled her faith in this man that she loved with all of her heart and soul. "Sam, I expect it is just a fear of the unknown, as you say, but praying about it wouldn't hurt none either." She sighed resignedly. "If all goes well, when do you figure you'll be wanting to cart us off to that heathen-infested part of the country?"

A smile lit up his face as her response once again reaffirmed her willingness to follow him wherever he led.

⌖⌖⌖

They had fallen in love almost at first sight. It had happened in upstate New York where he had become involved in a clothing factory venture with a gent from Syracuse. Although Sam was at first an absentee partner in the business, his colleague had sent a wire to him in Virginia requesting his immediate presence because of what he'd referred to as "a predicament." As it turned out Sam's partner had gotten himself and the business into a cash-flow situation as a result of his love for playing cards at the local honky-tonk. Sam, being a born-again Christian, had no desire to remain in partnership with the fella after finding out he was a gambler. It was then that he discretely bought him out and solved both their problems.

Sam was himself a gentleman with firm roots and substantial holdings in the Shenandoah Valley, and he had no desire to remain in the Syracuse area and tend to what was now solely his business...especially after laying eyes on the previously unseen clothing factory.

Oh, it was a clothing factory all right, but the clothes it turned out were ladies unmentionable undergarments. Once he had found that out, he was at first furious about how he'd been duped into investing in a sight-unseen business that dealt in such a scandalous product. But not being averse to turning a good profit, he calmed down long enough to realize some distinct possibilities and started looking for a buyer with maybe less propriety than he.

During the time while he searched for the right person upon whom to unload his undesired assets, he made time to attend one of the local churches each Sunday morning. Having a strong desire to listen to good preaching he was pleased to find a church and pastor to his liking. As fate would have it, that's not all he found that was to his liking. It was there that he first noticed, and then later met, Miss Judith Van Sheckle...the soon-to-be Mrs. Sam Bartlett.

He was instantly taken by her tantalizing personality and very ladylike manners. She was a little on the extroverted side, while at the same time extremely cordial and considerate. Her beauty was a sight to behold. She was of average height, about five-two or three. Her hair was a shade of auburn that reminded him of a newborn sorrel playfully kicking up its heels in the

13

slanting rays of the early morning sunlight. Her eyes were a deep blue and portrayed an undeniable tenderness. The facial structure was long, but not too thin. Her nose and mouth were absolutely perfect.

They hit it off right from the start, and their romance quickly blossomed into one of the whirlwind variety. It was barely a short two months before he proposed and she accepted, and they were married in a similarly whirlwind fashion.

What with her being a bit of an upper-crust debutante, she was at first unwilling to completely give up her accustomed lifestyle and succumb to his attempts at luring her back to the wilds of Virginia. He therefore did the only thing he could under the circumstances—he sold his holdings in the Shenandoah Valley. With more time now available to him and unable to readily find a buyer for the factory, he resigned himself and, despite his misgivings, concentrated his efforts on making a success of the factory.

Sam and Jay—as he liked to call her—were a happy couple right from the start. She quickly realized that there was more to life than debutante balls and ladies' teas in the afternoons. She grew to love Sam more and more as time went by, and those affections allowed her to devote her every waking moment to making him as happy as she was capable of doing.

About a year went by, during which time he put up with the factory as best he could. But despite honest and well-intentioned efforts, he finally came to the conclusion that making ladies' undergarments was definitely not for him. With that in mind he decided to have a talk with Jay about it, and after locating her in the parlor, he mustered up the necessary courage.

"Ah…Jay," he said sheepishly, while standing in the doorway.

She looked up from her Bible, and then seeing the seriousness in his eyes, tucked the bookmark between the pages and closed it lovingly. "Yes, Sam. What is it?"

He crossed the room while clearing a frog that had suddenly decided to occupy a prominent spot in his throat. He then dove right in. "I've decided that I'm not at all cut out to cut out women's clothes." He smiled one of those genuine smiles of his. "I'll bet I couldn't say that again three times real fast."

"No, I suppose not. But why did you say it in the first place?"

"Well, because I've decided to unload the factory for a song and go do something I'm better…" he smiled that smile again before continuing, "cut out for… pun intended." He watched closely for her reaction.

15 ➡

She frowned slightly. "And just what might that be?" she asked suspiciously.

He had already made up his mind to not beat around the bush. "My interests lie in raising horses," he said confidently.

Her surprise was complete. "Raising *what*? Boy, just when you think you know a person," she said from under raised eyebrows.

"Sorry I didn't tell you before about this. It's just that I never saw the need before now."

"And now you do?"

"Ah…yes, yes I do."

"Go on."

"Uh…I've been reading the newspapers and…" He inhaled deeply while trying to get it all just right in his mind.

"And what?"

He looked her square in the eye, exhaled heavily and blurted, "And I see a real need for the right man to set up a horse raising endeavor in Independence, Missouri!"

As her love for him won out, she allowed her expression of disbelief to change to one of resignation. "And just why do you feel *you're* the man for the job?"

Sam thought he saw what he hoped was an encouraging look in her eye. Hardly daring to believe that it might mean what he hoped it could, but at this point figuring he had nothing to lose, he excitedly said, "Well, just because I guess." He swallowed dryly. "Jay, I've been reading where folks are leaving out from Independence by the scores, and just good common sense would tell a gent that all those wagons need either horses or oxen to pull 'em."

He sat on the arm of her chair and took her hand in his. "Jay, I know I'm asking a lot, maybe even too much, but we've done well with the business and can afford to take a bit of a beating on a quick sale. We could then buy a herd down in Kentucky or Tennessee somewhere and drive 'em to Missouri. With a fair-sized investment we could buy a piece of land with a ranch already on it and set up housekeeping. That'd give us the start we'd need, and we could commence right in with breeding the stock for selling to the folks in the wagon trains."

As she watched his eagerness, she likened the excitement in his eyes to that of a little boy.

"What'dya say, Jay? I promise to take care of you out there."

"How about our child? Do you promise to take care

of our child as well?"

His expression changed to one of slight bewilderment, then quickly transformed to one of total happiness as the realization of what she'd just said clicked in his brain. "You mean…you're…we're gonna—"

"Yes, darling, we're going to have a baby."

CHAPTER

Two

The move to Independence hadn't proved to be a particularly difficult one. Sam had purchased a buckboard and had been especially careful to keep Jay as comfortable as possible during the trip. They'd not only been lucky enough to have located a suitable herd for sale in Kentucky, at a fair price, but were fortunate to've found and hired on four drovers to help get them all the way to Missouri.

The drive proved to be slow and exhausting, but it was made without any more than the usual mishaps that were a normal part of such journeys. Only a minimal number of the herd had been lost to predators, and by the grace of God the Indians had left them alone.

As soon as they had arrived in Independence, Sam wasted no time and through the local bank had readily found what he felt was an adequate spread. He and the owner struck an agreeable deal, and it changed hands in a matter of just two days.

Sam was not only a diligent and hard-working sort of man, but him being an honest Christian didn't hurt him any either when it came to furthering his reputation as a man who'd be willing to give a "down-and-outer" the shirt off his back if he was in need and couldn't afford one of his own.

His business flourished as folks just kept on coming and going on their way through Independence. The excitement and enthusiasm of all the families heading west was a blessing to him, and he was able to at least temporarily satisfy himself with just knowing that he was being a part of them fulfilling their dreams of settling the western frontiers. He soon realized that he envied some of them from time to time, but not wanting to stir up Jay, he kept those feelings to himself.

ﺑﭽﺑﭽﺑﭽ

"Sam?"

His attention returned to their conversation across the breakfast table as he realized he'd been daydreaming. "Oh…sorry, Jay. Guess my mind was off somewheres else."

After having rid herself of the last of the tears, she held tightly to the dishrag and smiled feebly. "Which isn't too unusual lately," she said. She allowed her weak smile to disappear completely as a seriousness took over while she placed her hand atop his. "Sam, darling, I followed you all the way out here from New York, and that turned out to be a good choice. I guess I could continue to follow you, leastways until you lead me astray, that is."

19 ➡

He smiled as he looked into her eyes. "The Lord has surely blessed me," he said as he leaned toward her. Their lips met in a kiss filled with warmth and affection. "Thank you," he said after they'd parted. "I promise to take real good care of you out there."

ﺑﭽﺑﭽﺑﭽ

It had been a busy time for the both of them since the decision had been made to make the trip west. Sam had a ranch and a flourishing livestock business to sell, as well as wagons to buy. Jay, on the other hand, had spent the entire time laboring over which household items to take along and which ones to leave behind. Although they'd been married barely five short years, she'd felt it necessary to save mementoes, knick-knacks, pieces of yarn and anything else she had found a nook or cranny in which to fit her triflings. She was the type to not throw anything away, and there were mountains to sort through. Not only was she a pack rat of sorts, but she rightly reasoned that it just didn't make any sense to her to start completely all over again. So after a serious discussion with Sam, she found herself willing to compromise on the condition that he purchase an extra wagon in which to haul what items she could manage to squeeze into it. Besides, they could sell it after they arrived at their destination, wherever that turned out to be.

Sam, being eternally grateful for her agreeing to make the trip at all, eagerly consented to the second wagon. He felt that it was the least he could do. He figured he would be able to hire a driver from one of the young men who would already be making the trip. All he had to do now was find just the right person, if in fact one existed.

About three weeks had gone by since the decision to leave had been made. It wasn't until then that Sam had been able to find a buyer for his stock business and they'd agreed on an equitable price. His efforts to sell the ranch had not as yet proved fruitful, and he was forced to face the reality that maybe the ranch wouldn't sell before they were ready to leave. With that in mind, he made the necessary arrangements with the president of the bank, Jacob McMasters.

Jacob being a fellow Christian made it a whole lot

easier for Sam to trust him with his legal matters, and after filling out a legal Power of Attorney, he turned the sale of the property over to him. Sam would be in touch after reaching their destination and would get word back as to where to send the proceeds once the sale had been made. With that worry out of the way, he concentrated his efforts on finding out as much as he could about the formation of the next train.

The word around town was that it would be leaving in less than a week. Because the size would be limited, spots would be handed out on a first-come-first-served basis. Anyone interested in joining up needed to make arrangements with the wagon master to solidify a spot in the final line-up.

Sam asked around and learned that the wagon master was a fella by the name of Hector Yallow. Folks said that he was the one to see. It seemed that anyone who had an acquaintance with him held him in high regard as a no-nonsense kind of person and a fair man as well.

Sam was finally able to catch up with him outside the mercantile. The description he'd been given fit the grizzled old-timer to a tee: weather-beaten leathery features, short graying beard, hat folded up in the front and walked with a slight limp that favored the left leg. "You Mr. Yallow?" Sam asked as he approached him on the boardwalk.

Hector Yallow stopped and eyed the younger man until he decided to reply by first spitting a squirt of brown tobacco juice in the general direction of the street. "Heck Yeah, at yer service," he said, and wiped some dribble from the stubble on his chin.

Sam extended a hand. "Pleased to meet cha. My

name's Sam Bartlett. I'm looking for a spot in your wagon train."

The wagon master took his sweet time while he assessed Sam and digested the request. "Ya any tougher'n ya look?" he finally said, and spit another stream of brown juice.

"You any tougher than *you* look?" Sam shot back. A perplexed look flicked across the man's eyes, and Sam wondered if he'd made a mistake by electing to give the gent a dose of his own medicine.

The dubious expression was quickly replaced by a crooked smile, and he reached out and accepted the still-outstretched hand of the upstart whippersnapper. "Nope. Fact is I'm just a big ol' cuddly pussycat. Pleased ta make yer acquaintance, Mr. B," Heck said from behind a now-genuine smile as he applied a firm grip and pumped the hand vigorously.

"That's...*Bartlett*."

"I know that. I just don't cotton ta memberin' folk's names is all. It's a whole lot quccker ta just put an initial ta their features."

He released Sam's hand, and Sam wondered if any bones had been broken. "In that case, what do I call you?" he asked as he clenched and unclenched it a few times just to be sure.

"Done told ya...Heck Yeah. That's short for Hector Yallow. The name come from somewheres over in Europe. Never did 'preciate it none." Heck spit again. "But I reckon a fella's gotta do with what the good Lord provides him with."

"Amen," Sam said, nodding his understanding.

"You a religious fella, are ya?" Heck asked.

"I'd say that'd depend on what your definition of

religious is. If you're asking whether I'm saved by grace and washed in the blood, then I'd say I'm religious." Sam wondered where this was all headed. "But if you're asking—"

"Well, hallelujah. Now I ain't got no worries 'bout us gettin' along. I know Jesus my ownself," Heck said, ending any further need for clarification.

Sam felt relieved and asked, "Good. Does that mean I get a spot in the train?"

"Yep, that it does. Ain't never turned down a good Christian family and never will long as I still got a breath left in me."

"Thanks, Heck, I appreciate the consideration. Now that we got that settled, just where is your train heading? Some folks say you're going over the Rocky Mountains, and some say you'll be stopping just short of 'em."

"Well, it being late August already, we'd have no chance a climbin' them mountains and gettin' to the other side before the snows was clean up ta our eyeballs."

Another small brown puddle formed in the street dust.

"Nosiree. This here particular train is gonna be stoppin' short. We'll be leavin' come this Thursday mornin' right about sunup. We'll be meetin' out at the west edge a town."

"Sounds good to me. Oh…one other thing, I have *two* wagons. I hope that isn't any trouble for you."

"Nope, no trouble atall. They's still two more spots left open after yers. Just be sure that they're both sturdy and in good enuf shape ta make the trip without holdin' the rest of us up."

Toward a New Beginning

Sam remembered that he needed to hire a driver for the other wagon. "Do you happen to know of anyone who might be interested in driving my other wagon? I'd be willing to pay him for his trouble."

Heck swept the sorry excuse of a hat off his head, revealing a receding hairline. He reached into his back pocket, pulled a mostly red handkerchief and used it to rub his forehead dry of the sweat that had collected. "Let me ask around. I just might be able ta help ya out there." He then wiped the inside rim of the hatband and replaced the hat back onto his head, tilting it just a mite to the right in the process. He then stuffed the handkerchief back into his hip pocket.

Sam figured there was no other reason for keeping the man from whatever it was that he'd been doing and said, "Well then, I'd say that that just about completes our business."

"Peers like."

"I reckon we'll be ready to go by Thursday morning then. In the meantime if you come across someone—"

"I'll do just that," Heck said, spit and grinned.

Their business completed, the two shook hands and went their separate ways.

Sam was eager to find Jay and tell her the good news. Their ranch was just on the outskirts of town, and he made good time getting home.

"Jay!" he called as he pushed through the doorway and into the living room.

"I'm in here...in the bedroom."

He entered the bedroom and greeted his son first. "Hi, Tom. You being a good boy today?"

"Uh huh," Tom said and held his arms up and out to his pa.

Sam lifted his son and held him balanced on a forearm. "We got us a spot in the train," he said to Jay. "We're leaving this coming Thursday at daybreak." The look in her eyes was the same one he had seen before when it had become evident that they were leaving New York to come to Missouri.

"That soon, huh?" she asked and tiredly pushed her way up from her task of sorting through the personal items in the chest at the foot of their bed. She then approached her husband and said softly, "Put Tom down, Sam. I really could use a comforting hug right about now."

Sam lowered his son to the floor and took her in his arms. He pulled her close.

"I'm scared, Sam," she said as she buried her face against his chest.

He patted her back tenderly and closed his eyes as he wondered if they were indeed doing the right thing.

CHAPTER

Three

Sam hitched up the team while Jay put the final touches on getting young Tom ready and saying her farewells to the ranch, vowing to never forget the fond memories it held for her.

Sam pulled the schooner to the front of the main house and loaded his family. They completed the short trip to the rendezvous long before the sun had peeked its orange brightness above the eastern horizon.

Heck had been true to his word and had found someone to drive the extra wagon for them. He'd come up with a young fella of seventeen by the name of Darrell Henderson. Sam had met with the boy the evening before and had come to the conclusion that despite being a bit on the peculiar side, he was an all right sort of a youngster.

≫≫≫

Darrell was tall and lanky, well over 6 feet, with the slenderness of his frame giving the false impression that he was taller than he actually was. On his head perched a shapeless brown hat, worn pushed back and allowing an unruly shock of blond hair to dangle over one of his intensely blue eyes. He wore a slightly tattered, gray, long-sleeved shirt and a pair of gray woolen trousers that were held in place by a set of brown suspenders.

"The wagon master said you was lookin' for a driver. That right?" the boy asked from behind an unwavering gaze that Sam figured could only have come from a well-directed upbringing.

Sam focused his attention on the youngster's face rather than his clothes. "Yeah, you applying for the job?"

"Depends."

"On what?"

Darrell lowered his gaze and scuffed the toe of his boot in the soft dirt, then started drawing small circles with it. "On whether or not me 'n your horses'll git along."

"That doesn't make any sense."

"Does ta me."

"You're saying—"

"I'm sayin'…if I don't git along with the bunch I'll be drivin', then I ain't drivin' 'em, simple as that." He then rested his gaze on the huge Conestoga that occupied the area at the side of the main house. The canvas sides had been tied up, revealing the items that had been stored inside. "That the Conestoga they'll be pullin'?"

"Sure is. It's loaded with furniture and things that the wife seems to think she just can't do without. There's a schooner right behind it that'll be carrying me and my family."

The boy nodded his understanding. He then reached back and latched onto the tail of the dirty blue handkerchief that hung from his right hip pocket. He pulled it and wiped the sweat from his brow, pushing the floppy hat even farther back on his head in the process. "I wanna meet the horses," he said matter-of-factly. He straightened the hat before replacing the handkerchief.

"Never heard it put quite like that before. Folks generally say they'd like to *see* the horses."

27

"That's most likely 'cause they don't know no better. I figger horses are 'bout the same as most people; Some're alright and some ain't. They all got their own notions ta deal with."

Sam liked what he was hearing. There seemed to be a simple-minded kinda freshness about this youngster that was setting real good way down deep inside. "You think you can handle that big of a wagon with a six-up pulling it?"

"Yep, long as they like me and I like 'em right back."

Sam grinned at the straightforwardness of the fella. "You say you want to see the horses, huh?"

"What I said was…I wanna *meet* the horses, but I reckon I'll meet 'em when I see 'em."

"Well, c'mon then."

Darrell followed close behind, keeping his gaze intent on the animals as he and Sam approached the corral. He caught up and asked, "Can I have my pick?"

"Uh…sure. I don't see why not. Doesn't make any difference to me. I like 'em all. Picked 'em out myself."

They reached the fence, and Darrell stooped his way between the rails. "Did you ask any of 'em if they wanted ta make the trip?" he asked as he patted the rump of the nearest animal.

"Eh…well, no…I didn't. You reckon that should be a consideration, do ya?"

The youngster glanced back over his shoulder. "Could be," he said simply. He then began to meander in for a closer look-see.

He spent the next few minutes wandering among the animals, patting rumps, pulling up lips, checking front teeth and running a hand down a front leg from time to time, occasionally raising one to gander at the condition of the bottom side of the hoof.

A puzzled look came into Sam's eyes when the grading of the horses didn't stop there. He furrowed his brow as he watched the kid talking softly to each of the horses in turn. He was too far away to hear exactly what was being said, but he was amazed to see each react in its own way. Some would bob their head, while others would shake it. Still others would wiggle an ear or maybe flutter their lips with a rush of air. Some would even paw at the dirt. He was spellbound by what he was seeing, and he felt mighty stupid even considering what he was thinking.

Finally, the talking done, Darrell patted one last rump and climbed back through the fence. He then placed a booted foot on the bottom rail and, while continuing to look at the animals, said, "Good bunch a horseflesh ya picked out."

"I already know that, but do they like you?"

"Some do. Some don't."

"Do enough of 'em like you to make up a team?"

"Yep, sure do. I'll take both a them two bays. The one over there with the blaze on her face," he pointed at the one he meant, "and that one with the stockin' on her left front." He pointed that one out also. "That big chestnut, the good-sized sorrel and that other sorrel." He continued to point out each of them in turn as he spoke.

"That's only five," Sam reminded him.

"Yeah, I know. I'm still thinkin' on the last one."

Sam waited patiently for him to make his final choice.

"OK. Against my better judgment, I'll hitch up the gray mare."

"Why are you thinking it's against your better judgment?"

"Well, I figure she's a real good horse…might even be the best of the lot, but she's in foal."

"What? How do you know that?"

"She just told me. But she really wants ta make the trip, and I reckon that's good enough for me."

Sam was feeling more than just a little befuddled as he raised his hat between a thumb and index finger. After scratching his scalp with the three remaining fingers, he replaced the hat and watched the youngster as he headed toward the wagons. He wondered at the boy's sincerity as he followed him. There was nothing to indicate that he was trying to get his goat, but it was just a mite hard for a grown man with even a speck of common sense to buy into the fact that a fella could not only talk to horses, but would even want to. Sam quickened his pace.

"Them horses tell you anything else?" he asked after catching up with him just short of the wagons.

"Yep."

Sam wondered what that could have been while the youngster took his time checking over the Conestoga, being meticulous in his inspection of its condition.

The Conestoga wagon had been developed back in Pennsylvania as a freight hauler. It was especially suited for travel over bad roads and had a capacity of up to six tons or so. The floor curved up slightly at each end to prevent its contents from shifting around inside. It was an ideal selection for hauling the Bartlett's furniture.

"Looks to be in pretty good shape," Darrell said after completing his walk-around. "Believe I'll take on the job if you're of a mind," he said, stating what Sam figured he already knew.

"Yeah, I'm of a mind. Now what about wages?" Sam eyed him suspiciously, expecting the worst. "How much you figure the trek's worth?"

"I figger we'll decide on that once we get to where it is we're going. I'm wantin' ta make the trip anyways, so I'm figgerin' you're doin' me a favor as much as I'm doin' you one. I ain't one ta be robbin' folks what're doin' me a favor."

That made good sense to Sam, and he stuck out his hand to seal the bargain. "Sounds like we got us a deal then," he said and smiled at his new driver. "So, what do you prefer folks call you?" Sam asked as the youngster accepted the offering.

"Well, I reckon most folks has kinda latched onto callin' me Stretch."

"Seems fittin' enough. You can call me Sam."

"Well now, who's this? I thought I heard you talking to someone out here."

Stretch quickly snatched the hat off his head and flushed a crimson red as what was most likely Sam's missus had taken him by surprise.

"Oh, hello, sweetheart. This is Stretch. He's agreed to drive the Conestoga for us."

"Pleased to meet you, Mr. ah...Stretch." She extended her hand and waited for the inexplicably nervous young man to accept it.

"I-I, ah…" He timidly reached out and managed to make contact with her hand by barely touching the fingertips.

"Not much of a handshake if you ask me," she said as she glanced at Sam.

"Best I can do, ma'am, under the circumstances," Stretch said, and nervously fingered the brim of the hat as he cast his eyes toward the ground.

"And just what kind of circumstances might those be?"

Still keeping his gaze lowered, he continued to fidget with the hat before answering, "Well...ma'am...it's just that...well...what with you being a female and all—"

"That's what I thought." She looked at Sam. "Are you gentlemen just about finished with your business out here?"

"Yeah, pretty much."

"Good. Supper's real close to being put on the table, and you, Stretch, are going to accept my invitation to stay and help us eat it."

"But, I—"

"But, nothing. You come along now and wash up." She unexpectedly sided up to the terror-stricken boy and hooked her arm around his elbow. She lifted the front of her dress with her other hand so it just cleared the ground and repeated the command. "Come on now," she said, and tugged on his arm.

It seemed to Sam that the poor boy was a candidate for heart failure. The terror in his eyes was way more than any fella should have to endure. Sam remained behind and grinned as Jay towed Stretch toward the front of the house. They stopped by the door, and she unhooked her arm from around his. Sam grinned as she pointed out the pitcher of water and washbasin that rested on the table next to the doorway. She then disappeared inside to finish preparing the meal.

Sam covered the distance to the washing table. He remained silent as he stood next to Stretch and washed his hands and face in the tepid water. After drying with the towel provided, he handed it to the boy and locked his gaze on the youngster's eyes. "You have a little trouble around women, do ya?"

"Yeah, you might say that. Never did have no call ta be friendly with one of 'em and—"

"Well, you might as well get used to it. Jay's a friendly sort, and I can't imagine you being able to avoid her this entire trip."

Stretch plopped the towel on the washing table and sighed heavily. "Yeah, I know. Reckon I might as well go get me another dose a her," he said before pulling off his hat and running a pitchfork of fingers through his hair.

They entered the house, and Stretch right away spotted little Tom with his arms wrapped around Jay's leg. "You didn't tell me you had a *boy*," he said with a measure of delight that enabled a smile to spread across his face. "Now boys, I ain't got a problem with." He hung his hat on the peg provided by the door and squatted down to Tom's level. 33

Tom, being none too bashful around strangers, unlatched himself from Jay's leg and came to see who this new person was. As Sam looked on approvingly and Jay went about completing the task of getting the meal laid out on the table, Stretch and Tom did their best to become friends. They seemed to hit it off real good. They talked and played with some of Tom's toys until Jay announced that supper was indeed ready.

"You two put those toys away. It's time to eat."

The toys were placed back in the box where they'd been packed for the trip, and Stretch reluctantly approached the table, his nervousness returning. Sam indicated the chair to his left with a pointing finger.

"You sit there."

Jay put Tom in his usual spot and sat down opposite Sam.

"Dear Lord…"

Stretch quickly placed his hands in his lap and bowed his head.

"Tomorrow is a special day for us as we set out in search of our new home in this vast country You've created. Father, I ask that You watch over us and protect us while we travel." He paused as Tom banged his spoon on the tabletop.

Jay reached over, took it from him and patted her son on the top of his head.

Sam continued, "And Lord, be merciful in Your dealings with us and help us to make the right choices and decisions. And finally, Father, I thank You for this food that You have provided and for the wife that fixed it. Oh yeah…and thanks for this skinny boy You sent us to drive the Conestoga who surely needs to eat it, amen."

Stretch was obviously unsettled as he cleared his throat in nervous discomfort.

Sam took notice and asked, "You ain't much of a Christian are you?"

"Well…eh…no, I reckon I ain't."

"There's no sense feeling embarrassed about it, Stretch. All it takes is a little desire to become one. Heck, who knows? It could happen when you least expect it."

Sam glanced at Jay and caught her nearly imperceptible nod. He returned his attention to Stretch, who had wasted little time and had by then stuffed his mouth about as full as was humanly possible.

Stretch chewed the mixture with exaggerated effort, swallowed almost painfully, raised a forked hand in front of his face and nodded. Finally, after managing to swallow just enough to leave room for a sensible response, he said, "Might could, I reckon." He swallowed again. "But right about now I'd say it'd be a whole lot more sensible to say that I'm way more interested in doin' justice ta these here vittles."

CHAPTER

Four

Sam reined to a halt next to the Conestoga. He waved a greeting and climbed down. "Morning, Stretch. How'd you sleep?"

"Slept just fine, thanks. Looks like it's gonna be a fine day ta hit the trail." He inhaled deeply of the cool morning freshness. "I surely do 'preciate me a fine mornin'," he added and tipped his hat to Jay. "Mornin', Mrs. Bartlett. That young'un still sawin' 'em off?"

"Good morning, Stretch, and yes, Tom's still asleep."

"I 'spect he'll be awake soon enough. In fact just about any time now, I'd say." He pointed. "Looks like Heck's comin'."

Heck reined up a short distance from the Bartlett wagons and quickly sent word out for all the drivers to assemble for a short meeting. Sam passed the word on to the family in the wagon next to them and waited for the fella to pass it on to the next family. Sam then fell in step with him as the two of them, along with Stretch, headed for the spot that had been designated for the meeting.

"Morning. My name's Sam…Sam Bartlett. This here's Darrell Henderson. We call him Stretch."

Pleased ta meet cha, Sam. Name's Kyle Hendricks." He nodded in Stretch's direction. "Howdy, Stretch. Me 'n the missus and young'uns is happy ta make yer acquaintance, the both a ya in fact."

Sam wondered at the man's drawl. "You aren't from around here, are you?" he asked.

"Nope. Me 'n mine hail from the hills a Tennessee.

Been sittin' here nigh onta two weeks now just waitin' fer the next train ta form up. We been itchin' ta mosey, but just naturally figgered it'd be best ta wait fer more folks ta join up with afore we lit out."

"That's most likely a smart decision on your part. I've been hearing stories about Mexican banditos robbin' folks along the trail and would think a wagon on its own would be easy pickings."

"Yup. That's 'bout the way I had it figgered my ownself."

They arrived at the gathering, and Sam made eye contact with the wagon master and nodded a greeting. Heck returned the gesture, spit a stream of brown juice into the grass at his feet and commenced to wipe the dribble from his chin whiskers.

Presently, it seemed that just about everyone had arrived, and Heck started sayin' his piece. "I called all a ya together before we get started ta let ya know what some a my rules are."

He waited for the murmuring to die down.

"I can see from the reaction that some a ya ain't perticalar fond a rules."

Again the murmurs made the rounds. He held up a hand until things quieted down again.

"Well, fond of 'em or not ain't the issue here. I got 'em and yer about ta get 'em as well. So just keep yerselves simmered down and let me make 'em clear to the bunch a ya before someone here goes off half-cocked. We got us a long trip comin' up…'bout five or six weeks, I'd say. There's most likely gonna be times when there'll be some dangers lurkin' around an about."

This time the murmuring was short-lived and died down on its own.

"When that happens, I'll be orderin' ya ta circle up. Course I know some a ya ain't got the foggiest what that means, but ya will shortly. Right after we get strung out on the trail, we'll be practicin' makin' a circle. That way when we need ta do it fer real you'll have a pretty good idea about what's goin' on. Any questions?"

No one spoke up, but Sam heard a couple of mumbles. He glanced around in an effort to see who might be the ones that could be of a hardheaded nature, but he was unable to put a finger on anyone in particular. He returned his attention to Heck.

"We'll also be circlin' up each time we stop fer the night. The horses'll all be kept inside the perimeter, as well as the humans. If someone needs ta leave the confines during the dark hours, I'm issuin' orders right now that you'll hafta let someone know where yer headed and when ya expect ta be back. Is that clear?"

A fella of about 30 or so stepped forward and hooked his thumbs into the top edge of his belt. "Does that mean that when a fella needs ta go off and find a bush, he needs ta be lettin' the whole world know about it?"

"That's exactly what it means, that or any other reason. Don't none a ya make the mistake a takin' this too lightly. We got chances a meetin' up with them Mexican hombres what's been robbin' folks out there, plus the fact that some of the Injuns has been gettin' riled lately 'cuz of all the white men what's been squattin' on their land." He eyed the group of concerned faces before continuing, "Once we get away from Independence and out into what I consider the wilds, we'll be postin' guards ever' night after we stop.

Each and ever' one of the men will be asked ta take a turn now 'n then. That's all a part a bein' in a train, and I ain't bein' partial ta hearin' no grievin' about it neither. If there's anyone here what ain't willin' ta do his share ta protect the others..." he paused to look around at the faces, "then that fella better just call it quits right here 'n now and save hisself a whole passel a trouble. Is that makin' it clear enough to ya?"

While Heck looked around, Sam did the same. His gaze came to rest on a group of three fellas that had scornful looks on their faces. His attention was drawn away from them as Heck continued, "OK, that's 'bout all I gotta say fer now. Just keep in mind that there can only be one man in charge a this whole shebang. I reckon it goes without sayin' that you folks hired me ta be that man, so I'd appreciate it if I was given a free hand when it comes ta doin' what's necessary ta give us the best chances of makin' a successful crossin'."

After a short pause, he continued, "With that in mind, we're gonna string these wagons out now, and I'm gonna be the one ta assign positions in line. Now, I know that you may or may not cotton ta who I put cha next to, but just trust me that I know what I'm doin'. If yer patient enough, it'll come clear to ya after we been on the trail fer a ways." He then took one last gander around the circle of faces. "OK, as long as there ain't no other questions what needs answerin', I'd say ya all best be gittin' on back to yer families and listen up fer my instructions."

The group was anxious to get on the trail and dispersed quickly. Sam and Stretch made a final check of their harnesses and climbed onto the seats to await their orders.

Toward a New Beginning

"Sam," Jay said softly as she placed a hand on his forearm.

He looked into her eyes. "Yeah."

"Pray for us, please."

"Sure." Sam looked over and spied the boy sitting aloft in the front of the Conestoga. "Stretch!" he called above the noises of the wagons closing in around them. "Come over here for a second!"

"Yessir!" Stretch hollered back and climbed down. When he had reached the side of Sam's wagon, Sam looked down and said, "Jay here asked me to say a prayer before we get started. I figured you might wanna be a part of that."

"Sure, why not. I reckon it couldn't hurt none, long as you ain't askin' me ta be the one doin' the prayin'."

40
Sam grinned, figuring he'd be working on the boy soon enough to get that way of thinking out of his head. They all bowed their heads as they waited for him to begin.

"Dear Father, before You sits three died-in-the-wool sinners. We thank You for all You've done for us and pray that You'll watch over us as we start this journey into the unknown. Bless us, Lord, and keep Your protective hand on us. Help us to be better witnesses for You. And Father, I ask a special prayer for Stretch Henderson here." Sam took a sideways peek at the youngster and saw him fidget just a bit. "Father, help him to drive that big old wagon like he had good sense about him. In Jesus' name I pray, amen."

Before Sam could say anything to him, Stretch whirled on his heels and headed back to the Conestoga. As Sam and Jay looked on, they saw him brush a sleeve across his eyes.

"He'll be under conviction real soon," Jay said softly.

"Yeah, I know," Sam replied. "Might even already be. That boy's in for the surprise of his life once he accepts the Lord Jesus into his life."

Heck directed Sam and Stretch into line, positioning the Conestoga directly behind the schooner. They were near the middle of the formation, which suited Sam just fine.

Once everyone seemed to have a spot, Heck made one last ride the length of the train and counted the number they were heading out with. Satisfied that all 23 wagons were present, he returned to the front, reined to a halt and sat with his horse facing forward and his back to the formation. He sat there for a good moment or two before pulling his hat and bowing his head. It was plain to all that could see him that he was saying a prayer of his own. Once he'd finished, he replaced the hat and hipped around in the saddle. He took a moment to survey the sight behind him before raising his left arm high above his head.

Sam could clearly see the figure of Heck a ways off in the distance and waited for the expected signal that would start the line of wagons snaking its way westward. Finally, the arm came down in a forward motion. At the same time the order was given, "Let's move 'em out!"

As the lead wagons started rolling, the sounds of snapping reins and creaking wheels began to fill the air as one by one the teams were coaxed into motion. Sam's own team was prancing and tossing their heads in anticipation of what was to come. Finally, the wagon in front of him pulled away and it was his turn.

Toward a New Beginning

He turned to look into Jay's eyes and smiled as he said with a heartfelt tenderness, "I surely do love you, Mrs. Bartlett."

He lifted the reins above the backs of the team and quickly brought them down in a snapping motion. "Hup! Hup! Get up there!" he commanded and gave them their head.

CHAPTER

Five

Nearly all the drivers had at least a passable amount of experience handling a team. There were, however, a few who had little or no real understanding of trail driving, and for the first few hours they found themselves engrossed in learning the tricks of the trade.

The train had done its practice circle just as Heck had promised it would, and that went all right...well, sort of anyway. The enclosure hadn't been made near big enough, with the result being seven wagons were left outside the perimeter.

Heck, being a patient sort of man, had taken the opportunity to call the drivers together for a short meeting. He sat his horse in the center of the sorry excuse of what he'd hoped for and surveyed the gathering around him. "Well, you fellas—"

A female voice sounded from the back of the gathering. "And ladies!"

"And ladies...excuse me, ma'am." He acknowledged the female driver by touching an index finger against the folded-up front of his hat before continuing, "You can all no doubt see we kinda missed the mark on our first try."

The mumbling and nodding started up and lasted until Heck raised a hand. Once he had their attention again, he continued, "But I'm of a mind that we done good...considerin'."

"Considerin' what?" The question came from the fella at Sam's immediate left. Sam looked his way and saw a grizzled old man with a hawk-like nose and a leathery complexion. He was dressed in buckskin from head to toe. Well, leastways from neck to toe, the exception being his hat. It was fashioned from the hide of a raccoon with the tail still attached and hanging down the back. "Peers ta me…" He spit and tongued the chaw over to the other side of his mouth. "Peers ta me we ain't near come close. Peers ta me…" he looked around at the faces, "we could use someone up front what knows what it takes to make a respectable circle."

"You sayin' yer that person?" Heck asked the old-timer.

"Yep," he replied and spit again.

Heck eyed the man. "OK, eh…Mr. C, is it?"

"Yep. That it is."

"OK, Mr. C, you move yer wagon up to the front." Heck glanced around the gathering and continued, "When we circle up tonight you all just do yer best. If it works out that we fall short like we just did, don't fret none about it. Just pull the leftover wagons along the outside and double up around the perimeter. Fact is, sometimes that's the best way anyways."

"Why's that?" came the female voice again.

"'Cause that-a-way the Injuns cain't git inside so easy," Mr. C said and spit into the grass at his feet.

"Oh," she said with a trace of uneasiness.

After the agreements with Mr. C's assessment had died down, Heck continued with his instructions, "We'll be gettin' goin' again real soon, but first I wanna let you all know that we'll be stoppin' in a couple a hours fer eatin'. If the terrain and trail allow it, we'll draw up three lines abreast 'stead a stayin' in one long one. Anyone here passable with number figgerin'?" He twisted around in the saddle and looked the group over.

Stretch raised his hand.

"OK, Stretch, get yerself a spot in the dirt for figgerin' and listen real close."

Heck turned back to the main group of faces while Stretch used a palm to smooth out the dirt in a bare spot.

"We got us 23 wagons in this train. I want three lines bein' equal in length. How many does that put in each line?" Although he was looking at the group he was obviously addressing Stretch.

Stretch right away went to figgerin'. He started drawing some numbers in the patch he'd smoothed out, but before he could come up with the answer Sam whispered to him, "Eight, eight and seven."

45

"Eight in the first line, eight in the second and seven in the third," he announced proudly, and nodded his thanks to Sam.

"OK then. Stretch, count me out which of the wagons'll be leadin' each line and have them drivers stay here after the meetin'. The rest of ya will just follow the wagon what's directly in front of yer own and that'll take care a things."

Stretch found out which one of the wagons belonged to Mr. C and adjusted his count accordingly, putting that wagon up to the front and skipping it in his count as he figgered out the other two lead wagons. When he'd pointed out the number nine and number 17 wagons, those two drivers were asked to remain behind while the rest of the drivers went back to the train and prepared to resume the journey.

Sam introduced himself to Mr. C as they returned to their wagons, "My name's Sam Bartlett." He extended a hand and waited for a reply.

"Name's Cottonwood Charlie. Pleased ta meet cha." He spit and accepted the hand.

Sam liked the feel of Cottonwood Charlie's handshake and the look in his eye as well. "You been on these trains before, am I right?"

"Yep. Went on one up ta Or'gun once, but didn't much like it. Came back last year and decided ta try the Santa Fe Trail. Kinda like a dryer climate, if ya know what I mean."

Sam nodded his understanding. He'd heard stories about how wet and stormy it was up there in the northwest. "So, you figure on settling down at the end of this trail, or what?"

"Or what is all. I ain't completely decided yet, and most likely won't know 'til I see what's at the other end." Charlie spit and adjusted the coonhide hat for a better fit. "Just depends," he said and continued walking on past as Sam stopped beside his wagon.

"Who was that?" Jay asked as she watched the bow-legged figure continue on toward his own wagon.

"That, my dear, was Cottonwood Charlie," Sam said and climbed up onto the seat. He lifted Tom onto his lap and cradled the boy to him.

"Is he as colorful as he looks?" she asked.

"That and then some," Sam replied as he watched the man struggle aboard his own rig.

Stretch had remained behind to help Heck in case he had a need for any more number figgerin'. Once the meeting with the "line-leaders" broke up, he returned to the Conestoga and climbed up, tossing a salute and a smile to Sam in the process. Sam returned the gestures and waited for things to get underway again. It took a couple of minutes for everything to get settled, during which time Sam enjoyed the company of his son. Once the lead wagons started moving, he handed the boy to Jay and took up the reins. When it was his turn, he snapped them along the horse's backs, and the wagon jerked forward.

As the morning dragged on Sam had more than just a little trouble keeping the team on task. Oh, they pulled the schooner all right, but he was forever having to prod and correct them. It was a trying and tiring morning and it passed not without taking its toll on his disposition. Plain and simple, he was getting cranky.

With the blazing sun just about straight up overhead, Heck came riding down the line and announced a break for eatin'. Sam was relieved that he'd soon be getting a break from the strife of dealing with the headstrong team.

47 ➡

The arrangements that had been made for the "line-leaders" to lead each of their sections into a three-abreast formation went off without a hitch. Sam and Stretch were in the second section, and Sam dutifully followed the wagon in front of him until they reined to a halt. He kicked the brake handle forward and wrapped the handful of reins around it, using a half hitch to secure the bundle of leather straps. He then sat calmly for a few seconds to enjoy the respite.

"Tough morning," Jay said softly and placed her hand on his forearm.

He sighed heavily. "Boy, that ain't the half of it. If I have to go through that day after day, I'm for turning back right now."

"Promise?" she asked with a subtle glimmer of hope. She knew full well that he had no intention of turning back. So instead of waiting for an answer, she gathered her dress and petticoats and gave him a raised-eyebrow, questioning look as if to say, "Well, are you going to help me down or not?"

"Oh. Eh…sorry, honey. Wait just a second and I'll help you down." He hurriedly got down and walked around the rear of the wagon. Once he'd reached the other side, he guided her feet as she made her way down to safe ground.

"Why don't you go let down the tailgate and set out that box of lunch items?" she said, and placing the flats of both hands in the small of her back, began to stretch out the kinks as best she could.

Tom had been asleep on the mattress they'd laid out in the bed of the wagon. He'd been jolted awake when the wagon had stopped jostling him and was peering around the corner of the canvas covering. "Wanna eat, mama," he said sleepily and rubbed his eyes with both fists balled tightly.

"It's coming, son," she said as she unsuccessfully tried to smooth some loose strands of hair back into their rightful place.

Just then Stretch approached the rear of the wagon. "Nice, easy morning, wasn't it?" he asked.

Sam bit his tongue and proceeded to let down the tailgate. He slid the lunchbox back to the edge of the gate and held his arms out toward his son. "Come here, Tom."

The boy stumbled and fell over a few things that were stacked in the way, but he managed to make it to his pa's outstretched arms. Sam lifted him down, and after watching him go off to play with a stick he'd found lying at his feet, he turned to face Stretch. "If you had an easy morning of it I'm real happy for you." He hooked his thumbs in the top edge of his belt and sighed a huge sigh. "My morning wasn't anywhere near enjoyable."

Stretch was genuinely concerned. "Why's that?"

"Well, to tell you the truth, I don't rightly know. There's just something about this team that makes it near impossible to get them to work together. It's like…well…like they ain't liking one another or something. It's real hard to put a finger on but I'm of a mind that something just ain't right."

"Mind if I was ta have a look-see at what the problem might be?"

"No. Go right ahead, more power to ya. Might even be that they'll *tell* you what the problem is." Sam was being sarcastic because of the hard times they'd put him through all morning.

"Never can tell," Stretch said with a smile and headed off toward the team.

Sam busied himself with helping Jay get the lunch together. Once it'd been dished out, he took a plate for himself and one for Tom and slid down with his back against a wheel. He coaxed the boy to him. "Come on over here, Tom. Time to eat."

Tom didn't need any more prodding than that. He dropped the stick and scurried over to his pa. The two sat side by side in the grass and waited for Jay and Stretch to join them. As Jay approached and found a spot alongside them, he called out to Stretch, "You 'bout ready to eat?"

"Yep. Fact is I am…I truly am," came the eager reply. Stretch left the team, and finding his plate of food on the tailgate, snatched it up. He squatted between Sam and Mrs. Bartlett and eagerly grabbed up a piece of the cold chicken.

Sam purposely cleared his throat, "Ahhmmm."

"Oh yeah, I forgot," Stretch said and let the drumstick fall back onto the plate. He licked his fingers and removed his hat.

Sam said a grace that asked not only for a blessing on the food but an answer to the problem with the team as well. He prayed for a better disposition so he'd remain calm when the horses tested his patience. After saying amen, they dug into the chicken and biscuits the Lord had provided.

"You figure out what the problem is with those knotheads?" Sam asked while gnawing on a wing.

"Yep." Stretch also was busy with a mouthful and didn't say anything more.

Sam eyed the boy and noticed he wasn't anywheres near slowing down on his eating. "Well, what is it?"

Stretch motioned toward the team with the piece of chicken he was clutching and swallowed hard, making room for some words. "Tell ya in a minute, soon's I fill up the bottom of this empty spot I got in my belly." With that said, he chewed off another bite and followed it with about half a biscuit.

Sam decided it wouldn't do much good to hurry the youngster, so he ate in silence and waited for the news, good or bad. What was amazing to him was that Stretch could put away food the way he did and still be as skinny as a fencepost. "You always eat like that?" he asked, a teasing smile crossing his face.

"Yep, 'specially when I'm hungry, like now." He turned slightly to face Jay. "Sure are a good cook, ma'am," he said and waved the chicken leg toward her.

"Why thank you, Stretch, but I think you'd be willing to eat anything right about now."

"Now that's a true fact," he said happily and shoved in the remainder of the biscuit.

Once things had slowed down and it could safely be said that Stretch had gotten the bottom of that empty spot filled, Sam tried again. "So what did you figure out about that team?"

"It's really purty simple." Stretch laid his plate in the grass and patted his stomach. "I think I'll live now," he said contentedly and smiled his thanks to Jay. He then turned his full attention to Sam. "You was exactly right. The trouble's that the two you got leadin' ain't liking one another." He paused to let that register while he lowered himself down onto one elbow. "My suggestion would be to leave the bay on the left front but move the sorrel to the left rear, switchin' her with the brown gelding. That way they'll be away from each other and not even able ta see one another." He pulled a blade of grass and started to use it as a pick for his teeth. "That'll solve yer problem."

Sam was not entirely sure that the solution could be as simple as that. "That's it? Just rearrange those two?"

Stretch lay back in the grass and locked his fingers together behind his neck. "Yep. Wake me when it's time ta head out."

Sam wasn't quite done with the problem solving yet and dug a little deeper. "So, how'd you figger out the answer, ask the horses?" he asked sarcastically.

"You don't wanna know."

Sam took care of rearranging the sorrel and the brown. Once he'd finished, he found a comfortable spot against a rear wheel. The sun had passed straight up just enough to afford a slim sliver of shade along the side of the wagon. He propped his back against the wheel and stacked his forearms on his pulled-up knees. He rested his forehead on his arms and let his eyelids fall for a little much-needed shut-eye. About two seconds after they blinked shut he was forced to deal with the realities of being on the trail.

"OK! That's it! Time to hit the trail!"

Sam accepted his fate and rose. He readied himself before resuming the confrontation with the bull-headed team by looking toward heaven and asking the Lord to give him the needed strength to get through the day. He then hefted Tom up into the wagon and handed Jay up to her spot on the seat. He waved an acknowledgment to Stretch and climbed aboard.

The wagon ahead started rolling as Sam unwound the bundle of reins from around the brake handle. He snapped them along the backs of the team and was pleased to see them strain against the harness with no more than a "Git up now!" from him. That was just the beginning of a very pleasant afternoon for Sam Bartlett.

The team performed wonderfully well and maintained their distance behind the wagon ahead with little or no help on his part.

"Seems to be going quite a bit better," Jay said offhandedly.

"Yeah, yeah, I know. You don't need to say anything. I guess maybe that boy does know a thing or two about horses," he conceded.

Jay's grin indicated that she agreed with him.

The afternoon passed quickly with Jay spending the lion's share of the time in the bed of the wagon entertaining their son. Sam enjoyed listening to the sounds of their laughter as he drove the team westward.

The clouds had turned from a grayish white to a brilliant orange and were just beginning to tinge purple when Heck called a halt. "Circle 'em up!" he hollered repeatedly as he rode the length of the line, waving an arm in a circular motion above his head.

The day's progress was ended, and Sam was more than just a little thankful. Even though the day had turned out to be a whole lot more tolerable than it had begun, he was still bone tired from their first day on the trail.

The circle was made and none too soon to satisfy Sam. Cottonwood Charlie had known what he was talking about, and did a real good job of leading the forming of the enclosure. It turned out to be darned near perfect.

53

➡

There were a few trees around, and Sam and Stretch were able to collect enough dead wood to build a small cook fire. Sam tended to his team while Stretch got the fire going. After unhitching his own six-up, he busied himself with unhitching Stretch's team and was thankful when the youngster had completed his task and arrived to help out.

"How'd it go with the team this afternoon?" Stretch asked and smiled a wry grin that most likely meant he already knew the answer.

"You really needing me to tell you, or are you just trying to rub it in?"

"Just rubbin' it in," he said with a grin as he led the team away.

The evening meal was wonderful. Jay had outdone herself, and before eating it, Sam asked the blessing and thanked the Lord for the good day they'd had.

Shortly after most of the folks had finished eating, a main bonfire was built near the center of the circle. Folks started gathering to discuss the day's progress and do some planning for tomorrow's journey. This was also the time when new folks were met and new friends were made. As eager as Sam was to get over to the main fire, he instead shooed Stretch on over there and took the time to help Jay clean up after the meal and organize things in the wagon for the night's rest. Tom was plumb tuckered and hit the sack right after eating. It wasn't more than a minute or two before he was sound asleep.

As Sam and Jay approached the circle of brightly lit faces, the conversation was indeed about the day's progress. Heck was talking, and Sam sat down cross-legged next to Stretch and pulled Jay down beside him.

"I figger we done 'bout 14 miles today. Which ain't a record, but it's surely a good ways."

"What cha figger we kin do on a average?"

Sam looked in the direction of the question and saw the face of the fella from Tennessee that he'd met earlier that morning. But try as he might, he couldn't remember the fella's name.

"That all depends, Mr. H," Heck said and spit toward the blaze.

The mention of the fella's initial sparked Sam's remembrance. *Hendricks…yeah, that's what it is,* he said to himself.

"On what?" Hendricks asked.

"On whether or not we get a rainstorm. On whether or not we get slowed by mud. On whether or not we get slowed by the heat. On whether or not we get slowed by the cold. What I'm sayin' is that there ain't no way a tellin' this time a year out here on the plains." Heck looked around at the nodding heads, and then continued, "You folks all need ta realize that this time a year is a mite iffy along the Santa Fe. Why, one day could be just like it was today…all calm and peaceable, then the next could blow up one a them twister fellas what can snatch a whole wagon clean up off the ground."

"That's a true fact," Cottonwood Charlie said. "I seen it afore with my own two eyes. Course I ain't never see'd a whole wagon picked up, but I see'd a cow go flyin' by once. And that's the truth, so help me Hannah."

No one disputed what was being said. Instead the next fella tried his hand at tellin' an even bigger whopper. And so went the evening. The yarn spinnin' and lie tellin' were some of the best Sam had ever heard. It went on for right about an hour until the fire was finally allowed to die down and folks said their goodnights and headed off to their respective wagons.

55

No guards were posted that night because of the wagon train's relative close proximity to Independence. This however would be the only night that guards would not be assigned for the remainder of the trip.

Sam and Jay said their goodnights to Stretch and left him sitting cross-legged in front of the smoldering remains of the fire. They retired to the comforts of the inside of the schooner where they undressed and changed into their nightclothes.

Once they were situated and nestled down for the night, Jay whispered to her husband, "Sam?"

"Yeah."

"I think I'm truly glad we decided to make this trip."

Toward a New Beginning

He smiled to himself. "Yeah, me too."

She snuggled in as close as possible and laid an arm across his chest. He looked out through the opening to the rear and watched as a streak of light traced its way across the sky. A gentle smile crossed his face, and he clasped her hand in his.

They both became lost in the togetherness of one another and the commitment of what they'd decided to face. They fell asleep with each of them wondering what was in store at the end of their journey.

CHAPTER

Six

The first week or so went well for the hearty souls in the wagons. There were the usual inconveniences: wheels needed greasing, horses needed shoeing and children needed paddling. But mostly things went along pretty much as expected.

The fourth day out being Sunday, they'd held a meeting that morning before hitting the trail. One of the men had given of himself and preached from the Bible on family living and loving thy neighbor. He'd done a passable job, and folks were satisfied with his effort.

Stretch also had attended the meeting, and since that time Sam had been noticing that he seemed to be having a different outlook on a number of things in general. Besides that, he was managing to scrape together enough self-confidence where he was almost entirely at ease around Jay.

The evening bonfires had already become an anticipated event to the members of the train. Of course there were a few exceptions, but most folks looked forward to the enjoyment and fellowship of being around other families for that hour or so. On two separate occasions, the thunderstorms came and washed out the fire, sending everyone scurrying to the protection of their wagons. But all in all, those get-togethers were a blessing.

Sam, Jay and Stretch used the evenings of fellowship to get to know folks. There were the Appletons, George and Fay, from Virginia. They were a young newlywed couple and were heading for their first home. Then there was Harry and Agnes Carter, who had the wagon right in front of Sam's. They had a 12-year-old son named Joshua who seemed to be more of a handful than a fella needed to have around him. Sam figured he was a good enough rascal, but just a little misguided was all. In front of the Carters, were Bill and Birdsong Hawkins. She was a full-blooded Comanche, and although folks had wondered about it, they hadn't asked him how he ever come to marrying an Indian. Bill was a fella that preferred wearing a buckskin shirt and britches. He also opted for moccasins on his feet rather than boots. He topped it all off with a floppy-brimmed buckskin hat with a feather trailing out the back on a short length of rawhide. He insisted that folks call him Wild Willie, as opposed to Bill.

Going back the other way in the train was a couple in the wagon right behind Stretch that were well into their forties. Mabel and Jacob Greenberg had three teenage youngsters, two sons and a daughter. The boys were named Danny and Ronnie, ages 15 and 14, respectively. The girl, Mary Jane, was the oldest and Stretch's age at 17. She was a pretty little filly and about as bashful as a 17-year-old could be. And that's sayin' something, considering how bashful Stretch was toward females. Her being raised around two younger brothers you'd think she'd have learned how to deal with the closeness of young men, but she hadn't.

⚹⚹⚹

Toward the end of the sixth day, the train halted at the banks of a tame-looking river. This being the first ford they'd be making, Heck called a driver's meeting and went over the procedure for getting the wagons across safely. Once he felt confident that everyone was clear on the procedures he wanted to use, they returned to their wagons and prepared to make the crossing.

Although the waters of the slow-running river were barely high enough to tickle the underside of a horse's belly, Heck still insisted on having outriders on either side of Cottonwood Charlie's wagon with their ropes secured to the wagon for safety's sake. When he made it without mishap and drove his wagon up the far bank, a cheer went up from the remainder of the travelers and they began making the crossing, each in turn.

Them being a ways back in the train gave Sam and Stretch ample time to check over their equipment and fill the water barrels that were lashed one on either side of the wagons.

59

Stretch eased the Conestoga down the bank and into the water just enough to facilitate easier filling of the barrels. He used a large cooking pot as a dipping tool and had the job completed in about two shakes. Once he'd finished, he tossed the pot into the back and waded toward the front of the Conestoga. Pausing to get a good handhold before pulling himself up, he glanced toward the bank and noticed Mary Jane Greenberg standing with her back against a cottonwood watching his every move.

As soon as she saw that he'd seen her, she blushed crimson and hurried off toward her folk's wagon.

Stretch also turned a few shades of red and readjusted his hat to hide some of his discomfort. He then climbed aboard and waited his turn for the crossing.

He did, however, take the time to sneak a peek or two at the wagon behind, but was disappointed when he didn't see her again.

The outriders had latched onto Sam's wagon and were steadying it across. Feeling braver than usual, Stretch twisted around in the seat and risked an all-out look at the Greenberg wagon. This time he wasn't disappointed. Mary Jane was leaning out from her position in the back of their wagon and looking straight at him. As soon as they spied one another, they both quickly jerked upright behind the protection the wagons afforded and looked straight ahead. Unbeknownst to the other, a broad smile crossed each of their faces.

The outriders tied onto the Conestoga, and Stretch told the horses that it was their turn to make the crossing. They responded favorably and crossed the river without any difficulties. Once up the far side he climbed down to watch the Greenbergs make the ford. The two boys waded across, grateful for the opportunity to cool off in the stream. Mary Jane, on the other hand, elected to remain in the back of the wagon.

The crossing went well enough, but Stretch could tell by the body language of Mr. Greenberg's horses that there was a possible problem with the team. This became readily apparent when the right-side lead mare reared up, displaying her displeasure with the whole thing. She settled back down after a few stern jerks on the rein from Mr. Greenberg, and the ford was completed without any further trouble.

Stretch watched as the team lunged up the bank. He decided to let Mr. Greenberg in on what he might do to fix his problem, and approached the wagon as it came to a halt. "Ah...Mr. Greenberg, sir?" Stretch pulled his hat and waited for the man to acknowledge him. At the same time he was pleased to see Mary Jane stick her head around the back of the wagon and look his way.

"Yeah, boy. What'dya want?"

"Well sir, it's just that I wanted ta tell ya that I could see that comin' a mile off."

"See what comin' a mile off?"

"Why, that lead mare a yours, of course."

"What about her?"

"It's just that she ain't got no hankerin' ta be in the water, and I'd switch her around so's she weren't able ta rear up if I was you."

"You sayin' yer some kinda expert when it comes ta horses, are ya boy?"

61

"Nosir, I ain't. It's just that—"

"Thanks for the advice boy, but no thanks. That mare's been my favorite for a number of years now, and I'm figgerin' she'll do for a spell longer. Her rightful place is up front, and that's where I'll be keepin' her."

"Suit yerself. But I hope I don't get the chance ta say I told ya so when she causes you 'n yours some heartache." Stretch then tipped his hat to Mary Jane who'd climbed out of the back of the wagon. "Ma'am," he said as politely as he could, in spite of the heated flush that had suddenly covered his cheeks. He then did the same to Mrs. Greenberg seated next to her husband. She smiled an acknowledgment, and he turned and left for the Conestoga, thankful for the relief he suddenly found himself experiencing.

By the time the last of the wagons had made it

across it was late enough to circle for the night, and Heck issued the orders. Guards were posted to walk the perimeter and were instructed to remain just outside the circle's enclosure. The particulars of how the watches would be set up, as well as their duration, had been settled around the main fire after the first day's travel. Three men would be used at a time and were to keep watch for about two hours, when the next bunch would relieve them, and so on until morning.

Although this created a hardship for those who were called upon, it was something that needed doing and was generally accepted by everyone as part of their duties. The only ones who seemed to have a problem with it were the same three that Sam had noticed with the scornful looks on their faces that first morning when Heck was dishing out some of his rules.

As it turned out the three were a gent by the name of Noah Baxter, his oldest son, Wayman, and youngest, Rip. They were, it seemed, pretty much content to keep to themselves with little or no contact with the rest of the folks in the train. Oh, they'd speak whenever spoken to, but they were hard-pressed to ever start up a conversation on their own. Sam figured they just weren't the neighborly sort and decided to leave them be.

A commotion had started up over at the Baxter wagon, which was right behind the Greenberg's. Sam and Stretch meandered over that way to see what all the fuss was about. As they approached, they could tell Noah appeared a mite upset about something.

"What'dya mean it's my turn again? I just done a turn a couple a nights ago."

"Look, Baxter..."

It was Heck doing the talking, and Sam could see

he was doing his levelheaded best to keep from losing his temper with the man.

"That was on our second night out from Independence, and since then ever God-lovin' one of us has had a turn. Now we're startin' over again, and yer elected. And that's the end of it," he added with the fire starting to boil up in his eyes.

"In the first place, Yallow, don't you be confusin' me with the likes a them Bible-thumpin' hypocrite friends a yers. I ain't God-lovin' and never will be, and that goes for my boys here, too." He gestured toward his sons with a wave. "And in the second place, it'll be the end of it when *I* say so." He struck a defiant posture by folding his arms across his chest and looking scornfully into the eyes of the wagon master.

Heck stuck a finger in his ear and wiggled it vigorously. "Well, that bein' the case," he said as he removed the finger, looked at the end of it and wiped it on his trousers leg, "That bein' the case, you'd best be decidin' that this conversation *is* at an end 'cause 'bout the next thing what's gonna happen is that I'm liable ta ferget that I'm a Christian and jump right in the middle a you."

"I figger that'd be a big mistake on yer part, Yallow. 'Cuz that'd rile my boys here and that'd give you a powerful lot ta deal with." Baxter smirked confidently.

"That's not the way I see it," Sam said matter-of-factly. "Nosir, not at all. I figure I'm kinda partial to getting all the way to the end of this journey, and that means I'll be needing Heck here to do the leading. Keeping that in mind, I'll be taking his side in this, and I don't think I'll have any trouble at all whipping the daylights outta those two still-wet-behind-the-ears pups of yours."

As Noah started to reply, Sam raised a finger to his lips and said, "Shhh. I'm not quite finished yet. After sizing up these two sons of yours, I figure I could whip a whole corral full of fellas just like 'em and still manage to hold the gate closed with my other hand, if you know what I mean?" He then walked over next to Heck and looked straight into the now insecure expression on Baxter's face. "Now I'm finished. So, if you got something else to say, say it. Or you can just go on and do what's expected and keep your trap shut."

Noah whirled angrily and mumbled something unintelligible as he departed.

"Thanks, Mr. B, but I coulda handled him my ownself," Heck said.

Sam remained silent while he waited for the two Baxter boys to decide if they wanted any part of him or not.

Finally, they made the smart decision and followed after their pa.

"That bunch could be trouble one of these days," he said softly, more to himself than anyone else.

CHAPTER

Seven

The next day marked the end of the first week on the trail. They'd been averaging about 15 miles a day and were right on schedule as far as Heck was concerned. Water and good grass had been plentiful, and the animals remained in fine shape. Late afternoon found the column approaching a river that was nowhere near as tame as the one they'd forded the day before. This one was rain-swollen and running fast. Heck figgered there must've been a rainstorm somewhere up in the mountains and the effects were just now reaching out there on the plains. He called for a three-abreast formation so they could get together to ponder the situation.

Once the three lines of wagons had halted at the river's edge, Heck got all the members of the train together and listened to suggestions and recommendations from anyone that wanted to have a say in the goin's-on. Right at first the general feeling was to go ahead and try to ford across a wagon or two and see how it went. The alternative was to wait a while to see if the swollen waters would subside. After a bit more discussion Sam came up with the idea of maybe sending out riders both north and south in search of a more passable crossing. That seemed to be the most reasonable thing to try first, and it was decided on with just a couple of minor objections being voiced.

Heck asked for volunteers and settled on Wayman Baxter and another fella by the name of Jack Walker to do the scouting. Shortly after they'd left, the circle was made and the camp settled down. The cooking fires were built up as the travelers waited for the return of the two men.

Just as the sun had given it up for the day and dipped its last speck of orange brilliance below the western horizon, Jack returned. Sam motioned to Stretch, and they followed him as he rode by, heading for the campfire Heck shared with Cottonwood Charlie.

They eased up to the conversation and squatted on their haunches as they listened to Walker's report. His assessment was that their chances weren't any better as far north as he'd ridden, which was about two to two and a half miles, as best as he could figure. Heck thanked him for the effort and sent him off to go get a bite and rest up. The rest of them remained around the fire and talked about Jack's report while they waited for Wayman to return. It wasn't long before Noah showed up.

66

"That boy of mine get back yet?" he asked gruffly.

"No, he ain't," Heck replied curtly.

"Well why not? That other fella come back already. Why ain't Wayman back yet?"

It was obvious to Sam that Heck was in no mood to listen to what Baxter had to say.

"Don't rightly know, Baxter. Maybe he's just sick and tired a hearin' your mouth and decided ta just keep right on goin'."

"That ain't one bit funny, Yallow. I'm concerned about my boy, and you ain't got no call ta be belittlin' me because of it."

Heck softened noticeably. "Yeah, you're right. I just ain't in no mood for listening to ya is all. I got problems of my own and am just as worried about yer boy as you are. I don't know why he ain't come back yet, but if it'll make ya feel any better, you have my permission ta head out lookin' for him."

Noah nodded slowly while giving the offer some thought. "Might just do that," he said pensively and looked at the western sky. "There's about a half hour of daylight left. That'll be enough time for me 'n Rip ta progress a good ways. Yep, I believe that's just exactly what we'll do. Be back 'bout a half hour or so after dark."

"Rip!" They heard him holler as he walked away.

❧❧❧

Wayman had ridden the better part of two miles. He was not having any luck, as everywhere he tested was way too deep and way too swift for just a horse and rider, let alone a whole passel of wagons. Not seeing any sense in going any farther, he'd made the decision to return with the bad news and pulled his horse's head around. In doing so, he came face to face with four Indian braves sittin' on their ponies and blocking his way. Where they'd come from he had no way of knowing, but that was the least of his worries. He knew enough about Indians to recognize these fellas as Comanche. He also knew he had no chance of outrunning 'em. That prompted him to take his next best option, and he raised an open-palmed hand in a sign of peace. "Howdy," he said.

The foursome was barely 40 or 50 feet away and took only a few seconds to reach, then surround him.

Amidst guttural sounds directed at one another, they began fingering his shirt, hat, saddle, saddle blanket and just about anything else they had a mind to.

Toward a New Beginning

Wayman wasn't liking the way things were going, and tried once again to talk to them on the off-chance that at least one of them spoke passable English. "Me friend," he said and jabbed a thumb into his own chest. "Me come in peace. No want trouble." He surveyed the braves and realized that they had no guns that he could see. This gave him a couple of options: Either he could draw his pistol and try for all four of them, which wasn't likely to be successful, or he could make a run for the river at the first chance that came along.

"Shut face...white-eyes," one of the braves said bluntly. "You give horse to me." He pointed to Wayman's mount with the business end of his tomahawk.

"But—"

"I tell you...shut face!"

The anger flared in the Indian's eyes, and Wayman knew he'd best be doing what was being requested. He carefully eased from the back of his horse, keeping a wary eye on the fella all the while. Once on the ground he surveyed his chances and decided on a try for the river. His opportunity came right away as the Comanche angrily grabbed the bridle, which in turn caused the horse to rear.

Wayman bolted and took off in a dead run. He reached the river all in one piece and dove into the swirling current. After sputtering his way to the surface, he began to swim as hard as he could. He was a real good swimmer, but the Comanches were just a split second behind him and were waiting for him as soon as he surfaced.

Almost immediately a searing pain hit him as a lance caught him in the fleshy part of his left thigh. The pain was significant, but he continued his frantic attempts to escape. The current was indeed as swift as he'd hoped, and he was thankful for it as he rolled over onto his back, clutched at the pain in his leg and allowed the swirling torrent to carry him downstream.

To his dismay he saw that the Indians were riding along the bank, keeping pace with his movement. He forced the pain in his leg to the back of his consciousness, rolled over onto his belly and began to swim.

Despite the discomfort it caused him, his efforts were soon rewarded, and he gradually approached the far side where he was eventually able to grab ahold of a tree branch that hovered just above the water. He hung on with all the strength he had left in him and rested as he watched the Indians on the far side testing their intent by riding their ponies into the swiftly moving waters to about chest level on the animals and retreating up the bank. Finally, they gave it up and rode up the bank one final time and out of sight.

Wayman figured he had his breath back well enough and released the branch. Instantly, he was swept away again. This time he was able to concentrate on making it to the bank without worrying about his pursuers.

The water was deep right up to the edge, and he was unable to find the bottom with his feet. He could feel the current tugging at the lance that was still stuck in his leg. The water being as cold as it was rendered the leg numb. He was glad of that because he felt very little pain as he bumped along the steep bank.

Finally, his feet made contact with solid ground, and he grabbed onto a mesquite bush that leaned out over the water. It scratched his face, but he was able to maintain his hold while he managed to work his exhausted body about halfway out of the water. He lay there for a couple of minutes and rested. Presently, he decided to deal with the injured leg and struggled the rest of the way out of the water and up the bank. He rolled painfully onto his back and scooted backwards until he was able to prop himself against a handy tree trunk.

There was only a minimal amount of blood, but he knew that as soon as the coldness went away so would the numbness. That meant the pain would return, and most likely the bleeding as well.

He continued to examine the wound and discovered the tip of the lance was sticking clean through to the under side. That meant that it'd missed the bone, and that meant there was a good possibility that he could pull it out.

Of course there was the possibility open to him of getting out his pocket knife and whittling the shaft off to a more manageable length, then try to make it back to the wagons, or...the other option really didn't appeal to him at all, but he figured it was the best way.

He made up his mind, poked his index fingers between the edges of the hole in his trousers leg and pulled the tear even wider. He then took ahold of the lance with both hands and began preparing himself for the worst. Realizing that this was gonna hurt more than just a little, he figured he might not be able to maintain consciousness and could easily bleed to death if he fainted. He reached into his hip pocket, retrieved his handkerchief and tied it as tight as he could around the leg just above the wound. He then picked up a stout-looking stick, about an inch or so in diameter, and placed it between his teeth. The beads of sweat popped out on his forehead as he took ahold of the offending lance. He sucked in a deep breath

70

and held it. He then made sure he had a good grasp on the shaft, clamped down on the stick and yanked with all his might.

As the blackness closed in around him he fought to remain conscious and continued to pull. Finally, he felt the lance come free, and fainted.

بهي بهي بهي

Noah and Rip rode along the river's edge as they continued to follow the signs. The light of day was fading quickly, making it difficult to see the tracks. Noah was a good tracker, but was hard-pressed to see the imprints. He hauled up, dismounted and handed his rein to Rip. He walked slowly along the riverbank, allowing a closer inspection of the signs. Finally, the trail came to a spot where it seemed three or four other horses had approached. He strained his eyes at this new development as he tried his best to recreate the scene, but had to admit there just wasn't enough daylight left. He glanced around and spotted what he figgered he needed. He walked over to some bushes and gathered together a small bundle of sticks. He pulled his handkerchief and carefully wrapped it around one end of the bundle. He then dug into a shirt pocket, found a match and lit the crudely-made torch.

The sticks were completely dry, and so the fire didn't last long. But even from just the brief illumination, he was able to piece together a good account of what had gone on here. While holding the torch close to the ground he studied the sign and was able to make out the prints of the unshod ponies as well as the boot marks where Wayman had dismounted and made a dash for the river.

Toward a New Beginning

The handkerchief quickly burned through, and the remnants fell to the ground. He tossed the smoldering sticks into the blackness of the swiftly moving water and stamped out the burning cloth at his feet. He made his way to the very edge of the river and quickly searched for any sign of Wayman's body. Satisfied, he climbed the bank and accepted the rein from his son. "Looks like he made it to the water," he said to Rip, but more to himself.

Noah rested his gaze on the foreboding black expanse of water and realized the slimness of any chance of survival for anyone that might have tried to swim the raging torrent. He then mounted up and led the way as they resumed their slow-paced ride while calling softly for Wayman.

After about a quarter mile or so, they gave in to the futility of the situation and headed back for the wagons. Little did either of them know that at the very point where they gave up the search Wayman was lying directly across the river unconscious.

CHAPTER

Eight

Wayman awoke with a start. The pain in his leg was less than he'd remembered it being during his waking moments throughout the night. The sky was a peaceful pre-dawn gray, and there was not a hint of a breeze. He propped himself up onto his left elbow and reached his right hand, testing the tourniquet. He ran a finger under the handkerchief and was satisfied that it seemed to be just about the right tightness. The wound was wet with a minor amount of fresh blood, but nothing that caused him any undue concern. He painfully worked himself up to a sitting position and tested the leg by trying to bend the knee. It was immediately apparent that that wasn't such a good idea. The knee refused to bend, and the pain intensified. He winced and fell back into the grass. Once the discomfort subsided, he struggled to a sitting position, propping his back against the tree. He looked around and spotted the Comanche war lance a short distance away. He reached out and took ahold of it. The effort sent another pain shooting into the leg.

He knew that if he was to have any chance of making it back to the wagons, he'd best be figuring out a plan of action. With that in mind, he used the lance as a brace and worked his way to a standing position. He then gathered his courage and attempted a step with the bad leg. It buckled, and he collapsed in a heap. A blackness threatened to consume him as the pain again shot through the leg. He gritted his teeth and whimpered helplessly.

Toward a New Beginning

Wayman knew he was in a bad way, but he also knew he had to find a way to get back to the others. He glanced around and spied a spindly tree nearby that had branches suitable for fashioning one of them under-arm crutches folks used when they were crippled. He slowly and with great effort began to drag himself toward it.

✯✯✯

The dawning morning back at the camp remained filled with the same apprehension felt the night before when Noah and Rip had returned. Noah had told them about finding the unshod pony tracks mixed in with those from Wayman's horse, and how it had looked like he'd tried to escape into the river.

Heck decided a trip to the spot was in order, so he, Noah, Rip and Cottonwood Charlie headed out just after sunup.

As they rode along the riverbank it was readily apparent that the waters had subsided significantly during the night. The level seemed to have lowered a good three feet or so. Heck felt a ford made later that morning was indeed possible, mainly because the swiftness of the waters had also decreased, although it was still far from what he'd like to see for a guaranteed safe crossing.

The ride to the scene of the encounter was a relatively quick one because no tracking was needed. Once they arrived, Noah pointed out and explained the different signs as he told the story of what he thought had gone on there.

Charlie, being a passable tracker his ownself and havin' more'n just a time or two of past dealin's with redskins, agreed with Noah's assessment, and they mounted up and continued along the river's edge in hopes of finding any indication of where Wayman might have exited the water, if in fact he had managed to escape and was still alive.

They'd traveled nearly a quarter of a mile when Heck spotted the figure on the opposite bank. "Well now," he said and drew rein. "Would you just look at that?" He pointed toward the lone figure hobbling along the bank, leaning heavily on the stick he had propped under his armpit.

Wayman was relieved to see the rescuers and waved an appreciative greeting. He lowered himself to the grass and waited for them to figure a way across to his side.

75

Heck rode into camp and let everyone know that they had managed to find Wayman, and that although his leg was in a bad way, he would not die from the wound. He put them at ease by letting them know that Noah, Rip and Cottonwood Charlie were escorting him back along the opposite side of the river.

The apprehension disappeared as the members of the train packed up and made ready to make the crossing and resume their journey. Once the camp was broken and everything was packed away, the fires were extinguished and the teams were hitched up to their respective wagons. There was no lack of volunteers to help with hitching up Charlie's team and the Baxter team as well. Birdsong Hawkins would drive their wagon while Wild Willie drove Charlie's rig. Jacob Greenberg took over the Baxter wagon, takin' Mabel with him and turning his over to their son Danny, who was quite capable. With all the wagons manned, they proceeded to the river's edge, keeping the same order as before.

With the current still being a mite swifter than he'd like, Heck instructed both outriders to stay to the upriver side of the wagons to better keep them on line against the force of the rushing waters. When they were in position, Wild Willie carefully drove the first wagon into the water. Once the outriders had fastened their ropes, he whipped up the team and they headed across.

The going was slow but the wagon made good contact with the river bottom. There'd been some concern at first that maybe the depth of the water would cause it to have a tendency to float. To the relief of everyone looking on, that wasn't the case, and Willie made it safely across. The usual cheer went up, and the second wagon carefully made its way to the river's edge.

The crossing went well and soon it was Sam's and then Stretch's turn. They both made it without mishap.

Stretch stood on the opposite bank and watched as Danny tried to coax his team into the water. The right-side lead mare was definitely not wanting any part of the swift current and was showing her objections by refusing to enter the water. He watched as Danny pulled the whip from its holder and cracked its length above the mare's head. Mary Jane appeared from inside the wagon and took the seat between her brothers. It was plain to Stretch that she was not at all comfortable with what was going on.

"Use the whip, boy!" Mr. Greenberg hollered just off to Stretch's left.

Stretch looked his way, and their eyes met.

Greenberg once again shouted his instructions to

his son. "She'll do alright, boy! Use the whip like you mean it!"

Danny raised the whip and took charge of the situation. The mare responded and reluctantly waded into the water. The outriders tied up, and they started the crossing.

Stretch again glanced sideways at Mr. Greenberg and noted his smug smile. The smugness intensified as if to say… *Told ya I knew what I was talkin' about.*

Stretch bit his tongue but the word appeared in his mind anyway…*Fool.* He returned his full attention to the scene in the river.

The mare was not at all taking to the current as it beat the water against her side. She tossed her head and half-reared as she protested the treatment she was being forced to endure. Danny did his best and kept her marginally under control with the use of the whip and a firm hand on the reins. Inevitably, she finally lost her footing and plunged into the surging waters.

The wagon was just past the centerline of the crossing where the water was at its deepest. The mare thrashed around, succeeding only in getting herself hopelessly tangled in the harness. This caused the remaining three horses to panic as they were pulled downriver.

The wagon didn't have a chance. As soon as it changed direction, the outriders were next to useless, but they gave it their best shot as they wrapped the ends of their ropes around their saddle horns and hauled back on their reins.

"Let it go!" Heck hollered.

They hastily unwound the ropes and flung them into the river.

Toward a New Beginning

The schooner careened wildly until it finally rolled over.

Mary Jane and her brothers had jumped just as the wagon had begun to tip.

"She cain't swim!" Stretch heard Mr. Greenberg shout as the girl hit the water. "The boys'll do alright, but Mary Jane cain't swim!"

Stretch was an excellent swimmer and had no second thoughts. He hastily sat down and pulled off his boots. He rose, shucked out of his jacket and, while running toward the river, grabbed the brim of his hat and tossed it just before he dove for the water. He surfaced quickly and looked for Mary Jane. Unable to make out much of anything, he swam as hard as he could until he finally neared the overturned wagon. When he reached it, he also came face to face with Ronnie.

Stretch had to yell to make himself heard. "Where's Mary Jane? You see her after she hit the water?"

Despite his fear, Ronnie managed a teeth-chattering, "Over th-th-that way." He pointed. "I s-seen her headin' over th-th-that way…just a little b-bit ago."

Stretch pushed away. "Stay with the wagon," he said and continued downriver. "God, please help me to find her." He didn't realize it, but he'd said the prayer out loud. He raised himself as far out of the water as he could and steadied his gaze ahead. For a darting instant he thought he'd caught a glimpse of her blonde hair, but still a pretty good distance away. He renewed his effort and began to swim as hard as he knew how. In just a matter of moments he heard a gurgling. "Help!"

Once again he took the time to rise up and look ahead. This time he for sure saw her and knew she'd seen him as well; she had a hand extended toward him.

"Help me!" she said. "I can't swim! Oh please, help me!"

He struck out and reached her just as they passed through a tree branch that extended out over the water. He wrapped his arm around her just under her armpits, and knowing she was now safe, took the time to rest before attempting to make shore.

"Am I gonna d…?" she asked, as the water covered her mouth, obscuring the words.

"You'll be alright. I've got ya now." He kept his voice calm and under control, not wanting her to get any more upset than she already was. "I'm a real good swimmer. Good enough for the both of us, in fact. So you just lay back and enjoy the ride while I get us over ta the shore." He could feel her shuddering and knew she was crying.

Just then Danny caught up to them. He rolled over onto his back and squirted a stream of water from between his teeth. "Nice day fer a swim…huh, sis?" he said.

She didn't answer.

Danny could see that Stretch had things well under control and headed for the bank that was by now no more than ten feet away.

Stretch pulled Mary Jane the rest of the way to the shore and was grateful when Danny grabbed ahold and helped pull them out onto the grassy bank. All three sprawled onto their backs, exhausted.

"Somebody gonna help me?" The plea came from the river. They all sat up and watched as Ronnie floated by, still holding onto the wagon. The mare had somehow managed to get untangled and had righted herself. In fact, all four of the horses seemed to be doing well. The wagon, however, was still lying on its side.

Stretch and Danny looked at one another and grinned. "Might as well, I reckon," Stretch said.

"Yeah, I reckon," Danny agreed, somewhat reluctantly.

They headed for the water and jumped in. While Danny went after Ronnie, Stretch focused his attention on helping the men who were keeping pace along the bank. Grabbing onto the ropes they tossed out to him, he managed to attach one around each of the two lead horse's necks. It was a simple process after that to get the wagon back onto dry land where it was found to be none the worse for wear.

Stretch was pleased to see that Mary Jane was right where he'd left her. She smiled her thanks. "Thanks for what you did," she said, and wiped a wet dress sleeve under each eye.

"You're welcome. You know you coulda been kilt."

"You too."

"Yeah, I reckon."

"I owe you my life."

She started to cry, so he sat down in the grass next to her. He mustered all the gumption he could find and took her in his arms while he let her get it out. He liked the feel of her as she shuddered against his chest. Her hair smelled fresh and clean, and he was secretly glad that she was crying so he could hold her.

She raised her head and looked into his eyes. "Your name's Stretch, ain't it?"

"Eh…yeah, it is. I-I been noticin' you too," he said and felt a tightening in his chest that was like nothing he'd ever felt before. He gazed into her blue eyes as she shivered and sucked in a gasping breath. "You cold?" he asked, and rubbed his hand up and down her upper arm.

"Yeah, a little."

He watched her form the words and for the first time ever he had a desire to kiss a girl. "I…eh…we best get goin'. You're ma 'n pa'll be worried sick about you." He started to rise.

"Wait," she said and pulled him back down.

She placed a palm on each side of his face and pulled him toward her. Their lips met, and he had a fleeting guilt-filled feeling that maybe he should pull away. But the feeling was just that, a fleeting one. They both enjoyed the awkward kiss. It was the first for either of them.

"Mary Jane!"

They hurriedly cut the kiss short and jumped to their feet. "Yes, Pa!" she answered as she tried desperately to smooth out the front of her dress. "Over here!"

It was pretty obvious that Mr. Greenberg was happy and relieved that his little girl was safe and sound. "Oh, honey," he said and threw his arms around her. "Thank God you're OK."

"God and Stretch here," she said and touched him lightly on the arm. "He saved me, Pa. He saved my life."

"I'm beholdin' to ya, son. I'll never ferget what ya did today. Thank you." He reached out and took ahold of Stretch's hand and pumped it repeatedly while he continued, "I'll never be able ta repay you fer savin' my Mary Jane here. If there's anything I got that I can give ya, or anything I can do…well, you just say the word."

"As a matter of fact, there is one thing. You can switch that lead mare like I told ya."

"You'll not get any more argument outta me. Not after what I seen today. You were right all along, boy."

"Oh, and there's just one other thing."

He squinted a suspicious eye at the boy. "And just what might that be?"

"With your permission, I'll be payin' my respects to Mary Jane from time to time, eh…sir."

Jacob continued to eye the boy with a sternness that finally forced Stretch to swallow hard. A twitch jerked at the corner of Greenberg's mouth as he turned toward his daughter. "And just where do you stand on all this?"

She reached out and hooked her arm around the crook in Stretch's elbow. She spread a gleeful smile and moved in closer. She hugged the arm to her and said, "I'd say I'm standin' right here next ta my fella, that's where."

The remaining wagons all made it across the river with no further mishaps. Jacob had just finished switching the lead mare when the rescue party appeared with Wayman.

A meeting was held to discuss Wayman's confrontation with the Comanches and the problems facing the Greenbergs now that they'd lost nearly all of their food and belongings. Birdsong Hawkins was mildly distressed that it was Comanches that were causing the trouble for the wagon train, but no one held the fact that she was a member of that tribe against her. The discussion centered on the precautions that were now necessary to protect the train from attack or intrusions. It was decided to double the number of men walking the perimeter at night.

As an added measure, Heck laid out a new rule that no one would be allowed to wander from the train by himself, day or night. Some folks thought this was getting a little extreme, but it was a steadfast rule laid out by the wagon master and was not open for discussion. It was also decided to have mounted outriders patrolling along the length of the train during the day. They were to remain a ways off so there would be plenty of advanced warning if trouble were spotted.

Birdsong had more than just a little knowledge about healing herbs and such things, and volunteered to look after Wayman. Wild Willie suggested he be laid out in their wagon so she could keep a close eye on him. Although Noah didn't much cotton to no heathen Injuns carin' for his boy, he realized his shortcomings when it came to doctorin' and agreed to the arrangement. So a place was made for Wayman in the Hawkins' wagon and Noah kept his mouth shut.

83 ➤

The Greenbergs were inundated with offers of assistance. They were given food and clothing, and were offered anything else they had a need for. Jacob and Mabel were overwhelmed by the generosity of their fellow travelers, and Jacob expressed their gratitude by saying a prayer of thanks and understanding that touched every heart present. Once the amens had died down, a fella would have been hard-pressed to find a dry eye anywheres around. But that's probably because Noah wasn't there at the time.

Stretch and Mary Jane had a talk with her ma and pa about letting them share the Conestoga during each day's trek. With her riding with Stretch, it would help to alleviate the overcrowding in the Greenberg wagon. That made a whole lot of sense, and Jacob agreed under the condition that they take Ronnie as well. Mabel smiled understandingly as she watched their daughter and her newfound beau head off toward the wagon with Ronnie tagging along close behind.

CHAPTER
Nine

The next week or so came and went without any more trouble to speak of. The outriders reported seeing an Indian or two every once in a while, and that always caused more concern than it turned out to be worth. They seemed to be keeping tabs on the train and just letting the white men know they were around. There was never any indication that they had any intention of being hostile. Birdsong let Heck know that the trailing Indians were not Comanche, but Arapahoe, and some day very soon they would approach the wagons and let their wishes be known.

The usual daily routine continued as the folks in the train went about their business of heading west toward their new homes. They crossed the prairie at a good pace, and by the end of the 13th day they had covered nearly 200 miles. Heck told everyone that as far as he could recollect, they were within two or three days of reaching the Arkansas River. Once there, they would follow it until it turned nearly due west. From there it would be a simple matter of just stickin' to it until folks found a spot that appealed to 'em and decided to settle down.

This news encouraged everyone, and even gave some of them a false sense of security. One who was not to be fooled was Birdsong. She knew the Comanches would return sooner or later and cause trouble if they had a mind to.

The nearly two weeks on the trail had brought the people in the wagons closer together, and they were fast becoming good friends. There was a sense of togetherness developing that was not only a necessary way of doing things, but rewarding as well. Stretch and Mary Jane were growing fonder of one another with each passing day. The biggest problem they were faced with was figuring out ways to get shed of Ronnie so they could steal those "magic moments" alone together. At times, that involved anything from fooling him into thinking that his pa wanted to see him, to letting him drive the team while they walked together hand-in-hand behind the wagon. Of course, that meant walking right in front of the Greenberg wagon with Mary Jane's pa watching them with an unobstructed view of the goin's-on. There was a time when Stretch forgot himself and slipped an arm around her waist, only to have that indiscretion met with the loud crack from Mr. Greenberg's whip. He quickly removed the arm and, twisting around, tipped his hat to him. Jacob returned the salute and suffered an abuse from his wife as she instructed him to, "Just leave them two young'uns be."

Sam and Jay had never been happier. He'd taught her the finer points of driving the team, and she eagerly accepted the challenge, which allowed him the freedom to spend time with his son. Of course, there were instances when Tom was sound asleep; those were the times they spent together discussing what their plans would be once they arrived at their destination. It was agreed that they would settle somewhere within easy distance of a populated area, rather than some far-off remote location where neighbors would be a scarcity.

George and Fay Appleton were just about as happy as any two newlyweds could be. He was forever doing for her and she for him. Sam tried hard to remember if he and Jay had ever been as "clingy" as those two seemed to be, but just couldn't come up with a time. Jay said she thought it was wonderful that they felt the way they did about one another, but Sam was of a mind that it was bordering on unhealthy for two people to be that close all the time.

The Carters, who had the wagon right in front of Sam and Jay, were getting just about at their wit's end with their son, Joshua. Stretch saw this as an opportunity to get rid of Ronnie once in a while. He pushed hard each evening for Josh and Ronnie to become friends and maybe spend more time together. That panned out to enough of a degree to allow him to steal a kiss from Mary Jane every now and then.

The Baxters, as well as the Hendricks, kinda kept to themselves and didn't bother anybody. There were times when Sam would try to strike up a conversation with Noah, but the old man just wasn't receptive.

Birdsong did a wonderful job of caring for Wayman's leg by keeping the herb mudpacks changed on a regular basis. They did the trick, and the wound responded to the tune of healing much quicker than folks had thought possible.

Wayman was not only grateful for the progress with his leg, but also the interest folks had seemed to take in his well-being as well. It was just a matter of time before he started opening up and became friendly with folks around him. This wasn't setting too well with his pa, but Wayman didn't give a hang one way or the other. He figured he was a grown man and could take on any kind of disposition he pleased.

The rainstorms appeared on a regular basis, coming

about every other day or so. Everyone welcomed them as a respite from the hot, humid afternoons.

The morning that marked two weeks on the trail saw a low-level fog strip hanging about 15 or 20 feet off the ground. As the sun chinned itself on the eastern horizon, it bounced its early morning brilliance off the underside of the fog, casting a beautiful pale orange and pink glow over the landscape.

"Sure is a beautiful morning," Sam said as he and Jay stood with an arm around each other's waist, taking in the beauty of God's creation.

She snuggled her head against his shoulder. "Um hmm," she said contentedly. "I don't think I'll ever get tired of seeing sunrises. Each one is different from the last."

Before he could respond, the sound of approaching horses reached their ears. They looked up and were surprised to see a small band of Indians riding their way.

"Go to the wagon," he said solemnly and gave her a slight push. He rested his hand on the butt of his pistol as he watched the approaching riders' every move. They rode to within a few yards of him and pulled their ponies to a halt. In short order, he was relieved to feel the presence of other men from the train as they sided up to him.

"Do you speak English?" Heck asked after taking a step forward from the others.

The Indians looked at one another until one of them began making some guttural sounds and started waving his hands around.

Charlie recognized some of the signs and stepped forward next to Heck. "Peers ta me these here fellas are Arapahoe. He's tellin' us they're here wantin' ta be our friends." Charlie watched some more, then translated again, "He's sayin' they ain't been able ta find any buffalo and are gettin' low on vittles." He paused and watched some more. "He's askin' if we got any food they can have that'll feed their women and young'uns 'til they come across a herd."

"Tell him that we'll spare what we can. No, wait." Heck turned to face the men behind them. "Any of you fellas got a problem with sharing what we have in the way of food?"

"I ain't sayin' I'm likin' it, but by the same token I don't figger we got no choice," Noah said. "I reckon if we don't give 'em what they's askin' for, they'll most likely just come and take it anyways."

"That the way you see it, Charlie?" Heck asked.

"Reckon so, Heck. These fellas are seemin' peaceable enough, but don't let that fool ya none. They're just as treacherous as any other Injuns you can name, 'specially if their squaws and papooses is hungry."

"OK, then. Tell him we'll give 'em what we can spare."

Charlie signaled the white-eyes' decision. The reaction was one of smiles and approving nods.

"Tell 'em ta get down and come on over to the camp," Heck said and started for the train.

Charlie conveyed the message, and the Indians dismounted. They assumed a meek demeanor as they led their ponies toward the wagons.

Once they entered the circle, they were greeted by the sight of every single woman and child, who were able, pointing either a rifle or handgun their way. The fella who'd been doing the talking got Charlie's attention by placing a hand on his arm. He asked him to tell the people to put the firesticks down. They would not cause anyone any trouble.

"You folks all lower them guns. These here fellas are nervous that someone will take a notion ta commence ta shootin'. He says they ain't here ta do no harm, and I'm of a mind ta believe him." He watched as most of the guns were lowered. However, a few weren't. He raised his voice a notch or two and tried again, "I said...put them guns down. One shot outta any of ya, and we'll most likely be bitin' off more'n we can chew. I'm figgerin' that these fellas are just an advance bunch that was sent ta ask fer food. I 'spect there's a whole passel of 'em just over one a them hills. I 'spect they's just layin' out there, listenin' for the sound of one a ya pullin' off a shot. Now put 'em down, I said!"

This time all the guns were lowered. Birdsong was the last to lower hers. She was a Comanche, and the Arapahoe were hated enemies of her people. She watched with hate-filled eyes as the smelly Arapahoe passed by in front of her. A distasteful sneer curled her upper lip as her eyes met the gaze of the leader. She continued to stare after him as he passed by. His head turned, and he glared at her over his shoulder. Finally, she could stand to look at these Arapahoe dogs no longer. She turned away and headed for her wagon.

Wild Willie watched as she hurried away. He quickly followed. He found her seated in the grass with her back propped against a wheel of the wagon. "You havin' a problem with them Arapahoe?" he asked, already knowing the answer.

"Yes. Me no like to see faces of Arapahoe dogs," she said, and angrily pulled a handful of grass and thrust it away. "They not fit to live." She jerked her head around to look straight into his eyes. "We not give them food," she said and narrowed her eyes into an icy stare.

"Well, I reckon if that's the way ya feel about it, then that's how it'll be."

"Good." After she said that, she realized that he was on her side, and the coldness eased from around her eyes. She closed them and the tears started as she remembered the time so long ago when her mother and brother had been killed in the Arapahoe attack on their village.

He knelt and took her in his arms. He held her and stroked her hair while she dealt with her sorrow.

Words were unnecessary.

The members of the train gathered together what food they felt they could spare and brought it to the area where the Indians waited patiently. Each time more food was added to the growing pile, the leader would nod his thanks. In anticipation of being successful in their attempt to get food from the white men, the Indians had brought along some buffalo robes to use for securing the items.

When the last of the food had been laid out, they spread the robes and placed the items in the centers. Bringing the corners together, they tied them securely with lengths of rawhide. After tying two bundles together with yet another short, but heavier strip of leather, they hefted them onto the backs of their ponies with a bundle hanging on either side. They thanked the white-eyes with nods, smiles and some hand signals before swinging up onto the backs of the ponies and leaving the circle of wagons.

"Hope that's the last we'll be seein' of them fellas," Heck said, as he and Sam stood together watching them go.

"Amen to that," Sam said.

CHAPTER

Ten

The next day was a bad weather day right from the start. The sky had clouded up overnight, and the members of the train awoke to a cold, steady drizzle. There was a brief respite during the afternoon, but that was short-lived as the thunderheads billowed up and the storms swept across the open prairie one after the other. Some of them were on the violent side with the rains coming down in horizontal sheets that blasted into the travelers head-on. The lightning bolts flashed incessantly as the seemingly endless choruses of cannonading thunder did their part to contribute to the severity of the storms. With the rain continuing to beat down, sometimes in the form of hail, Heck finally called a halt, and the wagons circled for the night, albeit about an hour earlier than usual.

With the constant downpour being pushed by the driving winds, fires were out of the question. So the travelers did the best they could under the circumstances and were forced to eat a cold supper.

Sam dug out a good-sized piece of canvas from the Conestoga, and he and Stretch built a makeshift lean-to that extended out from the side of the schooner. Once it was finished, Jay, Mary Jane, Tom and Ronnie joined the two men, and they all settled down for cold chicken and leftover beans. The canvas shelter did little in the way of keeping them dry, but it was better than nothing at all.

Finally, just after sundown, the storms eased a bit

and the swirling winds died down. Sam noticed the change, and while there was still some light he dug out the dry firewood he kept in the wagon for just such times. He found a suitable high spot under the lean-to and built a fire on it. In no time at all the warmth of the small blaze did its job, and the shivering and teeth chattering began to ease and eventually came to an end.

The next day was a whole lot better during the early hours, but by late afternoon the thunderclouds had again developed into violent storms, and Heck again called an early halt. They circled in the lee side of a large cottonwood grove that had a small stream meandering through it. Although these storms didn't seem to pack the rain like those of the day before, the thunder, lightning and winds more than made up for it. Folks huddled together and dealt with the adversity as best they could.

Sam and Jay did their best to soothe Tom and keep him occupied. The sounds of the storms frightened him, and whenever a lightning strike was close enough for the flash to appear blue and the sound to emit a nerve-bending crackle, rather than the rolling rumble of a far-off bolt, he would jerk with a start and begin to cry.

The storms continued throughout the afternoon. The rains were intermittent, as was the hail. Some of the canvas coverings on the wagons couldn't stand up to the pounding, and the occupants were forced to evacuate them and double up with other families. One such victim was the Hendricks family.

"Sam...Sam Bartlett!"

Sam worked his way to the front of the wagon and peered out. "Yeah!" he hollered, while managing to keep his hat on his head by clamping a forearm across the top of it. The hailstones pelted his face, and he shielded his eyes with a cupped hand placed just above them. Finally, he spied Mr. and Mrs. Hendricks and their two young'uns. He didn't hesitate. "Get in here! Get them young'uns outta that storm and in here under cover!" He reached out and took hold of the girl and lifted her into the wagon while the boy waited his turn. Once the two children were safely inside, Mrs. Hendricks climbed aboard, followed by Kyle.

"Oouu wee," Kyle said as he pulled his hat and hugged his wife who was already hugging the children. "Thanks fer yer hospitality. That storm's near tore our wagon ta pieces. Hope it makes out well enough ta be drivable tomarrah." He then stuck his head out through the opening and took a gander. "Nosiree, just don't seem ta be lettin' up none out there," he said once he'd pulled it back in.

"You alright?" Jay asked, looking at the children.

Both youngsters nodded, and Mrs. Hendricks spoke, "We sure are beholdin' to ya fer helpin' us. Ain't partial ta bein' a burden ta our neighbors, but—"

"You're not being a burden," Jay assured her. "Not at all. I would expect you to do the same for us if the shoe were on the other foot, ah...Mrs. Hendricks. By the way, what is your name? We've been traveling this train together for two weeks now, and I still don't know your given name."

"Mainly that's 'cause I ain't used ta bein' right friendly with folks 'til I knowed 'em fer a spell, but seein's how we're gettin' cozy tagether...my name's Ethelda Mae." She extended her hand.

Jay took it and looked into her eyes. "My name's

95

Judith, but those who're my friends call me Jay. And I'd like it very much if you'd call me that."

A smile crossed Ethelda Mae's face. "Alright, Jay. I'm right pleased ta make yer acquaintance," she said with her smile continuing to grow wider. "These here young'uns is Kyle Junior and Charlette."

Jay nodded and smiled at the two shivering children. She found a blanket and passed it to Ethelda Mae. "Here, put this around them before they catch their death."

The nest buildin' was interrupted as a panic-filled voice could be heard from somewhere outside. "What's that all about?" Sam wondered out loud as he made his way past Kyle to the rear of the wagon. He peered out through the opening and gasped. "It's a twister!" he said excitedly.

"What's a twister?" Kyle Junior asked.

"Come here and look for yourself."

The boy leaned out the back end of the wagon. His eyes grew to nearly twice their normal size. "Golly," he said in pure amazement. "I ain't never see'd nutin' like that afore. Golly."

"C'mon, everybody out," Sam said and pushed back the flap. "We need to find us a low spot to lay down in. If that twister decides to head this way, we'll be in for a heck of a time."

"What'dya mean?" Ethelda Mae asked. "What'll it do ta us?"

Sam had already climbed out and had started lowering kids down to the ground. "If it gets near enough to these wagons, it'll pick 'em up like pieces of paper and toss 'em wherever it gets a notion. And it'll do the same with people, too. Now come on." He glanced over his shoulder. "It looks like it's figuring on heading straight for us. Come on! Hurry! I'll go get Stretch and the others. You all head over by the stream and lay down flat in a low spot. Get in the water if you have to." With that he turned, leaned into the wind and headed for the Conestoga.

"Stretch…Stretch…get outta there! There's a twister coming this way! Head for the stream!" he hollered as he reached the wagon.

Stretch emerged and climbed down the back of the wagon. "Where is it?"

"Right behind you!"

"Oh my God. Mary Jane! Ronnie! Get outta there and fast! It's *here*!" As Mary Jane showed herself, he grabbed her around her middle and none too gently pulled her out of the wagon. Sam did the same with Ronnie, and they ran as fast as they could toward the stream.

When they reached it, they slid down the slight embankment along the edge of the water and watched the fury of the tornado as it approached. It was now within a hundred yards of the wagons, and all hell was starting to break loose. The trees were twisting and turning savagely, the wagons were rocking violently, and the sound of the approaching tornado blocked out everything except a man's thoughts…and prayers.

Sam was sure more than one person up and down the line was praying as hard as they could, so he joined in. He spoke the prayer out loud, but no one but God could hear him, not even himself. "Dear God, help us to survive this storm. Be merciful in Your dealings with us and spare us from Your wrath." He took the time to glance at Stretch and Mary Jane. He had his arm across

97

her back and was pulling her into the protection of his own body. Sam did the same to his son and beloved wife before continuing, "Father, at least spare these youngsters. None of 'em's had much of a chance to know what life's all about. Spare them, Father. I ask this in Your precious Son's name, amen."

As he finished, he cast a gaze at Jay and saw that she was looking at him. The expression in her eyes was one of fear, yet she'd found the strength to smile grimly. He returned it half-heartedly. Neither of them knew if this would be their last moment together on this earth.

Just as quickly as the funnel had lowered from the heavens, it left the ground and disappeared into the clouds. The winds immediately died down and the deafening noise subsided. Sam raised his gaze, as did the others. "Well I'll be," he said softly and rose up onto his knees. He looked into the heavens and said simply, "Thank You, Lord."

The inhabitants of the train appeared almost reluctantly from their places of hiding and went about the task of sizing-up the situation. The twister had left the majority of the wagons in tatters. Nearly every canvas top was torn, shredded or missing all together. Sideboards had been worked loose on a few of the older wagons, and more than one wheel had been broken. A good portion of the stock had panicked and ran off, but by the grace of God, none of the travelers had been killed or even seriously injured.

With the condition of the train being what it was, Heck decided to lay over for as long as would be necessary to repair what needed fixin' and get the train back in traveling shape.

The travelers pitched in and did what they could with what little light was left, but as night fell they were forced to call off their efforts and spend a nearly sleepless night wondering what the next day would bring.

CHAPTER

Eleven

The dawn broke under clear skies and a general feeling of despair as folks went about the task of putting their lives back together. No one had come through the storm unscathed. However, some had been more fortunate than others, yet they worked just as hard as those who hadn't been so lucky. All available extra canvas was dug out and stacked in a community pile for anyone with a need.

Wayman Baxter, bad leg and all, did his part by doing the cutting for the women as they sewed new wagon tops for the ones that had been destroyed. The rest of the women were given the tasks of running herd on the children and tending the meals. The men were kept busy with rounding up the stock and repairing the wagons.

Sam lifted a wheel onto an axle of the Hendricks' wagon. He twisted and shoved until he felt it bottom out against the stop. Ronnie balanced on the far end of a tree limb they had lain over a log and were using to lever the corner of the wagon off the ground.

Stretch stood nearby with retaining washer and nut in hand. A noise drew his attention and he looked up to see an approaching wagon. "Lookee there," he said and pointed.

Sam glanced over his shoulder. "Get that washer on here and let's fasten this wheel down. Then we'll go see who the visitor is."

Stretch pushed the washer into place and followed it with the nut. He picked up the wrench and hastily snugged the nut to a proper tightness. After a final tug he looked at Ronnie. "OK, that'll do."

The youngster jumped off the limb, allowing the wagon to come crashing down with a vengeance, but it held together. Sam then took ahold of the top of the wheel and gave it a good shake. "Yep, that'll do," he said as he wiped the grease from his hands with the rag he'd pulled from his hip pocket. He tossed it to Stretch. "C'mon, let's go," he said.

They arrived just as most of the other folks were getting there as well. Heck greeted the driver, "Howdy, stranger. What brings you out here all by yer lonesome?"

"Is this Hector Yallow's train?"

"Yer lookin' straight at him."

"My name's Harold Jenks...*Pastor* Harold Jenks. Mind if we get down?" he asked and began to climb down.

A woman's face appeared from inside the wagon, and she made her way to the edge as well. He assisted her to the ground. Next came four boys. They formed a line, obviously in order by age from oldest to youngest. "This is my family," he said proudly. "Maggie here's my wife." He placed a hand on her shoulder, and she smiled a dutiful smile. "Her real name's Margaret, but Maggie's what she prefers. And these are my boys." He walked around behind them and placed an open palm on the top of each one's head as he said their names, "Matthew...Mark...Luke...and John."

"What brings you folks all the way out here, Pastor?" Sam asked. "This ain't real hospitable country, especially when a wagon's out on its own."

"We were meaning to join this train before it left

Independence, but were delayed in arriving. Then when we finally did get there, we were dismayed to find that you folks had already left. We started out almost three days behind. It took this long to catch up."

"Well…" Heck dug an index finger into the inside of his cheek, pulled out the chaw and let it fall to the ground. "I reckon…" He paused while he gnawed off a fresh chaw. "I reckon you caught up now, so I figger yer welcome ta pull in line and ride along the rest a the way if it suits ya."

The pastor patted John's shoulder. "Thank you, Mr. Yallow."

"You just go on and pull your rig in line right at the tail end."

"Whatever you say, Mr. Yallow."

"The name's Heck. And I'd appreciate it if ya was ta call me that. Mr. Yallow was my daddy's name." Heck turned to face the others. "Let's get on back ta gettin' this train in shape ta roll," he said.

"You folks have trouble?" Pastor Jenks asked.

"Yeah," Heck replied over his shoulder. "Had us a near disaster with a tornada yesterday."

"Anyone hurt?"

Heck turned to face him. "A few bumps an' bruises is all. Mostly it was the wagons what suffered the most."

Pastor Jenks pulled his hat and quickly scanned the faces. "You folks mind if I ask the Lord's blessing on this train?" Without waiting for a reply he began to say a prayer for the safety of the people in the train, the sturdiness of the wagons, the well-being of the children, the continued health of the horses and just about anything else he could think of that might pertain to getting the train safely to its destination.

When he'd finished and the "Amens" had died down, Sam and Jay were making their way back toward the wagons. "Mite on the windy side, wouldn't you say?" he said matter-of-factly.

"What'dya mean?" she answered, while looking around but not noticing any breeze to speak of.

"Kind of a long-winded prayer...not that I mind what a pastor's got to say."

She smiled up at him and taking his hand in hers circled his arm around her shoulders. "Well, good thing I'd say, because pastors are supposed to be long-winded."

The remainder of the day was spent finishing up the reconditioning of the wagons. Pastor Jenks and his wife made the rounds, meeting every member of the train and getting to know each one's standing with the Lord. Overall, he was pleasantly surprised at the number of those that were truly Christian and had been saved by God's grace. However, he was particularly distressed when he tried to discuss salvation with Noah Baxter.

1O3 ➤

"I ain't partial ta hearin' no preachin', Preacher. So, just go on about yer business and just leave me and mine be."

"But don't you want to know without a doubt that when you die you'll go to heaven?"

"Now that'd be a real good question, Preacher. Mainly 'cause I ain't even sure there is a heaven...or a hell either, fer that matter."

"If you were to read your Bible you'd have that question answered for you, and a whole lot more besides."

"Well now...right there we got us two more problems. First off, I ain't got no Bible, and second off, I ain't never learnt ta read. So it wouldn't do me no good even if I did have one."

"There's other ways of learning about the Lord. I'd say your best bet would be to attend one of my services once we get settled in."

"Yeah, Preacher, I'll be sure and do that," Noah said and rolled his eyes as he turned and walked away.

The pastor sighed. "Sure is set in his ways, Ma. I'd say that's a project that needs my attention."

"I'd say so, Pa," she said, looking up at him.

He smiled down at her. "In the meantime, what say we finish meetin' the rest of these folks."

As soon as each wagon had been repaired, it was repositioned and added to the growing circle formation. When the last of the repairs had finally been made, everyone sat down to the first real hot meal they'd had in a while. After supper the main fire was started, and things were pretty much back to normal.

Heck informed everyone that they would be reaching the Arkansas sometime the next morning. This was good news to the beleaguered group of travelers, and spirits picked up considerably.

The talk around the bonfire eventually centered on the threat of future trouble from the Comanches. Nobody'd seen hide nor hair of any Indians, hostile or otherwise, all the time the repairs were being made, but that didn't mean they weren't around. Birdsong assured them that the Comanches would show themselves when it suited them and most likely not before.

꙳꙳꙳

The next morning arrived in all its glory. The sky was crystal clear, and there was not even the slightest hint of a breeze; it was promising to be a hot one. Breakfasts were made and eaten, and the dishes were dealt with while the teams were being hitched-up.

Shortly after the wagons had resumed their westward trek, to everyone's chagrin the Comanches made their presence known. They appeared almost ghostly atop small rises, from behind stands of trees and even boldly out on the open prairie. They would disappear just as quickly as they appeared, and the tactics served to keep everyone on edge.

The game of cat-and-mouse continued into the late morning until word was finally sent down the length of the train that the Arkansas had been spotted just ahead. A cheer went up, and the threat of the stalking band of Comanches was temporarily forgotten as the drivers urged their teams to a faster pace.

As they arrived at the river, the wagons were pulled into the three-abreast formation and halted along the bank. Although it was barely late morning, the decision was made to have an early lunch. Small cooking fires were built, and the womenfolk went about the task of preparing the meal while the men gathered around Heck for a briefing on what lay ahead.

Heck chewed off a fresh chaw and slipped the plug back into his shirt pocket. "I been right in this exact spot before." He paused, spit and wiped his mouth with the back of his hand. "There's about a day's push to the northwest along the river. Then she cuts west and makes a real big bend and heads kinda southwest. It'll be takin' the better part of a whole day just makin' it around that bend. Once we do git around it, we got us a decision ta stick to and might as well make it right now."

"What kinda decision?" Sam asked.

"Well, we can either head out 'cross country kinda west-southwest, or we can stay right alongside the river."

"What difference does it make which way we go?" Harry Carter asked.

"If we head out 'cross country, there's no guarantee about what the waterin' situation would be like, and—"

"How far is it across the open?" Sam asked.

"Anywhere from five to eight days, dependin'."

"On what?"

"On how fast we go, of course."

"What about keepin' to the river?" Noah asked. "What's that do fer us?"

"By stayin' along the river we add maybe a few days to the trip, but the good side is that we *know* we'll have water." Heck paused to let the options sink in. He allowed the murmurings and what-ifs to circulate and finally die down. "OK, what'll it be? You fellas wanna stick with the river, or head out 'cross country?"

Sam held up his hand for silence. "It appears to me that the most sensible thing to do would be to remain with the river. An extra few days isn't gonna make that much difference." Sam's opinion right away got the murmurings and what-ifs to going again, and he joined in, trying to make his position understood to Kyle.

Heck took charge. "Hold it down." When that didn't seem to do much good, he shouted, "I said...*shut up*!" Faces turned his way and became silent. "I know all you folks is in an all-fired hurry ta git where yer goin', but I'm here ta tell ya that I been both ways and am kinda partial ta stickin' by the river like Mr. B said. It could work out that we'd run inta plenty of water the other way, but I'm reasonin' that a sure thing is better'n a jab'n the eye with a sharp stick. I reckon I could just say which way we was goin' and be done with it, but I'd rather let you fellas decide on yer own. There's advantages ta both ways and disadvantages ta both ways. I'm fixin' ta take a vote here, and whichever way it goes I'll go along with. Does ever'one else agree ta do the same?" He looked around. "OK, good. Is ever' one of the wagons represented here?" He waited, and when it appeared that each of the wagons was indeed represented, he went on, "I'll be allowing just one vote per wagon, so you folks got about a minute ta decide which way yer wagon is votin', so get on with it." After giving them their minute, and then some, he continued, "Stretch, you do the countin'."

107 ➤

Stretch moved away from the group and sided up to Heck. He raised a hand to eye level and extended the index finger. Casting a sidewards look at Heck, he nodded as if to say, "Well, go ahead. I got my countin'-finger ready."

"All those who figger it'd be best ta head out the shorter way and risk gettin' scarce on water…raise yer hand."

Stretch carefully counted the upraised hands. When he'd decided on the total, he announced the findings, "Twelve!"

The show of hands went down.

Heck nodded. "Alright. Now, them what favor the

river way…raise 'em up."

Again Stretch made his count, starting with himself. Once he'd finished, he assumed a quizzical look. "Raise 'em up real high," he said, and started counting all over again. When he'd completed the count for the second time, he turned to Heck. "I got twelve for that way too, same's the first. That makes it a tie."

That was the signal for the arguing to start up in earnest. It was clear that there was a real problem going on here. Finally, Heck raised both arms above his head and got everyone's attention by once again shouting for them to shut up.

"Well, cain't say I didn't try ta let you fellas decide on yer own, but seein's how I didn't vote yet on one way or t'other, that'll be leavin' it up ta me ta do the decidin' after all."

"So what'll it be, Heck? Do we stick by the river, or do we head out 'cross country?" George Appleton asked.

Heck stroked thoughtfully at the stubble of gray beard with his thumb and index finger. He then lifted his hat and scratched his head. "I'm figgerin' I'll wait 'til after we make it around the big bend. Then I'll look at all aspects and decide which way is which." With all the yappin' startin' up again, he ended the meeting. "That's it fer now. Let's go eat some a them vittles what's startin' ta smell so good."

Jay had invited Mary Jane to share the meal with them. As soon as the men returned from the meeting, they made short work of the food that the two women had prepared. Jay made sure that Stretch knew that Mary Jane had helped with preparing it.

"You sure are a good cook, Mary Jane," he said, and

smiled his thanks.

"Thank you, Stretch, but I—"

Anything else she'd had a mind to say was interrupted by the dull THUD of an arrow slamming into the side of the wagon just above Stretch's head. He looked up. "What the…?"

Jay was instantly afraid. "Oh Sam," she moaned and reached out to Tom. She cradled him to her bosom and looked toward her husband with pleading eyes.

"Get under the wagon!" he shouted.

As everyone scrambled to reach the relative safety of the underside of the wagon, a blood-curdling "AIEEE!" sounded from the area along the river's edge.

CHAPTER

Twelve

It became immediately apparent that the wagons were being hit from two sides.

Sam fired at a figure over by the river. His aim was good, and the Indian threw up his arms, sending his weapons flying. He hit the ground, somersaulted and lay still. "Stretch! There's another pistol inside the wagon…just under the seat." He squeezed off another shot.

Stretch waved his thanks and scooted out from under the wagon. He headed for the front and climbed aboard as Sam watched his feet disappear above the bottom edge. After just a few seconds he reappeared with the pistol in his hand and a wide grin on his face. He ducked back under the wagon and forced Mary Jane down as close to the ground as he could get her. He held her there with a hand placed in the middle of her back as he took aim at a particularly aggressive brave. He squeezed the trigger and watched as the warrior spun around from the force of the bullet.

"Nice shot," Sam said, nodding his approval.

Stretch acknowledged him with a thin smile and a slight nod of his own.

It wasn't long before some of the other men came to join them, and it didn't take much after that for the attackers to break off and retreat to a safe distance. Things quickly settled down, and an eerie silence filled the air around them.

Sam reached out to his family and pulled them to him. He was a compassionate sort of man, and the tears welled up as he hugged them. Stretch, too, was holding Mary Jane, but his tears of relief remained on the inside.

Jacob came running right about then. "Mary Jane, you OK?"

"Yes, Pa. I'm fine," she said, then added in a soft whisper as she looked up into Stretch's eyes, "thanks to my fella here." She craned upward and kissed him softly on the cheek.

"Now that's just about enough of that sorta thing," Jacob said from behind a threatening finger. "You git yerself out from under that wagon. Why, I outta tan yer hide."

"Why? 'Cause I just kissed the fella what saved my life? I'll just bet that if you'd a seen him pluggin' that Injun that was fixin' ta git my scalp, I'd expect you'd be kissin' him yer ownself."

1 1 1
➡

"That right, boy? You save my Mary Jane?"

"Well, I—"

"Yeah, that's right," Sam said. "He darned sure did. Why, that girl of yours is lucky to be alive. That Indian was barreling down on her, and old Stretch here, just as calm as you please, took a bead on the savage and plugged him. Yessir, I'd say he saved her life alright."

A smile began to appear on Jacob's face. "That bein' the case, give him a kiss fer me, too."

Mary Jane didn't need to be told twice, and Sam grinned as she threw her arms around Stretch's neck and planted a kiss right smack dab on his lips. Sam judged that it wasn't any "Nice to see you again, Aunt Nellie" kinda kiss neither. Nosir. It was more of a "I'm truly thankful to you for savin' my life" kinda kiss.

Plus, he imagined that if a fella was to be on the inside of Mary Jane's brain right about then, he'd a found out that there was way more to the smooch than that. He figured it was probably her intention to convey the fact that it was really a "I sure do have a hankerin' to be your missus someday" kinda kiss.

When she finally pulled away and unhooked her arms from around his neck, Stretch was more'n just a little on the pinkish side. Fact is, there most likely wasn't a single redskin around that coulda held a candle to him if it came right down to deciding who was the redder.

"I…eh…" He flushed an even deeper shade. "Just doin' what I could," he managed to say, and crawled out from under the wagon, pulling Mary Jane along behind him.

As they stood before him with an arm around one another, Jacob gazed into his daughter's eyes. "Now I'd say that's showing some gratitude alright enough," he said, and spread a suspicious smile while rubbing a palm against the side of his chin. He looked at Stretch. "Fact is, me knowing my Mary Jane like I do, I'd say there was a sight more to that then just a—"

"Don't you never mind now," she cut in. "I'll be the one lettin' Stretch here know how I feel about him without you leadin' the way. You just satisfy yourself that I'm safe and sound and let it go at that while you head on back to the wagon."

Jacob started the chin-rubbin' again and allowed the hand to find its way around to the back of his neck, where he let it do some rubbin' back there as well. The grin widened. "OK," he said simply, and headed for his own wagon.

She threw her other arm around the front of Stretch's waist and hugged him tighter while snuggling the side of her face against his chest. The smile became a tearful one.

"Well now," Jay said, "it would appear that your father approves of Stretch here, although I can't for the life of me understand why."

Heck ordered the train to get under way. The lunch things were hastily packed away and the fires were hurriedly doused. He then gathered everyone together for a short meeting, during which he announced that from now on they would not stop without forming a circle. The discussion quickly deteriorated to a level of calling the Comanches vile names and accusing them of being heartless heathens with no regard for human life.

Noah was the worst of the lot. "Why, them yellow cowards even stuck a lance in my boy's leg and stole his horse. Not ta mention the fact that they left him out there overnight ta die."

113

Birdsong was hearing more than she cared to. "You do not know the Comanche!" she fired at Noah. "You cannot say these things!" She fought to hold back the tears.

"All I know is what I seen with my own two eyes. And as far as I'm concerned, they ain't worth the powder it'd take to blow 'em ta kingdom come." He was pleased to see a few nodding heads of folks that were agreeing with him. "And she ain't much better'n them that's out there," he added, feeling some safety in numbers.

"You best watch yer mouth," Wild Willie said as he came to his wife's defense. "How kin you say that when she took care a yer kin and nursed him back?"

"Just statin' a fact, is all," Noah said with a triumphant smirk. "A Injun is a Injun, plain 'n simple."

Birdsong jerked away from her husband's hold and lunged at Noah. She managed one glancing open-handed blow off the side of his face before anyone was able to catch up and restrain her.

Noah pointed accusingly at her. "See! See what I mean! They're all heathens!"

She struggled to break free, but Jack Walker had a good hold on her and didn't let go. "Just simmer down now," he said tightening his grip.

"Yeah. And that goes for you too, Pa." Everyone turned to see Wayman standing with a crutch braced under his armpit and the weight of his bad side resting on it. "You apologize to this lady here. She gave of herself and her time to see that I pulled through this mess alright, and I figger she's one heck of a good friend of mine." He hobbled forward until he was directly in front of his pa. They stood face to face for a few moments with everyone else keeping quiet and just watching to see what would happen next.

Birdsong tried again in vain to twist free.

"I ain't apologizing ta no heathen redskin, and that's the end of it. If any of you decides ta trust that Comanche woman, you ain't got the good sense God give a rock. Now—"

"Does that mean you've started believing in the Lord, Noah?" Pastor Jenks asked.

The veins were bulging in Noah's neck as he glared at the pastor. He spun angrily and headed for his wagon.

With the confrontation at an end, Birdsong began to simmer down, and Jack was able to loosen his hold

114

on her. Heck then broke things up, and everyone headed for their respective wagons. Although the air was filled with disgust and abhorrence for the way one of their own had treated Birdsong, they were all relieved to be leaving the site of the ambush.

Heck had no desire to be caught off guard again, so every man who had access to a horse, and was not needed to drive a team, was used as an outrider. Wild Willie turned their team over to Birdsong. Joshua Carter, even though he was just twelve, was big for his age, and his pa, Harry, had taught him to handle the team while they were back in Independence. So the task was turned over to the boy, and Harry joined the outriders. Danny and Ronnie borrowed a couple of horses and helped out. Despite his injury, Wayman was able to handle his pa's team and did so. That freed up Noah, who also enlisted Rip. Those driver changes upped the number of outriders to a very comfortable eleven, including Heck.

Heck assigned positions to each of 'em. There would be five on each side of the train, while he would remain free to wander from side to side as he pleased. They were instructed that if they spotted anything that even resembled a redskin, they were to shoot first and ask questions afterward.

As the train made its way along the river, an uneasiness hung over it that was thick enough to whip up a mess a biscuits out of. The smiles were gone from the faces, children were no longer allowed outside the wagons to walk alongside as had been usual, and every single wagon kept a rifle easily accessible. Conversations were kept to a minimum as the day wore on, with the travelers remaining vigilant to their surroundings.

Toward a New Beginning

Jay was doing her best to keep Tom entertained, but he was being uncooperative, and it took a lot of patience and effort on her part to finally be able to wear him down to the point where she was able to rock him to sleep in her arms. She continued to hold him the rest of the afternoon and into the early evening.

Sam had been watching her unwillingness to put the boy down and was growing increasingly concerned for her state of mind. She cradled him in her arms and rocked him to and fro while she hummed a tune, which although it was a mite familiar to Sam, he was having a time putting a name to it. "Why don't you lay him back there in the wagon bed?" he asked, tilting his head toward the area behind them.

She stopped her rocking motion and the humming as well. She smiled a weak smile. "But what if the Indians came and took him away? What would I do then?"

Sam was startled by the uncalled-for sincerity in her eyes and the earnestness in her voice. "Nothing will happen to him, Jay," he said softly, then added, "I promise."

"Are you sure?" she asked with a pleading look that for a fleeting instant made him wonder if she was losing her sanity.

"Yes, honey." He switched the cluster of reins to his left hand and placed his right arm around her shoulders. "I'm sure," he said sincerely and drew her closer to him. He vowed inwardly to ask Pastor Jenks to intervene and help him comfort her.

The wagons reached the beginning of the big bend in the river just as Heck had said they would. The drivers made short work of getting circled and making camp for the night. The evening meals were cooked over extremely small fires because it was felt that any large sources of light would only invite the Comanches to shoot arrows in that direction. The main bonfire was dispensed with that evening, and everyone except the perimeter guards retired early.

❧❧❧

"Sam? Wake up."

Despite being dead tired, he managed to open his eyes. "Yeah, what is it?"

"Time ta get up and take yer turn a watchin'," Kyle said and lowered himself down off the back of the wagon.

"I'll be right there. Just give me a couple of minutes to get my boots on and grab my rifle." He could hear Kyle walk away as he pulled his trousers-clad legs out from under the covers—all the men were sleeping with their pants on just in case the Comanches decided to attack in the middle of the night.

"Wha...what is it?" Jay asked as she rolled over. "Is Tom alright?" she asked with a startled realization that something might have happened to her baby. She popped upright and was relieved, with the help of the moonlight, to see him down by her feet, fast asleep.

"He's just fine," Sam assured her as he pulled on his boots. "I'm just getting up to go take my turn at standing guard."

"Will you bring him up here to me?"

He was puzzled by the request, but did as she asked. He vowed again to ask the pastor to have a talk with her as soon as possible.

Toward a New Beginning

Once the boy was settled in next to her, he kissed each of them on the forehead, and while touching a hand to her cheek, whispered, "I love you."

She grabbed ahold of his arm as he reached for his Sharps. "You be careful, Sam Bartlett. Don't take any unnecessary chances," she cautioned. "I'm not ready to get rid of you just yet."

He leaned over and this time kissed her on the lips. "Count on it," he said softly, and was gone.

"Kyle? Where are you?" Sam asked as he pushed the buttons through the proper holes down the front of his coat.

"Over here," came the soft reply from beside the wagon just ahead.

Sam could easily make out the figure in the bright moonlight. He covered the distance quickly. "Let's get away from here so we can talk."

Kyle nodded, and they moved away from the wagon with its sleeping occupants inside. Once they were at a safe distance, Sam asked, "How'd everything go? You hear or see anything suspicious?"

"There was a time, just a little while ago, when I was hearin' some mighty peculiar coyote howlin'."

"What'dya mean, peculiar?"

"Dunno. Just seemed a mite peculiar is all. It'd be one from one place, then one from another place, then one from another place. I dunno, just seemed peculiar that there never was any two of 'em howlin' at the same time. What would you make a sumptin' like that?"

Suddenly a coyote howled mournfully, and not too far away from the sounds of it.

"See, there it is right there," Kyle said as the two of them had turned to face the sound. "Now you just wait a few seconds, and I'll bet six bits up against a bent-up horseshoe that there'll be another one a soundin' from a different direction."

He'd no sooner gotten the words out when, sure enough, the answering howl came just as predicted.

Sam crouched slightly. "Looks like you win that bet," he whispered. "Sounds to me like those aren't coyotes. Just to be sure, let's go wake up Birdsong and see what she thinks about all this. Ain't no sense in going off half-cocked."

They made their way ahead two more wagons, and as they approached the Hawkins' wagon, she came sliding silently over the top of the tailgate.

"Good that you are here," she said as they came face to face. "I want to tell someone those not coyotes. That is Comanches telling other Comanches they will attack soon. Is good idea to make the people be awake so they not be surprised when they come to kill us when we sleep."

"Can you tell which way they'll come from?" Sam asked.

"Yes. The signals say they will attack first from over there." She pointed to the north. "Next they will come from that way." She pointed again. "Then that way." She pointed a third time.

"Thanks, Birdsong," Sam said with genuine sincerity. "OK, Kyle, you go round up the rest of the guards while we warn the folks in the wagons. Let them in on what's goin' on and have 'em all congregate over along the north side in case the Comanches decide not to wait. We'll get some of the other men to cover the other two directions. Make it quick. We don't have any idea for sure just how much time we have."

119 ➤

Toward a New Beginning

Kyle nodded and left hastily with a parting, "Gotcha."

Sam and Birdsong didn't waste any time. He went one way, and she went the other. In just a matter of a few short minutes the encampment was wide-awake, completely warned and ready for just about anything. With about two hours left 'til dawn, they waited with rifles in hand for what they now knew to be an imminent attack.

CHAPTER
Thirteen

Sam peered intently from his position behind the wheel. He noticed a flicker of movement out of the corner of his eye and jerked his head toward it. He scanned the area for anything that would verify what he thought he'd seen. He smiled knowingly as he hunkered down and rested the barrel of the Sharps between the spokes. He took careful aim and waited for the bush to move again. When it did, he squeezed the trigger. An instant after the rifle discharged, the clump gave a yelp and came to rest on its side.

"Good shot," Stretch said from his position about an arm's reach away.

"Thanks." Sam pulled the breech open and dug out the spent shell. He snatched a fresh one from the supply he'd lined up on the step, pushed it into the receiver and slammed the breech closed.

The pot-shotin' had been goin' on now for the better part of a half hour. As far as Sam could tell, no one in the train had been injured as yet. However, the Comanches were loosing warriors at a pretty good clip. Another shot rang out from over on the north side. Sam didn't take the time to look. Instead, he intensified his scrutiny of the small area he was responsible for.

The Indians had started this hide-n-seek game just after sunup. Charlie had said that it was their way of unnerving' the white men to the point of where they'd get jumpy and frazzled. When they figured the time was right, they'd attack in force. Then and only then would they know fer sure what they were up against.

Birdsong had agreed with his assessment, saying, "What Charlie say is true. Comanche will make the white men nervous. Then it will be easy for them to come and take whatever they want. Sometimes it takes a long time for this to happen. But the Comanche will always win."

The game of nerves continued for the better part of the morning. Shortly after nine or so, the Indians seemed to disappear as the area assumed an eerie quiet. After a few minutes, during which no shots had been fired, Heck and Charlie made the rounds, asking each lookout if they'd seen anything in a while. The answer was the same from each of them; no one had seen hide nor hair. Heck decided to find out from the authority on the subject just what was goin' on, so he and Charlie made their way to the Hawkins' wagon.

"What's this all about?" Heck asked as he looked into Birdsong's dark eyes.

She folded her arms in stoic reflection. "I think the Comanche are gone. I think too many are killed. I think they will wait for another time to come back."

"So you're sayin' it's most likely safe ta skedaddle outta here?" Charlie asked and, pushing his fingers up under the back of his hat, scratched the bald spot toward the rear of his head.

She unfolded her arms and gestured with a one-handed, sweeping motion. "I am say, the Comanche are no longer here, but is never safe for the white man in this country. If you want to make some tracks, then I think now is a good time." She once again folded her arms and waited.

"What'dya think Charlie? Should we give it a try?"

"'Peers ta me she outta know enough about her own people ta have a handle on how they'd act. Yeah, I figger this's as good a time as any."

"Sounds fair enough ta me. Let's get 'em hitched up and git outta here then." Heck turned toward Birdsong and touched an index finger to the folded-up front side of his hat. "Thanks, Birdsong. I'm beholdin' to ya."

Heck and Charlie spread the word that they were movin' out. Folks worked feverishly, and the train was ready to roll in near record time. The outriders were sent out with the usual orders to shoot to kill anything that moved. Charlie whipped up the lead team, and the train began to snake its way around the big bend in the river.

By late afternoon they'd completed that part of the journey, and Heck called a halt. They were now faced with a moment of truth; it was time to decide on a course of action. Heck had all the drivers meet at about midpoint in the lineup, where he once again spelled out their options. After a bit of discussion, it was decided that it made a whole lot of sense to leave the river and head out across country. That way they'd not only be able to cut a couple of days off their journey, but they'd be away from the river, which the Indians seemed to favor as a hiding place from where to launch their attacks. He reckoned that the cut across the prairie would amount to about a hundred to a hundred and ten miles, give 'er take. Of course, there was no way of knowing what their chances would be of coming across water along the way, so he ordered everyone to replenish their supply before they got underway.

123

Toward a New Beginning

The atmosphere was a solemn one as the outriders rode guard while the water barrels were being filled to overflowing. As each wagon finished stocking up on the life-sustaining liquid, it was pulled away from the river. Pastor Jenks was the last to reposition his wagon, mainly because he'd taken the time to say one of his long-winded prayers.

Once it was clear that everyone was ready, Heck waved his arm and shouted, "Let's head 'em west! And may God go with us!"

Those within earshot said a hearty "Amen," and the outriders fanned out. Charlie laid his whip out along the backs of his team and snapped it just above the ears of the left-side lead. The team strained against the harness, and the wagon lurched forward. One by one the others followed, and they headed into the vast expanse of open prairie that stretched away from the river.

Jay sat on the seat next to her husband. Her back was ramrod straight as she held her son in her lap and hugged him to her. Her mouth was set with grim defiance. She glanced down at the rifle on the floorboard. *Lord, forgive me, but I'll kill anyone who tries to take my baby,* she vowed and felt immediately ashamed for even thinking such a thing. "But it's true," she mouthed vehemently. She then pulled the boy even closer.

Sam noticed the extra attention she was again giving to Tom. "Why don't you just let him lay down in the wagon?" he asked as he saw her shift uncomfortably.

"He's doing just fine," she said without looking his way.

He decided to let it go for now, and after saying, "Suit yourself," he returned his attention to handling the team and watching out for Comanches.

The day's journey finally came to an end, and the circle was made as compact as possible. Household items were stacked in the gaps between the wagons, and sentinels were posted behind each of the fortifications. The fires were kept small, and the evening meal was eaten with a minimum of conversation. Those who stood guard had their food brought to them and ate in silent discomfort.

The strain of not knowing what the Indians would do next had taken a prodigious toll on the members of the train. Husbands and wives had begun bickering with one another, and children were becoming more unruly than usual from the effects of being cooped up.

After supper Sam decided it would be a good time to have his talk with the pastor. "I'm going to take a walk," he said as he rose from the warmth of the fire.

"You want company?" Stretch asked.

"Naw. I just wanna stretch my legs," he lied. "I won't be gone long, honey," he said to Jay. He leaned down and gave her a peck on the cheek. She showed no reaction, so he turned and headed for the pastor's wagon.

"Howdy, Pastor...Mrs. Jenks," he said as he approached the Jenks' fire.

"Hello, Sam. Out for a little walk I see."

"Yeah, you might say that...but...well...I was really needing to have a talk with you soon's your dinner's finished," Sam said as he watched the pastor push the remains of a biscuit into his mouth.

"Well then," Pastor Jenks said around the mouthful, "I'd say your timing was just about perfect, because that, sir, was the last bite of my supper." He pushed a hand against his knee and rose from the rock. He glanced behind him, and placing both hands against his backside, tried to get the circulation going again with a slight rubbing motion. "Not the most comfortable piece of dining room furniture I've ever had the pleasure of sitting on." He stopped rubbing his backside and added, "But I guess the Lord has His reasons for sending me and mine out here, and I'll just have to do the best I can with what He gives me." He looked down at Maggie. "Thank you for the meal, Ma. It was wonderful, as usual."

"You're welcome, Pa," she said and smiled appreciatively. "Now, whose turn is it to help with the cleanin' up?" she asked the semi-circle of youthful faces seated around the fire.

126

"It's mine and Mark's," John said, and reached for the stack of dirty dishes.

"Go easy on the water, boys," the pastor said.

"Yessir. C'mon, Mark, let's get 'er done." Mark scooped-up the ones that his ma and pa had used and the two boys went off to tend to their chore.

The pastor placed a gentle hand on Sam's shoulder. "Now Sam, what seems to be on your mind?"

"Let's walk," Sam said.

Once they were away from the fire, he began to explain his suspicions about the way Jay had been acting lately. The pastor listened intently as Sam told him how he'd talked her into leaving her family in New York and had carted her off to Independence. A tear welled up when he told about how he'd promised Jay faithfully that he'd take care of her and Tom if she'd agree to make the move with him.

When he'd finished, the pastor turned to face him. "You know, Sam? I think you're feeling some guilt because of placing your family in what has turned out to be harm's way." Sam opened his mouth to protest, but the pastor raised his hand between them and continued, "There's nothing wrong with feeling that way. I'm not real fond of having my family out here dodging arrows neither. But the fact remains that we *are* here, and we are now faced with finding a way to deal with it." He looked at Sam's downcast eyes. "Do you understand what I'm saying, Sam? We have to keep the faith."

Sam sighed heavily. "My wife and son are the two most important things in my life…next to God, that is," he added, remembering who he was talking to. "They're counting on me to bring them safely through this mess, and that's just what I intend to do, but in the meantime Jay could use some comforting from the Lord."

127 ➤

"Say no more. I understand fully, and you can rest assured that you're not the only one that's concerned about the condition of folk's faith around here. I've been noticing all the bickering and crossness towards the children. Tomorrow being the Lord's day, I think I'll be taking a few minutes to see if I can help get these folks back on the right track."

Sam extended a hand, and the pastor clasped it. "Thanks, Pastor. I hope you can do something for Jay before it's too late."

The pastor placed his other hand on Sam's shoulder and said, "I'll do my best, Sam."

Toward a New Beginning

The next morning was a copy of the one before, except without the Indians harassing them. The sky was clear without a speck of cloud to be found anywhere. Sam had just finished hitchin' the team and walked over to see if Stretch was in need of help.

"How you doing, Stretch? You just about got it done?" he asked as he approached the Conestoga.

"Yeah, purtnear," Stretch replied and pulled a strap through the buckle until it was as tight as it would go. Reaching for yet another strap he hesitated, then forgetting the task at hand, turned to face Sam. "Sam, I ain't one ta be nosy, but…"

"But what, Stretch? You can feel free to talk with me. Fact is you're darned near family."

"Yeah, I feel that way too, but…well…what's eatin' on Jay anyway?"

"Oh, that," Sam said wistfully. "That's something that's needing some attention alright. I think she's afraid for young Tom and is having a hard time dealing with those fears."

"So what're we gonna do about it? We cain't just let it keep on the way it is. I don't know if you've noticed the difference or not, but that breakfast she fixed this morning weren't fit for a—"

"Yeah, I know. I had me a talk with Pastor Jenks last night, and he says most all the folks in the train are acting kinda intense about things as well. He says he's gonna try his level-headed best to give 'em a sermon this morning that'll maybe get 'em back on the right track."

"Boy, I sure hope so. Many more meals like the one

we just had, and I'll be needin' ta marry-up with Mary Jane just so's I can get enough vittles in me ta keep from dryin' up and blowin' away."

Sam chuckled. "Hopefully we can get things straightened out before it gets to that point. But to look at you, I'd say you're in a whole lot better shape right now than you were a few weeks ago when we started this trip."

"That's exactly what I'm talkin' about." He patted his stomach. "These few pounds I've put on are settin' real good with me, and I'm figgerin' on hangin' onto 'em."

They both chuckled this time and returned to the business of completing the task of harnessing the team.

As each group completed the things necessary to get ready for the day's journey, they brought their Bibles and collected in the center of the circle. Guards were left posted on all four sides of the encampment with a request that the pastor preach loud enough for them to hear as well. Noah had no desire to listen to any hypocrite preachin' and volunteered to be one of the guards, saying he didn't much care if the preachin' was loud, soft or not at all.

Once everyone was present, Pastor Jenks stood quietly at the head of the congregation and scanned the faces before him. He was in no hurry and took the time to gaze into the eyes of each one present. He lingered for an especially long time on those of Judith Bartlett. Once he had everyone fidgeting and wondering what was going on, he said, "Let us pray."

Folks bowed their heads and again waited for the pastor to continue.

Finally, the words came. "Dear Lord, before You

stands a flock of frightened children… .Your children. As You can see, they are in need of encouragement and understanding as to why You sent them out here in the face of these dangers."

Sam tightened his arm around Jay's waist and was pleased to feel a slight response from her.

Pastor Jenks continued, "There are times in our lives, Lord, when we feel as though You've forsaken us, but…" He paused and raised his gaze. "Everyone look up here at me," he said. They all did as instructed. "But that time is not now. Does each and every one of you accept that?"

Jay started to speak, but decided against it and instead let the tears begin to flow.

"Because if you don't, then you might as well admit that you have no faith in what God is about. He is all-powerful, almighty and all-seeing. He knows you're here, and He also knows you are His children. If you don't accept that, then you might just as well renounce your Christianity."

The only sound Sam could hear was a fly buzzing around his ear. He brushed at it.

The pastor bowed his head, and the rest followed his example. He waited a good while, then said, "Yea, though I walk through the valley of the shadow of death, I will fear no evil: for Thou art with me; Thy rod and Thy staff they comfort me." He paused as those wonderful words of encouragement from the Twenty-third Psalm gripped every heart present. "Amen," he said softly and raised his gaze.

Jay let Tom down to the ground and Sam felt an elbow nudge into his side. He looked in that direction and came face to face with the grin on Stretch's face.

Stretch patted his stomach and the grin grew even wider.

Sam was thankful that the Lord had sent this man of God to join their train. He felt even more thankful as he felt Jay slide her arm around his waist. He looked down at her and thumbed a tear from her cheek as he mouthed the words, "I love you."

Pastor Jenks then resumed the meeting by preaching a sermon on the joys of being fulfilled through believing in Jesus Christ and that all things are possible when a person is a child of God. He stressed that peace of mind came only through understanding that God does not give His children a task or a situation that is too big or too intense for them to handle.

After listening to the blessing that the pastor had bestowed on them, Sam and Jay returned to their wagon with an arm wrapped around each other's waist and little Tom tagging along on his own two feet.

131

The wagons headed out toward the unknown once again, but this time Sam felt a reassurance that he was no longer fighting this battle on his own. His beloved wife was at his side once again.

The day proved to be a long one for the travelers. There was no stopping for the midday meal. Whatever eating was done was done while the wheels continued to roll westward.

When dusk finally did come to the prairie, the weary travelers had made almost 21 miles despite their late start. Folks ate their evening meal in relative silence, and after the guard situation had been laid out for the night, everyone else turned in.

Sam was dead tired and almost immediately fell into a deep sleep.

CHAPTER

Fourteen

Sam heard a faint scratching coming from somewhere beneath the wagon and figured it was a mouse looking for his breakfast. He shivered against the early morning chill and pulled the covers up under his chin. A coyote sounded its woeful call from somewhere off in the distance. He smiled at the realization that it was indeed a real coyote this time. He lowered the blanket, swung his legs out from under it and shivered again. He looked over at Jay, pleased to see that she was sleeping soundly. He pulled aside the rear flap and took in the hint of gray along the eastern horizon.

He glanced at the Conestoga as a shuffling from within reached his ears. He located his boots, pulled them on and found his shirt. He quickly put it on, covered it with his coat, grabbed his hat and made his way to the rear of the wagon. He quietly worked his way over the tailgate and lowered himself to the ground. Tom twisted, squirmed and finally turned over as Sam let the flap close behind him. He waited a few seconds to see if the boy would awaken. When he was sure that Tom continued his sleep, he headed for the fire pit and went about the business of kindling the morning fire.

By the time Stretch emerged from the Conestoga and joined him, the fire was good-sized and licking at the morning crispness. Stretch reached out to the flames. "Mornin'. Bit on the cool side this fine mornin'," he said cheerfully. "Might be a tolerable day for a wagon ride."

"Mornin', Stretch. You seem to not have any cares this morning."

"Just an Injun or two tryin' ta take my scalp is all. Other'n that..." He turned around and bent over, giving his backside all the chance it needed to get the beneficial aspects afforded by the flames. Satisfied that he was fast approaching toasty, he straightened up and, while rubbin' in the warmth, turned to face Sam. It was then that he realized that Sam was preoccupied with something other than the heat from the fire. "You see something out there?"

"Dunno just yet, might be," Sam said. He took a couple of tentative steps toward his wagon, and then stopped and squinted into the dawn. "Might wanna go get your rifle," he said softly.

Stretch headed for the Conestoga while Sam continued to the front of the schooner. He reached under the front seat and pulled the Sharps from its usual spot. He grabbed a handful of shells from the small box on the floorboards and stuffed them into his coat pocket. He reached for another handful just as a muffled moan reached his ears. He turned toward the sound and was able to make out the vague outline of a figure as it crumpled to the ground about 20 or 30 yards ahead. An uneasy shiver ran up his spine.

133

"Jay, wake up," he hissed into the wagon, then crouched behind the wheel for whatever little cover it afforded.

"Wha...what is it?" she asked sleepily.

"I think the Comanches are back. Keep your head down and watch out for Tom. Stay inside 'til I find out what's going on," he whispered hoarsely.

"Please be careful."

He remained bent over while he made his way toward where he'd seen the guard go down. As he drew near, he saw the figure attempt to rise and then fall back with a groan. "Stay down," he warned. He swallowed the lump in his throat as he continued to ease forward. Suddenly, a slight movement caught his eye. He froze and peered intently until he saw the movement again. Just behind the front wheel of a nearby wagon was another figure lying in the grass. He raised the Sharps and pulled the trigger.

The Comanche grunted and rolled over as the slug ended his days of raiding wagon trains.

"Forgive me, Lord," Sam said as he dug out the spent shell. He hastily loaded in another casing and made his way to the downed guard while the rest of the camp sprang to life. He knelt beside the figure and saw that it was Wild Willie. There was an arrow protruding from his midsection.

"Danged redskin got me when I weren't lookin," he said. He winced as a pain hit the wounded area. "Prop me up against that wheel over yonder and git on about yer bizness. I might be able ta pluck one or two of 'em off while I still got some pluckin' abilities left in me."

Sam felt sorry for his friend, but didn't argue. He got a good hold under his arms and dragged him to the nearby wheel where he sat him upright facing the inside of the circle.

Willie smiled through the pain and tipped his hat with the barrel of his pistol. He pulled his knife and rested it across his thighs. "Go give 'em hell," he said and shuddered his way through another spasm. He coughed and a red trickle appeared at the corner of his mouth.

"May God bless you, Bill Hawkins," Sam said softly and turned away.

He hadn't noticed until now and was surprised to realize that the camp was full of the sounds of yelling, screaming Indians mixed in with sporadic gunfire. He heard a scream, and instantly picked it out as belonging to Jay. He whirled and caught a glimpse of a figure disappearing into the front of their wagon. Panic stricken, he sprinted to the schooner, jumped onto the hub and climbed onto the seat. He pulled his knife and jerked aside the flap. Right in front of him was the naked back of a Comanche brave. Without a second thought, he plunged the blade in as far as it would go.

The Indian started to slump forward, but Jay raised a bare foot to his chest and pushed with all her might. He somersaulted backward over the seat and continued to the ground as Sam shuffled to get out of the way.

135 ➤

"You and Tom alright?"

"Yeah," she replied and brushed a fallen lock from in front of her eyes. "Where's your pistol?" she asked.

"Right here under the seat." He reached down and retrieved it. "Here, keep it handy. I'll be back just as soon as I can. In the meantime...stay put." He stayed just long enough to see her check the load. He felt thankful that he'd taken the time to instruct her in its use.

In his haste, he nearly fell off the wagon, but he managed to regain his balance as he reached the ground. He glanced at the Comanche at his feet, then looked out from the circle to where he spotted a naked figure hunkered down and coming in. He raised the Sharps and squeezed off a shot. The attacker progressively crouched lower and lower until he just kinda tipped over and lay still.

In the meantime Stretch was havin' troubles of his own.

"Stretch! Help me...Stretch!" Mary Jane hollered hysterically as a Comanche brave wrapped his arms around the upper part of her legs and hefted her up onto his shoulder. "Help me, Stretch!" she hollered again as she beat on the brave's back with her tiny fists.

"Mary Jane!" Stretch yelled and headed toward where he figured the plea had come. "Mary Jane! Where are you?" His heart raced as he rounded the corner of a wagon. His worst fears were realized as he spied a Comanche brave running away from the circle with her draped over his shoulder. "Mary Ja—" Blackness enveloped him as the tip of a Comanche arrow grazed his scalp, knocking him out cold.

Sam had seen the Indian overtake Mary Jane, heft her onto his shoulder and disappear between the wagons. He saw Stretch run to her aid, and feeling as though everything was under control, he returned his attention to the fight at hand. He took out another intruder just as the Indian was about to grab up one of the Hendricks' kids.

The battle raged for only about five or six minutes, yet it seemed more like hours. Finally, things eased up as the Indians retreated and disappeared behind a rise in the prairie. A lingering report could be heard as someone mistakenly figured he could make good on a long-distance shot. Once the gunfire had ceased all together, the moaning and wailing for the dead and injured took over.

Sam helped Jay and Tom down from the wagon and hugged them to him, thankful that they were safe. "You two OK?" he asked.

"We're fine. Let's go see where we can help out."

They went to where he had left Willie. As they approached, she shielded Tom's eyes from the sight. Sam was distressed to see two more arrows sticking out of his chest. He was slumped over, almost lying on his side. Four Indian braves were sprawled in front of him. One was lying across his legs with the knife stuck in his chest and Willie's hand still holding onto it. Sam checked the load in Willie's pistol that lay in the grass beside him. It was empty. It was plain to see that he had given a good account of himself before giving up the ghost.

Sam brushed a thumb and index finger downward **137** across the unseeing eyes, closing off the sightless stare of death. "Rest easy, my friend," he said solemnly.

They turned away from Willie's remains and crossed the circle toward the Greenberg wagon. They were disheartened by the sight of the dead and wounded as they passed them by. Jack Walker lay in a pool of blood, a tomahawk lodged savagely in his scalp. Wayman Baxter's wounded leg had busted open and was bleeding profusely. Heck had taken an arrow in the upper portion of his left arm, but seemed to be handling it well enough. He'd broken it off to no more than just a stub and was doing his best to comfort those who had been less fortunate. The arm dangled uselessly at his side with the blood dripping off his fingertips.

Birdsong was just about the closest thing the train had to a doctor, and she was doing her best to patch up those she could. Sam slowed as they approached her. She was applying a flat, square compress to a gushing head wound on the side of Harry Carter's head. "You will push tight against this," she told Harry and placed his hand against the bandage. She picked up a strip of cloth and carefully tied it around the wounded head. "You will not move. You will sit here," she told him and pointed at the ground. Harry nodded but didn't speak. She rose, turned and came face to face with Sam.

"Birdsong, I…Willie's…"

"Where is my man?" she asked, reading the remorse in his eyes. "Where is—?"

Sam pointed. "He's over there," he said softly and placed a gentle hand on her arm.

She looked up at him as a cloud of foreboding shrouded her.

"He's gone," he said with heartfelt tenderness.

She closed her eyes and stood quietly, allowing the full impact of the simple statement to enter into her. She swayed slightly and mumbled some words in her native tongue. A small blue and gray bird lit on the very tip-top of a nearby clump of brush and rattled off its song of life. Once she heard the delightful song, her spirit was at ease with the tragedy, and she allowed her eyes to open. "Did he die bravely?" she asked and looked into his eyes for the truth.

"Yeah, he sure did. You'll see that when you go over there."

Satisfied that he had spoken truthfully, she said simply, "Today I will make him pretty. Tomorrow I will light him on fire." She turned and slowly walked away toward the gruesome scene that awaited her.

Sam put his arms around Jay and his son as they stood together and watched her go. "She sure is a strong woman," he said and pulled them closer.

Pastor and Mrs. Jenks were also doing their best to comfort those who needed it, which was just about everyone. A true accounting of the extent of the damage would be some time in coming.

They reached the Greenberg wagon just as Mabel finished wrapping Jacob's right arm in a near-white piece of cloth she'd torn from one of her petticoats. "You alright?" Sam asked.

"Yeah, I'll get by." He glanced around. "Where's Mary Jane...and Stretch?"

"Last I seen 'em one a them heathens was hauling her off and Stretch was hot after him, over there between those wagons." Sam pointed.

"Are you saying he never came back?"

Sam was instantly fearful of the possibility that Stretch had been killed and Mary Jane was gone. "You stay here," he said to Jay. "I'll go see what I can see."

He expected the worst as he proceeded to the area where he'd last seen Stretch. He breathed a sigh of relief as he turned the corner between the two wagons and spied the boy sitting up in the grass holding a hand to his head. "You alright?" he asked as he knelt beside him.

Stretch looked around with a dazed, confused expression. "I dunno. What happened?"

"That's a good question. Last I seen, you were high-tailing it after a Comanche that had Mary Jane slung over his—"

"Mary Jane!" Stretch jerked his head around, trying to look in every direction at once. "Mary Jane!" he said again and attempted to get up. The effort sent a sharp pain shooting through his wounded scalp, and he fell back to earth. "Owww. What happened to my head?" His hand once again found the wounded area, and he explored it with tentative fingertips. He pulled the hand away and inspected it. His fingers were covered with blood. He looked up at Sam. "Am I hurt bad?"

Sam bent over and inspected the gash. "Don't look too bad. Might need some bandaging, but I think you'll live. C'mon, I'll help you up."

As Sam assisted him to his feet, the youngster's concern once again turned to Mary Jane, "Where's Mary Jane anyways?"

"Near as I can figure she got hauled off by them Comanches."

"But that can't be. It just can't be." He grabbed Sam by his shoulders and continued the plea, "Sam…we gotta go after her. We can't just let her go." He crumpled back to the ground and sobbed his anguish. "It's all my fault. I shoulda been there when she was in need. I let her down." He raised his tear-streaked face to the heavens and prayed in earnest for the first time in his entire life, "God, watch over her and keep her alive 'til I can find her." He lowered his gaze and pulled his shirttail from out of his trousers and wiped the tears. "I'll find her, Sam. With or without yer help, I'll find her."

Sam was nearly overcome by Stretch's genuine sincerity. "It'll be *with* my help, Stretch. I promise I'll help you get her back. But in the meantime we gotta deal with what went on here." He then told Stretch about the severity of the attack and about those that he knew of who'd been either killed or wounded. His voice quivered as he told of Wild Willie and his fight to the very end.

"How are the Greenbergs dealin' with Mary Jane's bein' gone?" Stretch asked.

"I don't think they understand yet that the Indians took her."

Stretch closed his eyes momentarily and sighed a deep sigh. "Well then, I reckon I got a duty to let 'em know," he said resolutely.

"I think that'd be a good idea. In the meantime, I'm gonna go see if I can help get some of these folks back on their feet. I imagine that after things settle down, we'll be having a meeting to decide our options and how we're gonna handle things."

"I'll come look ya up after I deal with Mary Jane's ma 'n pa, but I don't need no meetin' ta tell me what I'll be doin'."

141 ━▶

Sam slowly nodded his understanding.

The toll on the wagon train had been significant, but Sam had already seen the worst of it. There were numerous bumps and bruises, and a few more cuts and scrapes, but the only two fatalities had been Willie and Jack Walker. Although many were wounded, none of the injuries were thought to be life threatening, except maybe Harry Carter's head wound. It all depended on how well they could keep it from bleeding or getting infected.

Once the wounded had been bandaged and Jack was laid to rest in a shallow grave, Heck called a meeting to figure their next move. Folks had tried to talk Birdsong into letting them bury Willie right along with Jack but she was set on cremating him.

The meeting got under way with everyone present

except for two men who were posted to stand watch against the direction the Comanches had chosen when they'd pulled back.

Heck's arm was tied up in a sling, and the blood was showing through the cloth as he started to speak, "Looks like we got us a passel a trouble lookin' us straight in the eye. We got two dead, a sight more'n just a few folks wounded, and four young'uns missin'; Mary Jane Greenberg, Charlette Hendricks, Josh Carter and the pastor's youngest, John, and ain't none a that ta be taken lightly."

"So, what're we gonna do about gettin' our kids back?" Jacob asked.

Heck exhaled heavily. "I wish I could say we're just gonna run right out there and fetch 'em back, but that would not only be foolish, but most likely life-endin' as well. Them Injuns is on their home grounds and got a real big advantage over us. In the first place, we don't even know if they're still around and are gonna attack again, or if they done high-tailed it outta here and are miles away by now."

The meeting broke down temporarily as small groups of dissenting voices became prominent and each group tried in its own way to solve the mystery of what the Comanches were doing at that very moment.

"So when do you reckon we'll be knowing if they're still around or not and when will we be going after Mary Jane and the others?" The question came from Stretch, and everyone agreed with it openly.

Heck pondered his options for a few moments as folks waited for his answer. "Now that's most likely the easiest question I've been asked in a coon's age, Stretch. The answer is a plain and simple...*I don't know.*"

142

"What'dya mean, you don't know?" Jacob asked, the agitation evident in his expression as well as his tone. "That's my little girl out there. She ain't done nothin' ta be hauled off by them savages. Why...there ain't no tellin' what kinda abuse she'll be put through. She's—"

"Yers ain't the onlyest young'un out there, Jacob," Kyle Hendricks interrupted. "There's some others of us what's got a stake in this as well. My baby young'un's right beside a yourn. That means I'll be lookin' fer answers my ownself, but givin' Heck a hard time ain't gonna get it done." He looked around, and his expression conveyed the despair that was in his heart. His tone lessened in intensity as he continued, "I imagine the pastor and poor old Harry, with his cut-up head, is lookin' fer answers they ownselves. I reckon 'bout all we kin do right now would be ta trust in the Almighty and see what kinda hand He deals us."

There was a general chorus of agreement.

Pastor Jenks spoke after things had settled down again, "My son John is a good Christian boy, just as I'm sure the others who were taken are good Christians as well. They all know enough to trust in the Lord and put their faith in His hands. He will care for them until such time as we're able to launch a reasonably thought-out mission of our own to rescue them. In the meantime, we have no choice but to do as Brother Hendricks says and trust in the Lord to watch over them. If we run out chasing after them in a half-cocked manner...well, chances are we'll be food for the scavengers before the day is done. With that in mind, does anyone think they have a more reasonable way of approaching the problem?"

Toward a New Beginning

"They are safe." The words were soft and reassuring. As everyone looked toward the sound of the voice, Birdsong stepped out into the inner part of the circle. "They will not be hurt," she repeated.

"How can you say that?" Noah asked and rose from his haunches. "Far as I'm concerned you ain't no better'n them what just kilt some a our folks. Seems ta me—"

Birdsong fired an icy stare at the white man as she cut him off, "Some of our folks was my man. Some of our folks was my husband. These Comanche are not my people. My people are Comanche, too, but are of the northern tribe." She waved an arm in a sweeping motion that encompassed just about everything other than the south. "My people live in peace beside the Lakota Sioux. These Comanche are Penateka and live to the south. My people do not steal women and children. My people are not cowards who sneak in the night and kill without warning." She paused and bowed her head before continuing with an obviously heavy-hearted remorse, "My man is gone. I now have no more reason to continue this journey. I will help to find the children. If I die, I do not care. My man is gone. But you must understand I am not of the Penateka, but I know of their ways. These children will be kept in good health and will not suffer beatings. They are for buying things from other tribes. If a child is not kept unharmed, he will not be worth much in a trade."

The silence that followed was deafening.

Jay pushed between the two men in front of her. "I would think there's been enough accusations piled on this woman. She has just lost her husband, who, by the way, died protecting each and every one of you. Now if you, Noah Baxter," she pointed an accusing finger at him, "had any semblance of a brain in that thick skull of yours, you would realize that there's only been one perfect human being on this earth, and that was the Lord Jesus. Just because a person has red skin, black skin or brown skin doesn't give you the right to lump that person into a pot with all the others you don't like…for whatever reason."

Noah shifted his weight from one foot to the other and darted his eyes from one face to the next, looking for a sympathetic eye. He didn't find one. Not even from either of his own sons.

Jay smiled as she addressed what she saw, "Peers to me that you might be having some second thoughts about being an all-out bigot, that right? The best way you have of redeeming yourself is to understand that this young woman is ready to sacrifice herself for those that she considers her friends." She looked at Birdsong, reached out to her and brushed a lock of black hair back off her face. "She's willing to give of herself the same as Jesus did when He died for all us sinners. And you know something else, Noah Baxter? I'll just bet that if one of your boys had been taken in the raid, she'd be willing to help rescue him as well, although I can't for the life of me imagine why."

No one spoke as the truth in her words touched everyone present, even Noah. Every face was on his as he rested his gaze on Birdsong. "I'm sorry, I guess I just—"

His apology was cut short by the sound of a rifle shot.

"Here they come again!"

145

CHAPTER

Fifteen

This time around, as the men defended the train, they had a new incentive. Their children were the main targets of the Indians, and that just didn't set none-too-well with them or their wives. The women remained beside their husbands and kept the extra guns loaded so they could keep up a steady fire.

One of the wagons had been pulled well inside the circle, away from the others so the younger children could be hidden away. At the very height of the battle Tom had decided to stick his head out through the rear flap to see what was going on. A particularly aggressive Comanche had made it through the perimeter defenses, and seeing the boy peeking out, headed for the sought-after prize.

Stretch was down on one knee behind the Conestoga with Ronnie doing his reloading. He pulled off a shot and was disappointed to see that he'd missed. He cursed under his breath and reached for a freshly loaded rifle. As he turned his head to locate it, his peripheral vision picked up the movement of a figure running away from the center of the circle. The fleeing Indian held a kicking, screaming child in his arms. Visions of Mary Jane whisked across his mind. He jumped up, dropped the rifle, snatched the pistol from his waistband and began running as fast as he could. He covered the ground quickly, gaining on the culprit with each stride.

The Indian halted, dropped his prize and turned to face the oncoming threat.

Stretch didn't slow none and barreled into the Comanche. The few extra pounds he'd put on served him well and his momentum sent the both of them tumbling. Although still dazed, he recovered enough to work his way onto one knee while he shook his head, attempting to clear the cobwebs. As his vision cleared he saw that his opponent was pulling a knife.

The Indian glared with icy hatred, screamed and lunged. Stretch dove to the side, narrowly missing being cut. He rolled in the grass, and just as the Indian gathered himself to pounce, he remembered the pistol he had managed to keep ahold of. He pointed it and pulled the trigger three times in rapid succession. The Comanche collapsed not more than three feet away, and Stretch grinned his relief as he watched the wounded Comanche writhing in pain.

147

The youngster had begun to cry. Stretch glanced at him and saw that it was Tom who'd nearly been taken. This enraged him all over again, and he glared with loathing as he stuck the barrel of the pistol up the Indian's left nostril and eased back the hammer.

"Don't do it," Jay said from behind him. "He's already done for and Tom's alright, thanks to you."

"If I'd a knowed it was Tom he was makin' off with, I'd a kilt him 'bout three times by now."

"Thankfully, that won't be necessary. You best get on back to the main fight. I'll watch this heathen until this is all over."

Stretch still had the barrel of the pistol shoved up the Indian's nose. He gave it a push and watched the unwavering defiance in the fella's eyes. He figgered that he wasn't gonna get him to cow-down, and that Jay was right. He eased the hammer down and rocked back on his haunches.

"Now, give me that pistol and go help Sam," she said softly and reached out for it.

"Yes, ma'am," he said meekly, handed it to her and rose.

The fighting hadn't slowed much, so he headed off at a good-paced run. He slid to a stop on his knees beside Sam, picked up the rifle lying in the grass and pulled open the breech. "I'll load...you do the shootin'," he said, and after pushing in a fresh shell, slammed the breech down and handed it to Sam.

He drew a bead. "Nice job you did back there."

"Yeah, but I wish I'd a done the same for Mary Jane this morning."

Sam pulled the trigger.

148   "Nice shot," Stretch said as he accepted the spent breech-loader. "Where's Ronnie?" he asked, looking around.

"Don't know. I expect that after you left he went off to help his pa, leastways that's the way he headed." Sam squeezed off another shot and squinted his consternation at having missed.

The fighting lasted for just about five or six minutes—same as before—but this time the wagon train took only minor casualties. The gray mare that had been a member of Stretch's team, and in foul, took an arrow in the neck and had to be put down. And the newlywed, Fay Appleton, took an arrow in the folds of her petticoats. The women had a time locating and dislodging it, but once they did, other than having a small hole in the front of her dress, she was none the worse for wear.

The brave that Stretch had taken down turned out

to be a real ornery cuss. Even though he'd pulled off three shots at the man, there was just a single hole in the upper part of his right leg. Whenever someone tried to have a look at it, he would get belligerent and refuse to cooperate. Finally, they called for Birdsong to come and have a look-see.

As the prisoner watched her approach, his expression grew puzzled. She set the basket on the ground and loomed over him with her hands on her hips. She looked down with an expression of disgust. Seeing her attitude toward him infuriated him to the point of attempting to rise and put her in her place.

She pointed at him, and while looking at George Appleton, who'd been assigned to guard the prisoner, said, "You make him to sit."

George grabbed ahold of the rising Indian and pulled him back down, and none too gentle neither.

149

The fella glared at him and snarled something in Comanche.

George just smiled back and tipped his hat while he waited for Birdsong to take charge.

She then spoke in Comanche. "You will sit and keep quiet."

"Squaws do not tell a warrior what to do!" he snarled back at her.

"This one does. You will do as I tell you, or I will let you die from your wound."

He did not respond to this unexpected reply and remained silent as she knelt and began to examine his leg. He winced as she touched the wounded area.

"It is good that it hurts. You steal children…it is good that you pay for this with much pain."

"Why do the white-eyes not let me die? Why do

they send a woman to care for my wound?"

"I do not know," she said simply and busied herself with applying a remedy from the basket.

He watched as she deftly applied some herbs, and then wrapped a cloth around the thigh. "Why does a Comanche live with these white-eyes?" he asked when she had finished.

"My man was a white-eyes."

"Where is your man?"

"He was killed in the attack this morning," she said solemnly. Grief stricken, she turned and walked away.

The rest of that day was spent watching and waiting, watching for any sign of movement outside the circle and waiting for yet another attack. Toward evening, a lone rider appeared on the northern horizon, just beyond what would be considered effective rifle range. He sat motionless on his pony with a feather-festooned war lance propped atop his thigh and sticking straight up into the evening sky. He remained even after his image had faded from view in the falling darkness.

Birdsong had spent the afternoon dressing her man in his finest clothes in preparation before sending his spirit skyward in the morning. She'd finished with the ritual just after the sentinel had appeared to the north.

Sam arrived at her wagon just as she was putting the finishing touches on Willie. "He sure looks pretty," he said while looking at Willie's neatly parted, slicked-down hair. He'd remembered that she'd said she would make him pretty today and light him on fire tomorrow, so he just naturally figured that "pretty" was what she wanted to hear.

"Yes," she said softly. "He is pretty and is now ready

to go home to be with his ancestors. He will start the journey as the sun rises. He will rise with the smoke and travel with the sun as it makes its journey across the sky."

Sam waited patiently while she traced the lines on her man's face with a gentle fingertip. He felt that she was reliving some good times spent with him. Finally, she returned to the present with a slight jarring.

"You loved him, didn't you?" he asked.

"Yes, he was a good man."

"I will help you in the morning to send him on his journey."

"Thank you. Is good. I will let you."

He felt a need to change the subject and asked, "You see that Indian fella sitting his horse over there?" He pointed toward the sentinel.

151

"Yes, I see."

"Do you have any idea what he's doing out there?"

"Yes, I know."

Sam didn't push her. Instead he waited for her to straighten Willie's collar. Finally, she rose. "Come," she said. "I will tell you."

They walked slowly with no particular destination in mind. She seemed melancholy, and rightfully so Sam decided.

"This brave," she indicated the rider to the north, "is looking to see the spirit of someone."

"What'dya mean?"

"When someone is lost who is a very important member of the tribal council, another someone who is very close to his family must watch the place where he became lost. He must watch until he sees his spirit rise or he finds the lost one's body."

"You mean like a chief or something?"

She nodded. "It could be a mighty chief, a lesser chief or even a medicine man, but someone will be there until the wagons have gone and the body is found."

"Does that mean they won't attack anymore?"

"No. They will continue to attack until they have what they want."

"And just what might that be?"

"I think they want more of the children, but I am not sure. Maybe I can find this answer from the captured one."

Sam nodded. "Might not be such a bad idea to try."

She glanced toward his wagon. "You will go now to be with your family. I go to my wagon to be with my man and prepare some food for the captured one." She turned and was gone.

Sam returned to his wagon. Jay had fixed a hurried meal, and it was eaten just as hurriedly. Neither he nor Stretch wanted to be caught unawares and accepted the meager meal of cold biscuits and warmed-over beans as part of the price they had to pay. They polished off the meal and wasted no time as they returned to their lookout positions.

Birdsong gathered together some jerky and dried cornmeal cakes, which she placed in a small basket. She also put in some bandages. Satisfied, she went back to the prisoner.

By the time she arrived, the darkness was nearly complete, but she was still able to make out the guard standing nearby. "Would you please find some sticks to burn in a fire?" she asked. "I have bandages for his wound and some words to speak to this prisoner. I have need of the light from a small fire."

Danny had taken over for George. "You figger this skunk's worth buildin' a fire for?" he asked. "His low-down thievin' friends took my sister and most likely ain't lettin' her have the warmth of a fire tonight. Why, they probably ain't even feedin' her, neither."

"She will be treated well," Birdsong assured him. "They will not harm her."

She waited patiently while he decided whether or not to believe her.

"Yeah, I'll just bet," he said sarcastically and stomped off to find some firewood.

She watched him go, and then turned her attention to the Penateka warrior. "How is your wound?" she asked, placing the basket in the grass at his side.

"Ummm," he grunted and glanced at the basket.

His slight interest confirmed that he was indeed hungry. "I have brought food," she said.

He eyed her. "I will eat," he said simply.

"We will wait for the fire to be made, then I will share your meal," she said and looked in the direction Danny had taken. She changed the subject, "Was a chief lost today?"

"Yes," he replied quickly, then added, "Me."

"You are a chief?"

Now it was his turn to change the subject, "What tribe is your people?" he asked, knowing a true Comanche would never turn down an opportunity to brag about his or her tribe.

"I am of the northern tribe," she said. "My people are—"

"This is 'bout all I could come up with," Danny said and lowered his arms, letting the sticks roll off.

153

Toward a New Beginning

❦❦❦

It was getting late and the light of day was fading rapidly. Mary Jane watched through the slit as a fat woman approached, carrying what looked like some long-awaited food.

She quickly drew away from the opening and settled in a spot just as the flap flew open and the woman entered. She extended the flat pieces of bark and uttered something that none of the children could make out, but the meaning was plain enough.

Mary Jane accepted the two crude plates and passed one to the boys. The other she kept for her and Charlette to share. They all ate hungrily.

"This here stuff ain't half bad," Josh said around a mouthful of dried bread. "Better'n what Ma makes sometimes." He gnawed off a chunk of meat. "Why, I'll just bet—"

"That ain't no way ta be a talkin' 'bout yer ma," Charlette drawled through misty eyes. "You'd most likely be sayin' different if'n ya was ta lose her ferever." The misty eyes changed to tear-filled ones. She sobbed noisily as the two boys kept right on stuffing their faces.

"There, there now," Mary Jane said as she placed a consoling arm around Charlette's shoulders and pulled her to her. "You'll be back with your folks soon's the men of the train come and rescue us."

"Do ya reckon?" The question was more of a woeful plea than a question. "I don't know what my kin would do if I was ta be kilt by the Injuns. Boy...that no-account brother a mine would surely be sorry that he always called me his snot-nosed, heathen, brat sister. Bet he'd never call me that ever again." She wiped the palms of her hands across her cheeks and sighed her despair.

"Course not, 'cause then you'd be his *dead*, snot-nosed, heathen, brat sister," Josh said and tried his best to elbow a grin out of John.

But John was busy stuffing his mouth full of grub and didn't respond the way he would've liked. Nosir, just one little twitch at the corner of his mouth was about it.

"I'd say that's just about enough out of you, Mr. Ignoramus," Mary Jane said. "Can't you see that she's scared half to death and misses her ma 'n pa?"

John looked at Josh and said, "And not ta mention that it's just plain unchristian ta make fun a her, just 'cause she loves her ma 'n pa and you don't."

"Now, that ain't true. I love my ma 'n pa same's anyone. I just don't see no reason ta cry over spilt milk. We got us a predicament here that cryin' ain't gonna fix. It'll take more of a —"

"Shhh!" Mary Jane warned. "Someone's coming."

Fear surrounded them as the flap flew open. An Indian man ducked inside and looked into the frightened faces of the captives. In his hand he carried several lengths of rawhide. He centered his gaze on Josh and grunted something in an impatient manner that made it sound like an order. He grabbed Josh by the arm, spun him around and thrust him roughly to the dirt floor of the teepee.

Josh began to cry.

The Indian pulled the boy's hands together behind his back and bound them tightly. Next, he tied his feet. While Josh continued his blubbering, the Indian tied the three remaining captives, hand and foot. Once he'd finished, he inspected his handiwork with a tug here and there and grunted his satisfaction at each favorable inspection. He then made his way to the exit and, after casting a backward glance, snorted and ducked through.

Once the crunching footsteps had died away, an acute awareness of their situation overcame any composure that remained. John and Charlette lost it and began to cry. Mary Jane too wanted to cry as the hopelessness of their plight engulfed her. The tears welled up. She fought to keep them in, but finally lost the battle as they overflowed and ran down her cheeks. She closed her eyes and thought of her family.

CHAPTER

Sixteen

The sticks were dry and caught hold quickly. While Danny piled on more kindling, Birdsong rummaged through the basket and removed the food she'd brought. Once the fire was going strong and the food had been all laid out, she held a piece of hardtack out to Danny. He was hungry and smiled his appreciation before accepting it.

"I have food for the prisoner as well," she said. "Will you untie his hands?"

"You reckon that's a good idea?"

"Yes, it is a good idea. He must eat. His feet will remain tied to the wheel. He cannot run."

Danny nodded and clamped the biscuit between his teeth. He reached around behind the prisoner and loosened the bindings. He then squatted beside the blazing fire and went back to eating his biscuit.

The Comanche, Running Antelope, was thankful for the removal of his bindings. They had been tied very tight, but he had not complained; that would be a sign of weakness. He rubbed his wrists, slowly returning the feeling to his hands. Once he felt satisfied that the circulation was sufficient, he looked at the woman and said, "I will eat now."

She smiled and picked up a piece of hardtack as well as some jerky. She offered them to the Comanche chief. She was not at all averse to looking into the eyes of this man. He had a strong face and muscular body. She imagined that he was probably a good warrior. She glanced at Danny. He was busy eating his meal.

She nibbled on a piece of jerky and decided to try to find out more about this Penateka. "What is your name?" she asked.

"I am called Running Antelope," he said and took another bite. "What are you called?"

"I am Birdsong. As I have said before, I am of the northern people."

A hint of surprise widened his eyes. The reaction did not escape her notice.

"Are you a mighty chief or a sub-chief?" she asked.

"I am the adopted son of the mighty chief, One Eye. I am a war chief with many coups. I have counted coup on the Arapahoe, Kiowa and Cheyenne." His chest puffed out slightly as he told her of his accomplishments.

"I can see that you are a great warrior, but why are you adopted? Was your mother and father killed?"

"I was taken from them when I was still a boy. The Penateka came to my village and raided our people. I too was of the northern people."

This time it was her turn to feel surprise.

A trace of sadness crept into his voice as he told the story of his capture. "They stole many horses and took children as well. I have not returned to my people since that day."

She listened intently as he continued, wondering if he knew of any of the people she remembered. She asked questions and was pleased to discover that he was from the same hills and valleys as she. Their villages had been very close to one another. The excitement warmed her heart as she listened to him speak the names of tribal members that she recalled. She watched closely as he spoke and noticed a hint of sorrow darken his eyes whenever he spoke of his childhood days. She could see that he was not totally happy with his life and saw an opportunity to maybe enlist his help.

"I am happy we are of the same people. I see in your eyes that you were very happy as a child. I also see in your eyes that although you are a sub-chief, you are not truly happy with the Penateka."

"You have no right to say this!" he blurted angrily.

"I am sorry if I have offended you. Please forgive me." She bowed her head submissively.

The awkward moment was mercifully interrupted as Danny rose and retrieved some more sticks for the fire. They watched in silence as he tossed them into the dying flames, sending sparks swirling into the night air.

"I'm gonna tie him up," he said and retrieved the length of rope he'd removed earlier.

She told Running Antelope of the white-eyes' intentions. He did not complain as the rope was pulled tight around his wrists. He was appreciative that it was not tied nearly as tight as before.

159

Once the job was completed, Danny turned to Birdsong. "I'm gonna go get my bedroll. Heck wants me ta sleep the night where I kin keep an eye on this varmint."

She nodded and watched as he disappeared into the surrounding darkness. When they were alone, she asked Running Antelope, "Are you tied too tight?"

"No, I will be OK. Why are you worried about me? My people killed your man. My people have taken the children from your friends. My people have—"

"No!" The single word from her demanded his attention.

His gaze followed her as she rose and came around

the fire to where he was bound to the wheel. She lowered herself to the grass and looked into his eyes.

She spoke softly, "The Penateka are not your people. Your people are of the northern tribe. Your people are my people. You are my tribal brother."

They remained seated in the grass, looking into each other's eyes. He knew that what she had just spoken was true.

"Now I will fix your leg again," she said and reached for the basket of bandages.

ﭒﭒﭒ

Mary Jane awoke to the sound of a dog barking. Her body ached from the position that being bound hand and foot had forced her to assume during the night. She'd gotten only short snatches of sleep and was tired. Her mind was fuzzy as she looked around at the surroundings in the dim, gray light of dawn. The children were asleep. Charlette whimpered and squirmed in her discomfort. Josh was doing well enough, but jerked convulsively as he was no doubt experiencing a dream of some sort. John was calm and sleeping peacefully. She envied the boy as she watched his serenity.

She worked her way up to a kneeling position and attempted to arch the kink out of her back, but to no avail. She lowered herself onto her side and wormed over to the entrance flap. She looked out through the slit and saw a pair of legs right in front of her. Startled, she quickly drew back. She reasoned that it had to be a guard, and after regaining her nerve, she cautiously returned to the slit and peeked out again.

The legs moved to the left, and she was afforded a somewhat restricted view of the immediate area. She saw a few teepees, a smoldering fire pit and a contraption made of sticks that had what looked to her to be strips of meat laid out across the top of it.

Returning to her thin sleeping mat, she lay back down and stared off into space.

❧❧❧

Birdsong looked up as Sam and Stretch approached. She nodded a greeting and rose from her position of grieving beside her man. She turned to face them squarely. "He is ready to go to be with his ancestors," she said pleasantly.

"What do you want us to do?" Sam asked.

"I have gathered the wood."

He nodded solemnly.

"He is to be placed on the pile and a fire started. His spirit will rise into the sky with the smoke." She looked at Willie. "He has told me this thing. He told me before that once the flames have devoured his dead body, the spirit will have already left and he will be in a place he called…ah…"

"Heaven?" Sam asked.

"Yes, heaven," she said. A smile crossed her face. "He has told me of this place where he will go. He spoke well of it. I think someday I would like to go there, too."

Sam smiled and vowed inwardly to someday have a talk with her about the Lord Jesus and salvation.

"I will miss my man, but… ." A single tear spilled over the bottom edge of her eye and she quickly wiped it away.

"Birdsong, it is alright to weep for a lost one," he said and, reaching out, he pulled her to him. He held her tenderly as she shuddered her grief against his chest.

Stretch stood by and felt grief of his own as he wondered about Mary Jane. He wanted to join Birdsong in her sorrow, but he fought the urge. With the tips of his fingers, he wiped away the wetness that had collected at the corners of his eyes. *Oh Mary Jane, where are you?* he wondered.

⨝⨝⨝

The camp was coming to life as Mary Jane opened her eyes. The other captives were beginning to stir as well. She was amazed that she'd managed to sleep as soundly as she had. She shifted her positioning and wound up on her other side, relieving some of the numbness in her hip.

"Are you awake, Mary Jane?"

"Yes, Joshua, I'm awake."

"What'dya figure they'll do with us?"

"Oh…probably nothing," she lied.

"Mary Jane?"

"Yeah."

"Would you say another prayer?"

She smiled inwardly. She'd been praying all through the night. Each time she'd awakened, she'd prayed herself back to sleep. "Yes, Joshua, I will," she said affectionately and paused to gather her thoughts. When she felt at ease, she began, "Our Father, strengthen us in this, our time of need. Help Joshua here to remain strong and understand that Your love will carry him through this. Amen."

"Thanks, Mary Jane…and Mary Jane?"

"Yes."

"I'm real sorry for makin' fun of Charlette last night."

"Might not be such a bad idea if you was to tell her that when you get the chance."

"Yeah, believe I will."

As if on cue, Charlette awoke with a start. "Wha…what's that?" she asked and popped up to a sitting position. She looked around, and as she realized where she was, she began to cry.

"It's OK, Charlette," Josh said. "We're all in this together, and I won't let nothin' happen to ya."

She shuddered and forced a smile despite the tears.

"And I'm sorry 'bout makin' fun a ya last night."

Unable to speak, she nodded.

John too had awakened and sat up. He saw her tears and asked, "You OK, Charlette? This heathen givin' you a hard time?"

"I ain't no heathen. I'll have you know—"

163 ➤

"That's just about all I care to hear outta the both of ya," Mary Jane said. "Now shut yer faces and listen to what I got to say." She fired an angry glare at each of them. "In case you two haven't realized it yet, the only way we'll most likely stand a snowball's chance of gettin' through this is to stick together and trust in the Lord." She softened. "Course, I ain't yer ma, but I'm just about the closest thing you got right about now." She noticed the almost imperceptible nod from Joshua. "So stop bickerin' with one another and see if we can pull together toward a plan to love one another the same way Jesus loves us."

No one spoke. They all knew she was right.

Josh felt ashamed. "I-I'm sorry," he said meekly. "It's just that—"

No one had heard the approaching footsteps and they were startled as the entrance flap opened unexpectedly.

Toward a New Beginning

The morning sunlight burst onto Josh's face.

He was temporarily blinded by the brightness and turned away from the stark intrusion. "What the...?" he said.

The same man who had tied them up the night before entered. A wide grin spread across his face at seeing the boy's discomfort. He said something unintelligible and chuckled lightly. He knelt and pulled a knife from his belt. Scowling into the defiant face of Mary Jane, he growled, then chuckled again.

His breath smelled terrible as a blast of it hit her full in the face. She drew back from the putrid stench and turned her head away from him while she fought to keep the tears from appearing.

When he'd finished cutting their bindings, he gathered up the pieces of rope and left through the flap, leaving it open this time.

Mary Jane breathed a sigh of relief as she struggled to stand. "See how that works?" she said cheerfully. "That's what we need to do; stick together and try our best to not show fear. The Lord will protect us from whatever comes our way."

Shortly, the same woman as before brought more food. They eagerly accepted it, and she left without a word. This time Mary Jane remembered to say grace over the meager meal, and they ate in silence while each of them wondered what would happen next.

After they'd eaten, the young captives took turns peeking out through the entrance at the activities of the camp. There was a definite gathering of horses and assembling of people. As Mary Jane watched, they streaked stripes of bright colors on their faces and bodies. They even decorated the horses. She was fascinated as they drew circles, painted zigzags and even patted handprints onto the sides, necks and rumps of the animals.

Suddenly, the colors were forgotten as a particularly important looking man appeared from a nearby teepee. He was dressed in buckskin pants and wore rows and rows of beautiful colorful beads on his chest. On his head was a magnificent feathered headdress that extended down to the ground. He stretched both arms above his head and chanted something that got everyone to raising a ruckus. They whooped and hollered until he gestured with the hatchet-looking thing in his hand. That must've been some kind of a signal, because all of a sudden the entire group jumped onto the backs of the horses. They continued to whoop and yell until he also mounted and led them out of the camp.

165

→

☙☙☙

"Did you sleep well?" Birdsong asked Running Antelope as she, Sam, Heck and Stretch stood in front of the prisoner.

He elected to not answer. Instead, he chose to stare a fiery glare at his enemies. He was relieved, however, when one of the white-eyes reached behind him and released the bindings that had confined him throughout the night. He was further pleased when they untied his ankles and he was allowed to rise. His wound was painful, but by using the sturdy wagon behind him as a means of support, he managed to straighten to a standing position. He was pleased that no one attempted to help him.

Toward a New Beginning

"Your leg is good?" Birdsong asked, watching his progress.

"It has seen better times," he replied, continuing to eye the white-eyes. "What do they want?" he asked while gesturing with a tilt of his head. He continued to hold securely onto the side of the wagon with both hands.

"They want to know why the Penateka take the children. They want to know *where* the Penateka take the children." His grip slipped and he nearly went down. She'd seen it coming and was there in an instant with a helping hand and a supporting shoulder for him to lean on. "You will sit now," she said, looking into his eyes.

"I will stand," he corrected her.

"My northern Comanche brother will sit...please," she added softly, while conveying a genuine concern in her voice as well as her eyes.

"As you say," he conceded and allowed her to assist him to the grass.

She pulled the basket of bandages close beside her and started to unwind the bloodstained cloth from around his wounded leg. "Will you tell my friends where are the white-eyes' children?" She continued to unwrap the wound without looking up.

He winced as the pain became significant. "The Penateka...I mean...my people." She smiled but remained silent as he continued, "My people will sell the white-eyes captives to the Mexicans. They will be taken to the south for a long time and made to do the work of many."

"When will they do this?"

"I think maybe two or three suns will pass before the Mexicans will come."

"Will you say where the village is that holds the captives?"

"I cannot. That would betray those who have accepted me. It would place them in danger."

"These white-eyes have taken good care of you and will set you free if you will tell them where the children are being held. They do not wish to see you die. They are here only to ask for your help in return for your freedom."

Suddenly, any further conversation was impossible as the entire eastern horizon erupted in war whoops and yelling. Running Antelope's face broke into a wide grin. The Penateka had returned to once again attack the wagons. The three white-eyes scrambled away from him and hurried to meet the threat. Birdsong looked into his eyes, and a feeling of sorrow came into his heart as he watched the dismay cross her face.

167

"You must never forget that you are my brother," she said and was gone.

He watched her leave and pushed his pain aside as he slowly worked his way to a standing position. With great difficulty he made his way toward the sentinel that awaited him to the north.

CHAPTER

Seventeen

Birdsong was close behind as Sam and Stretch ran to their rifles. Heck had disappeared off somewhere unseen to do his own fighting. She took one last glance over her shoulder as she arrived at Stretch's side. She saw Running Antelope making his way out past the circle of wagons. Her thoughts went to him as she watched his escape. *May the gods go with you, my brother.* Her mind returned to the task at hand.

The children had been herded to the wagon toward the center of the circle and stuffed inside. Danny and another young man were assigned to guard them. Each took up a position under the wagon with rifles pointing out through the wheel spokes. The members of the train had done all they could to prepare themselves, and they waited for the impending attack. With every eye behind the fortifications trained on the line of Comanche horsemen, the wait stretched to nearly five minutes.

Jay glanced at the wagon where her son had disappeared from her view a few minutes before. She reached for Sam's hand, found it and gave it a gentle squeeze. They smiled into each other's eyes.

Suddenly, a yell went up from the line of Indians. The figures sat on their ponies and pumped their weapons high above their heads as a lone horse approached them in a wide arc from around the eastern side of the wagons.

Birdsong watched as the pony arrived at the area

toward the middle of the line of warriors. The chief sat on his mount with his headdress extending to below his pony's belly. It showed that he was indeed a mighty chief. She remembered his name and knew that One Eye had regained his lost son, but she also felt that she had lost her brother. She watched as the two clasped forearms in greeting.

The tension grew thicker as the members of the train gripped their rifles in anticipation of the impending attack. Finally, One Eye raised his feathered war lance, pulled his pony around and disappeared into the mist of the throngs of his people. The line of horsemen also turned and quickly disappeared behind the hill.

"What's going on?" Stretch asked Birdsong as a cheer went up behind the barricades.

"They are returning to their village," she said with a smile. "The chief's dead son has reappeared from the spirit world and they go home to rejoice."

"You mean that fella we had captured was the chief's son?"

"Yes. He is the adopted son of Chief One Eye."

Sam sided up to them while Jay scurried off to find Tom. "Birdsong, what'dya think our chances would be of following them Indians to see where their camp is? Should be easy enough to track 'em."

She nodded slowly. "I think it would be easy to find the village, but not so easy to get the little ones away from them."

"Yeah, but at least we could trail 'em and find out where Mary Jane is," Stretch added.

"Let's go have a talk with Heck and see what his thoughts are on the subject," Sam said.

The trio located the wagon master, and Sam laid

out his idea while Cottonwood Charlie listened in. Heck was not too fond of the idea, but Charlie was. Him knowin' a mite about Indians, he was able to convince Heck that the redskins would not be expecting the whites to follow, and that made their chances of being successful pretty good. Birdsong agreed, and it was settled.

Preparations were made and they wasted no time in getting started after the Indians. Charlie led the way with Birdsong, Sam and Stretch close behind. Charlie was the best tracker, so it figured he'd be the best one to head the bunch. Birdsong, knowing the Comanche ways, was a logical choice to tag along. Now Sam and Stretch were a different story altogether. Neither one of 'em had any good reason to be out there chasing down a bunch of thieving Comanches. Stretch was there just because no one was able to stop him from going after Mary Jane. Sam, on the other hand, just plain and simple didn't have any better sense.

As predicted, they had no trouble following the trail left by the Comanches. It led pretty much due south, with only a slight variation to the east. After about a half hour of steady riding, they topped a small hill, and Charlie raised a hand. He dismounted, and after motioning for the others to keep low, he walked his horse back to just below the crest of the hill, where he tied the gelding securely to a nearby bush. The rest of them had dismounted and tied up also. They all crawled forward and lay on their stomachs just below the crest.

Portions of the teepees were obscured by a good-sized stand of cottonwoods, with some willows mixed in. Although they couldn't see any, the presence of so many trees was a pretty good indication that there was water running through the area. There was also ample grass throughout that afforded good graze for the Indians' ponies.

"Not a bad place ta set up housekeepin'," Charlie commented as he removed his coonhide cap. He wiped the sweat from his balding head with the neckerchief he'd pulled from a hip pocket.

"Ummm…yes. This is a good place," Birdsong said as she too had noticed the favorable attributes of the site. But that's not all she'd noticed; in an area at the edge of the trees was a gathering of Penateka who were holding a celebration for the return of Running Antelope.

"Ain't no sign a Mary Jane," Stretch said.

"I don't reckon they'd be lettin' them captives have the run of the place," Charlie said, with a slight sarcasm in his tone.

"Yeah, I guess you're right. I was just hopin'—"

"Well, I'm afraid hoping isn't gonna get it done," Sam said and sighed a deep sigh that indicated he might have been feeling a little on the hopeless side right along with Stretch. "As far as I can make out, there's no way to approach that camp from any direction without being seen. I would expect—"

"I know a way," Birdsong said.

"And just what might that be?" Sam asked.

"After the sun goes to sleep and the darkness returns, I will walk in the village and learn where the little ones are being held."

"Ain't that a bit risky?" Charlie asked.

"What is risky for a Comanche woman to walk in a Comanche village?"

Toward a New Beginning

"Well now, I'd say that's a real good point, but the fact remains that you ain't a member of *that* particular Comanche village." He pointed a stubby finger at the camp. "If one a them was ta figger out that you was a stranger…why, who knows how big a ruckus they'd raise over that?"

"You are right, Charlie, but when it is dark and I do not go near any fires, they will see only another Comanche woman."

Charlie rubbed the stubble on his chin. "Hmmm. Ya know, she might just be able ta pull it off at that," he said and allowed a slight grin to appear. "Yep. Just might do the trick," he decided. "In the meantime, how 'bout we back off a ways and wait fer dark. Wouldn't do fer us ta get spotted out here in the open."

⇤

ᏺᏺᏺ

The children huddled around the entrance to the teepee as the sounds of horses reached their ears. There was more than just a little laughing and frivolity going on as the returnees pulled their ponies to a halt and slid down. As far as Mary Jane could tell, the center of all the carryin'-on seemed to be a man who had a bandage tied around his leg. He was helped down and assisted to a place in front of one of the teepees, where he was lowered onto some animal skins and made comfortable.

"Sure do wish I could understand Indian lingo," Josh said as he gazed out at the scene.

"I wanna see," John whined from behind Mary Jane.

"OK, but just for a little while," she said and moved aside slightly, allowing him to squeeze in beside Josh.

Charlette was not to be left out. "Me too," she said.

"Just wait a minute," Josh said as he continued to stare out at the Indians, while at the same time trying to shoo her away with a waving hand behind his back.

Food was brought to the man and he ate hungrily. He nodded periodically and talked sparingly around the food in his mouth as questions were asked of him. Wherever he'd been, he was surely happy to be where he was now, Josh figured.

Charlette tried again. "Can I see now?"

"Oh...alright. But just for a little while." He drew back and reluctantly surrendered his watchin' spot to Charlette. A wide grin spread across her face as she edged forward and peered out.

Mary Jane sat back from the entrance and tried to reason her way through what was going on. The fact that the Indian was wearing a bandage meant that he'd been wounded. That would indicate contact with the wagon train. Had he in fact been wounded, captured and tended-to after the attack on the wagons? If so...

173 ➡

The question rattled around in her head, but she was unable to come up with a reasonable answer. It just didn't make any sense for him to be captured and then set free while they remained prisoners in this smelly teepee waiting for God only knew what to happen to them. She needed to watch some more.

"That's enough, John. I need to see what I can to maybe help understand what's goin' on."

"Aw...Mary Jane. Just a little while longer... please."

"Move it now, I said."

He moved aside and crawled to his sleeping mat, where he sat facing the other three. "Don't never get ta have no fun," he mumbled through pouting lips. He then picked up an innocent pebble and flung it angrily against the side of the teepee.

As Mary Jane watched the Indian with the wounded leg, he turned his gaze toward her and smiled while nodding slowly. Another brave was seated next to him and was doing a powerful lot of talking and gesturing. It seemed to her that the animated conversation was pretty much directed at the teepee where she and the children were being held. It was as if the wounded Indian had just been told of the captives and was enjoying their plight.

"OK, that's enough lookin', Charlette," Mary Jane said and gently nudged her away from the entrance. "Let's all just stay back and see what's gonna happen next."

CHAPTER

Eighteen

Heck and Kyle peered into the water barrel lashed to the side of Kyle's wagon. "What'dya figger, Heck? We gonna have enuf ta make it to the Arkinsaw? Ain't much more'n, 'bout two…three days worth is all what's left in there," Kyle said as he peered once again into the darkness of the more than three-quarters empty barrel.

"Don't know fer sure, Mr. H, but one thing I do know…if we don't start takin' it easy on it, we ain't gonna have more'n 'bout a sip 'er two left over by the time we do get there. And that's only if we was ta git outta here purty durn quick. My figgerin' is that the longer we put off gettin' back on the trail, the more of it the horses'll be drinkin' up without us even makin' a lick a headway." Heck looked up into the cloudless sky. "Sure wouldn't hurt none if the good Lord was ta supply us with a real good frog strangler."

"Amen ta that," Kyle said. "But judgin' from the looks of it…" he too gazed into the expansive blue sky, "I'd say that ain't likely, leastways not right off anyways."

Heck pulled his hat and wiped his brow with the sleeve of his good arm. "Yeah, I'm afraid yer right about that." He sighed, replaced the hat and glanced at his tied-up arm. "Sure would be feelin' a whole lot better if I hadn't a took that arrow." He gingerly rubbed the wound before continuing, "We need ta spread the word fer folks ta start rationin' what water they got left. Tell 'em that drinkin' will be kept to a minimum and that the stock and the children got dibs over the rest of us."

"They ain't gonna necessarily 'preciate givin' most a the water ta their horses," Kyle said, shakin' his head slowly.

"Yer probably right about that, but I figger most a these folks is smart enough ta realize that without the horses bein' alive ta pull the wagons...well...amen. Just tell 'em what I said, and if any of 'ems got a problem with that, tell 'em ta come see me about it."

"Whatever ya say. But in the meantime, maybe we could send out a scout or two ta look fer some. Ain't no tellin' how long we'll be holed up here waitin' fer either the Comanches ta finish us off or our children ta get found."

176

Heck rubbed his chin while he pondered the suggestion. "That might not be such a bad idea at that. I reckon if Charlie and them other fellas ain't snatched them young'uns and got back here by sometime tomorrow morning, I believe I'll do just that."

᪪᪪᪪

As dusk came to the prairie, the foursome rode slowly toward the Comanche village. A plan had been decided on that would enable Birdsong to sneak into the camp. They had seen a finger of cottonwoods that extended a ways along the south edge that also kinda connected to yet another stand of trees a couple of hundred yards even farther to the south.

It was decided that she and Sam would circle around and approach from the west side of the farthest trees. He would wait there for her return while she used the cover to sneak in and see if she could find out where the children were being held. Once that was established, she was to get back out of the camp, and they would decide if a plan could be thought out that would get the children out safely. In the meantime, Stretch and Charlie would remain hidden in the scrub oak on the hill to the north until they were needed.

As the foursome drew to within a quarter mile of where they remembered the camp to be, Sam and Birdsong split off. They rode steadily, giving the camp a wide berth. It took the better part of a half hour, but they were finally able to spot the trees in the silvery moonlight and quickly covered the remaining distance. They reined up and dismounted.

"This is good place for you to stay," she said and handed him her rein.

"How long you figure you'll be gone?"

"I do not know. I will come back as quickly as I am able."

"You be careful. If you get caught—"

"Yes, I know." She smiled a smile that in the moonlight seemed to him to hold very little confidence. She turned and was gone.

He tied their reins around a branch that extended nearly to the ground. He then seated himself with his back resting against the trunk of a suitable tree and closed his eyes. He was not in the least bit sleepy or tired. He used the opportunity to talk with the Lord.

Birdsong quickly made her way through the small stand of trees and presently arrived at an open area that extended for about 25 or 30 yards. She paused to scan the open expanse. Satisfied that it was safe, she continued, but this time she assumed a bent-over posture and utilized a bouncing gait that ate up ground quickly. She arrived at the far side of the clearing and paused again, this time to catch her breath. Once she felt rested, she continued at what was a much more deliberate pace.

She had gone only a short distance before encountering the first of the Penateka lodges. She squatted in the moonlight and carefully surveyed the area. There seemed to be a minimal amount of activity on this side of the village. The majority of the people were gathered toward the other side, enjoying the comfort and togetherness of a large fire. She knew that if she tried to wander around the village in her half-Comanche, half-white-man's clothes, she would stand little or no chance of getting past the first person she met. She glanced around and spotted a blanket lying by the entrance to one of the nearby lodges.

She was extra cautious as she moved forward and finally ducked behind the protection of the lodge. She circled around until she was within easy reach of the sought-after prize. She retrieved it and threw it around her shoulders, leaving sufficient excess around her neck in case she found the need to use it to hide her face. Once she had prepared herself, she cocked an ear in the general direction of the fire and was able to faintly make out little clips of conversation.

The discussion was mainly centering on the return of Running Antelope and the capturing of the children.

She pulled the blanket up slightly so it covered her ears. She pinched it together in front of her mouth, held it securely in place and boldly walked out into the open.

As she neared the gathering of Penateka, a woman

turned from the area and headed straight for her.

"This is a nice night to walk," she said as she drew near Birdsong.

"Yes, I am pleased to enjoy the moonlight," Birdsong said in passing and lowered her face away from the woman. She glanced over her shoulder and was pleased to see her continuing away in the opposite direction.

Birdsong stopped next to one of the lodges and breathed a sigh of relief. She was still a good distance from the circle of Penateka, but near enough to clearly hear what was being said. She listened intently and learned that the children were indeed being held in the village. It was expected that the Mexicans would come sometime within the next two days. Once they arrived, the children would be sold for clothing and blankets. The people felt that with winter fast approaching, this would be a good trade. She was also able to discover where they were being held. She looked in the direction of the spoken-of lodge and with the aid of the light from the fire was rewarded to see a face peering out through the opening.

She remained a short while longer to catch a glimpse of Running Antelope. He was indeed a very important sub-chief and seemed to be well respected by everyone. She had a fleeting thought that she wished she had met him when they were both young and still up north with their own people. She had loved Wild Willie, but she also knew that she would have been happy had this adopted Penateka been her husband.

She decided it was time to leave and turned away from the fire. Her intentions were interrupted as she bumped into the returning woman she had passed earlier. She had been caught with the blanket away from her face and immediately lowered her gaze as she attempted to push past her while nudging the blanket up around her chin.

"What is your hurry, little one?" she asked as she hooked Birdsong's arm with her hand.

"I have to make water. Please let me go before I wet myself." Birdsong knew the excuse was flimsy, but it was the best she could do on such short notice.

"Which lodge are you from?"

"I...ah—"

"I think you are someone I have not seen before. Let me look into your face."

Birdsong slowly brought the blanket down. "I am a friend of Running Antelope," she said.

"Then come, we will go to see him."

"That is a good idea, but first I must make water."

"I think you are not what you seem to be. I think you do not know Running Antelope. And I think you do not need to make water." She then took Birdsong by the arm and gently pulled her in the direction of the fire.

Birdsong resigned herself to the fate that awaited her and let the blanket fall from her shoulders as they walked slowly toward the gathering.

The woman ushered her through the crowd and straight to a position in front of Running Antelope.

As the rest of the Penateka began to notice them, the talking dwindled until finally there was near silence.

Running Antelope looked up into Birdsong's frightened eyes.

"She says she is your friend. Do you know this woman?"

CHAPTER
Nineteen

The bright moonlight lit up the prairie well enough for a fella to make out individual blades of grass. Charlie pulled one and stuck it in his mouth. He glanced at Stretch's prone figure a short distance away and wondered how the youngster could sleep at a time like this. He was balanced onto one side using an arm as a makeshift pillow. He returned his attention to the camp below. The drone of voices had remained steady ever since they'd taken up their position shortly after separating from Sam and Birdsong. It was plain to see that the fella with the bandaged-up leg was still the center of attention.

Stretch snorted and rolled over. He then sat bolt upright and began spitting repeatedly while pawing at his mouth. "What the heck?"

"What's ailin' ya, boy?"

"Some kinda critter—" He spit again. "A bug er somethin' crawled right inta my mouth." The spitting continued long enough for the bug to be long gone and then some.

Charlie hadn't realized just why Stretch's episode with the bug had seemed so loud to him, but then it dawned on him, the noise from the camp had lessened considerably. "Might not be such a bad idea fer you ta pipe down a mite. Yer makin' 'bout enough ruckus to wake the dead." He turned his full attention toward the camp and was distressed to make out Birdsong in the firelight. He squinted his chagrin. "Dang. Looks like Birdsong's been found out."

Toward a New Beginning

The bug forgotten, Stretch crawled over beside Charlie and made his own assessment. "Yep. Sure nuf. Now what?"

"Let's keep an eye peeled 'til Sam shows up. Then we'll decide on our next move."

"Don't see no other way," Stretch said. "Maybe they'll decide not ta kill her, I mean what with her bein' a Comanche and all. Maybe we'll even git lucky an see where they decide ta hold her."

"Don't know if she's a Christian gal or not, but I reckon she needs ta be doin' a powerful lot a prayin' right about now," Charlie said.

"Amen ta that."

Birdsong looked into the eyes of Running Antelope. She did her best to keep her gaze strong and unwavering. The woman who had brought her nudged her closer to the firelight.

"She has said she is your friend. Is this true?" she repeated.

"Yes. She is my friend. Her name is Birdsong. She is of the northern people. She was the one who cared for me when I was wounded and held captive by the white-eyes."

A murmur spread throughout the gathering as each one present voiced their opinion about what she had done for Running Antelope.

"Why are you here?" The words came from the old man seated to the immediate left of Running Antelope.

Birdsong looked into his face. She knew instantly that this was the mighty chief, One Eye. Where his left eye should have been was nothing more than a dark cavity.

"I have come to find the captive children," she said.

"You are a brave woman. Did you come alone?"

"No. I came with some white-eyes." She noticed a sign of alarm wrinkle his forehead and decided to try to put him at ease. "My friends do not come to make trouble for the Penateka. Their only interest is to locate the captives and try to find a way to free them." She paused and lowered her gaze.

"Why do you not lie when I ask you these questions? A lesser person would not admit the true reason for being here. Maybe I will decide to kill you because you dared to venture into my village."

"A lesser person would not understand that telling a lie to a mighty Comanche chief will bring certain death. I have no reason to tell a lie. My friends will see that I have been taken and will return to the wagons. They are safe in the night."

183

Running Antelope leaned over and conferred with his adopted father. Their conversation was kept low and confidential, even though she could see those who were near attempt to listen in by leaning slightly closer. Finally, a decision was made and everyone straightened up.

"Running Antelope has said that you are a woman with a good heart. He says he will take you into his family...as his worker. He says he also wishes you to continue to care for his wounded leg." He looked at his son. "Is this your wish, my son?"

"It is."

"So be it. This woman now belongs to Running Antelope."

Birdsong was relieved that she was not to be killed for venturing into the Penateka village. She bowed her head in submission to the chief, accepting his decision. She then raised her gaze and looked into the eyes of Running Antelope. She liked what she saw. He was not showing any sign of domination over her or any indication that would suggest anything other than what the chief had ordered. She liked the face she looked into. It showed a strong character that pleased her. She felt safe belonging to Running Antelope.

༈ ༈ ༈

The serenity of the night had gotten the better of Sam, and he'd dozed off while he waited for Birdsong's return. He awoke with a start as an owl sounded its eerie call from the branches of a nearby tree. He rubbed the sleep from his eyes and wondered how long he'd been asleep. He looked at the position of the moon and figured he'd been out for the better part of an hour or so. *Wonder what's holding Birdsong up?* he wondered. *Woulda thought she'd have returned by now.*

He stretched, yawned and slowly got to his feet while brushing the leaves from the seat of his britches. He then gazed toward the direction she had taken and wondered again at her tardiness. He decided to go have a look, pulled his pistol and checked the load. He replaced it in his holster and headed off through the trees.

He remained cautious as he made his way through the sparse cover provided by the cottonwoods. When he arrived at the clearing that separated the two groves, he stopped and knelt behind the protection of the final tree. He surveyed the clearing and decided it was safe. He hurriedly crossed to the other side and again knelt. Satisfied that he was alone, he rose and continued into the grove.

He presently arrived at the outskirts of the village and ducked under the hanging branches of a particularly huge willow. He used the next couple of minutes to peer from the branches at the activity in the camp. It seemed to him that the majority of the Comanches were turning in for the night, but there was no sign of Birdsong. *Where in tarnation is she?* He'd almost said it outloud, but had somehow managed to keep it to himself.

Being somewhat restricted in his ability to see enough of the camp to make heads or tails out of the layout, he moved back and forth under the willow and looked out in different directions. This tactic worked pretty well, and with the aid of the moonlight, he was able to come up with a pretty good picture of what he was up against.

There was what appeared to be a thick stand of trees to the east that extended out beyond the edge of the camp. He figured that if he could backtrack a ways and head off in that direction, he'd have good cover for just about the entire distance to the northern end where it seemed most of the teepees were set up. He took one last gander at the camp and let the branches fall together. He then turned and headed out the backside of the huge tree.

Almost immediately he found a well-used trail that went in the direction he wanted to go. He began to follow it, thankful for the easy going it provided. He paused from time to time and listened into the night for any sound that would indicate danger.

The farther along the trail he went, the more he could hear the babbling of voices coming from somewhere up ahead. He could also see the orange glow of a brightly burning fire. He rightfully put the two together and

185

decided there was some kind of a get-together going on around the fire. He veered away from the trail and headed in a more direct line toward the activity.

No sooner had he arrived at what he felt was a pretty good watching spot than he was alarmed to see a Comanche brave suddenly appear from behind a nearby teepee. Sam instinctively ducked down right where he was. To his relief, he found himself behind a small bush that was sufficient to hide him if he remained perfectly still.

The Indian walked only a short distance into the woods and paused to relieve himself. Sam waited patiently until the brave had finished. As the man turned and headed back toward the fire, Sam breathed a sigh of relief and counted his blessings that that was all the fella had to do.

186

He settled in and scanned the area in the direction of the fire, but saw nothing that gave him any indication of what might have happened to Birdsong. There were mostly just men gathered around the fire. The fella they'd held captive was among them. Sam watched as he was helped to his feet and escorted away from the fire and into the nearest of the teepees.

Shortly after his departure, the rest of the Indians began to leave the area and disappear into the night.

"Looks like the party's just about over," he whispered softly. He continued to watch until the last of the Comanches had gone.

With his mind full of unanswered questions, he duck-walked backwards until he felt safe enough to turn and retrace his way back to the trail. He found it easily enough and followed it until he arrived back at the willow.

On his way through the groves of trees to where he'd left the horses, he took the time to reason what this might mean. It seemed to him that if Birdsong had been killed, there would have been a whole lot more commotion than he'd seen and heard. No, it made more sense that she'd been discovered and taken prisoner. *At least she'd be some comfort to the children,* he thought. He then said a brief prayer for her safety as well as the safety of the children.

~~~

From where they lay, there was no way Charlie or Stretch could hear even a smidgen of what was bein' said. They had to be content with just watching. Whatever was being said seemed to include another fella who was sitting next to the fella they'd had captured. When all was said and done, Birdsong was led away and taken to a teepee that was not too far away. That was the last they'd seen of her.

They remained on their guard while they waited for Sam to return. If there'd been even the slightest sign of one of them Injuns lighting out in their direction, they'd a been outta there like a shot. But things remained tolerable as the activity continued around the fire as if nothing had happened.

The whole thing was a puzzlement to Charlie, but he figured the longer they put off killing Birdsong, the better. "Sure don't understand why they just took her off to that teepee," he said while scratching the bald spot under the back of the coonhide cap. He got a little vigorous and the hat fell off forward. He picked it up while he continued, "Seems like they weren't none too upset about things. No sir, don't make a whole lotta sense ta me." He slapped the hat against his leg and fitted it back onto his head.

The two remained silent for a spell while they continued to watch the camp. Then right out of the clear blue, Stretch changed the subject, "Charlie?"

"Yeah?"

"You ever been married?"

"Yeah, but only one'st."

"Did ya like it? I mean...havin' a wife an all?"

"Nope."

"Why not?"

"Well, mainly 'cause she couldn't cook worth a plug nickel. Oh, she was a alright sort, but just didn't have no idea 'bout how ta get around a kitchen, or a cookin' fire neither fer that matter." He paused, remembering back. "That's about the closest I ever did come ta starvin' ta death. And with food all around me too."

"I'll bet Mary Jane's 'bout the best cook around these parts."

"Don't be bankin' on that, boy. Why, I knew a fella once that thought the gal he was sweet on was a real good cook, so he up and married her. It weren't more'n two...maybe three months before he was so skinny that he hired hisself out as a hitchrail."

Stretch had been listening intently until that point, figuring Charlie was telling him a true story. "Don't you ever—" Stretch halted in mid-sentence as one of the horses nickered. "Someone's comin'," he said softly and hunkered down in the grass.

"I didn't hear nothin'," Charlie said but drew his pistol anyway. "What makes you think someone's comin'?"

"You could say a little birdie told me, but then again I don't understand bird talk," Stretch whispered.

"Huh?"

"Never mind."

They listened into the night until, presently, they heard the sounds of an approaching horse walking slowly as it headed straight toward them.

Charlie beckoned through his teeth. "Pssst." When he had Stretch's attention, he motioned the youngster to spread out, thereby assuring that the approaching rider would have to pass directly between them. They waited with drawn six-shooters.

Once Charlie was sure it was Sam, he rose, and letting the pistol slide into his holster, said, "Nice evenin' fer a ride."

Sam's horse was caught off guard and shied, but he managed to pull the startled animal under control. "You sure don't think anything of giving a fella heart failure, do ya?" he said and swung down.

189

Stretch replaced his six-gun. "Did ya see her? Did ya see Mary Jane?"

"Nope. Plus I lost Birdsong, too."

"Yeah, we seen that," Charlie said.

"What'd you see?" Sam asked as he began to loosen the cinch from around the belly of the appreciative animal.

"Seen a Injun gal bring her inta that gatherin' around the fire, and after a spell of parlayin', seen her escort Birdsong off to one a them teepees. That's the last we seen a her," Charlie said. "So I reckon yer sayin' ya don't know nothin' neither, that right?"

"Yeah. I dozed off for a while, and when I came to, I realized she should've been back by then. So I sneaked my way up real close to the fire for a look, but that must've been after they'd already taken her to the teepee because I didn't see any sign of her."

"Did ya see Mary Jane then?" Stretch asked hopefully.

"Nope, or any of the others either. Ain't got the slightest idea where they're being held or if they're even in the camp at all."

≈≈≈

The ride back to the wagon train was a solemn one as each of the dejected trio was lost in his own thoughts about the recent developments. Stretch was the hardest hit by the failure to find the captives. His love for Mary Jane was growing by leaps and bounds, as was his need for her. In the privacy of the silent ride across the moonlit prairie, he prayed in his heart for her safety and wondered if praying about things really did any good.

CHAPTER

Twenty

The only one who didn't seem to have much of a problem with Birdsong's being captured was Noah. His exact words were: "Once an Injun, always an Injun. She probably just ran off and joined up with them heathens."

This didn't set well with the other members of the train. Even Wayman and Rip shunned him for a while. But with a more pressing matter at hand, Heck called a meeting to explain the water situation—not that it really needed explaining. They all had eyes and could see that at the rate they were going, the supply wouldn't last much more than another two or three days.

"We need ta go easy on what little there is left," he said, addressing the gathering. "Until we find more, we need ta assume that what we got is all we'll have 'til we get outta this scrape."

"And what happens if we don't find more?" Noah asked.

"That question don't need much of an answer, but I'll give ya one anyway, that is, if ya really want a description of what a human looks like with his tongue all swolled up so big it won't fit into his mouth no more."

Noah was just fixing in his mind what that might look like when the pastor spoke, "No thanks. That won't be at all necessary. The Lord will provide."

"Too bad that savage ain't here," Noah said. "She could do a rain dance or somethin'. Why, I hear tell—"

"Why don't you just shut yer face 'til ya got sumthin'

ta say what's worth listenin' at?" The words came from Kyle Hendricks and were accompanied by a scornful look that said he meant business. "I reckon I heard just about all I care ta hear outta you. That little ol' Injun gal risked her life an maybe give it up too, just ta help find them young'uns. The way I figger things, that makes her worth a whole passel more ta the survival a these families than you, or me, or any of the rest a ya that let her go in yer stead. Now I ain't much on speechafyin', but this here's somethin' what needs sayin'. So if I was you, Baxter, I'd be countin' my lucky stars and be down on my knees askin' the good Lord ta bring her back safe 'n sound, and with them kids taggin' right along behind her, too."

An uneasy silence followed as no one dared to speak for fear of getting Kyle started in on them. The stillness was finally broken as Wayman began clapping his hands, slowly at first, then as others joined in, faster, until the entire group was applauding Kyle's speech.

Noah fumed as he turned beet red. He sputtered helplessly while trying in vain to find the necessary words with which to defend himself. But there weren't any that were appropriate, so he did the next best thing and stomped off toward his wagon with the applause still ringing in his ears.

Once he had left, the hand clapping quickly died down.

Heck looked at Kyle's downcast eyes and said, "Not that I'm partial ta givin' a fella whatfor, but that was a right accurate speech from where I was listenin'."

"I'm sorry I felt the need ta say it," Kyle said. He looked at Wayman and Rip. "I'm 'specially apologizin' ta the both a you boys. I don't figger it made ya feel none too good, neither."

Wayman was the first to speak up, "My pa's been a bigot for as long as I can remember, and most likely way before that. I only wish I'd a been the one ta say what you just did." He placed an arm around Rip's shoulders. "You won't be gettin' no hard feelin's from us. That right, Rip?"

"Nope. Reckon I feel 'bout the same's you. And don't none a ya be worryin' 'bout what'll come of this. Pa's an alright sort. He'll be sore fer awhile, but he ain't a violent man. What he needs is a little a what most all a you folk's got."

"What's that?" Heck asked.

"I reckon I'm figgerin' he could use a real good dose a religion." He placed a hand on his brother's shoulder. "Me 'n Wayman here ain't never been what you would call church-goers, but we been keepin' our eyes and ears open on this trip, and there's a kinda peacefulness about folks what…what—"

"Love the Lord Jesus?" Pastor Jenks said with a smile.

"Yeah, I reckon that's exactly what I'm sayin'… them what love the Lord Jesus. And I 'spect that if you folks don't mind none, me 'n Wayman here'll be payin' closer attention whenever there's preachin' goin' on."

"We'd be happy to have you," Pastor Jenks said. "And don't give up on your pa, either. Just because he has a hard spot in him doesn't mean the Lord doesn't love him, too. You try your best to get him to come and listen to the preachin' right along with you. In fact, if you're of a mind, I'll be happy to come talk with him about it."

"How about we not push our luck," Wayman said.

193

Toward a New Beginning

"Some folks is just plain and simple sour, and I 'spect Pa's one a them. But that don't mean we won't work on him."

Heck stepped forward and pulled his hat. "Good. Now that we got Noah's road ta salvation all planned out, how about we do some plannin' about findin' water while we still can?"

After a short discussion, it was decided to take Kyle's suggestion and send two riders out in an attempt to locate a reliable source. George and Rip volunteered to make the ride. Fay was not at all happy about her husband's willingness to leave her, especially with the attacks seemingly coming at will, but she was a considerate woman and understood the urgency surrounding the needs of the wagon train.

With the knowledge that the Comanche village lay to the south, the riders were to be sent out to the north and northwest with instructions to not venture any farther than seven or eight miles. That way they would be able to return by nightfall or shortly thereafter.

George kissed Fay tenderly and headed out to the north. Rip veered off northwest, and both riders were soon out of sight. The prayers of the wagon train went with them.

※ ※ ※

Birdsong awoke to the familiar sounds of the Comanche village. As she lay on her sleeping mat, she remembered when those sounds had been common to her. But now, she was filled with an uneasiness that told her she was far from being out of the woods, that is, as far as being accepted by these Penateka Comanches was concerned.

She rolled onto her side and looked at Running Antelope's broad back as he slept on the far side of the lodge. There was no one else present. That meant he did not have a woman. The idea of being his woman appealed to her, but she quickly forced it from her mind. *My man is only two days gone and already I am thinking of another.* She then centered her thoughts on the things around her. She was pleased to see that the lodge was neat and well kept. His war bonnet was perched atop a lance, propped against one side of the enclosure. His other weapons of war were stacked neatly in another area, with his extra clothing piled alongside. She could not remember ever hearing of a Comanche warrior, who was without a woman, who kept his lodge as organized as this one. It pleased her. *He has a good heart and is not a lazy man,* she rationalized.

195 ➡

She rose from the mat and crossed to the opening where she knelt and peered out. Just outside was a young man who was standing guard. He had heard her approach, and with folded arms and a stolid expression, turned his head to look her way.

"You are so young to look so serious," she whispered and glanced back to make sure she had not awakened Running Antelope. "What is your name?"

Bear Cub ignored her question and turned his gaze straight ahead. She crawled out of the opening and rose. He unfolded his arms and turned toward her. He placed a hand against her shoulder and said through his stoicism, "You will not leave."

"I understand," she said looking into his eyes. "I will not leave." She placed the palms of her hands against the small of her back and twisted the stiffness away. "My name is Birdsong," She smiled into his face. "I would like to be your friend. What is your name?"

"I am called Bear Cub," he said while managing to keep his gaze forward and his stoic manner intact.

"That is an unusual name for a Comanche brave." She knew this would get him to talking. All Comanches enjoyed talking about how they had been named.

The beginning hint of a smile came to his lips. "Long ago when I was very young... ." He paused long enough to allow her to understand that that was indeed a very long time ago. "As I was walking with my mother through the woods, we came to a place where a bear had been brought down by hungry lions. They had killed the bear and had eaten her belly. My mother told me that we must leave quickly, before the lions came back. As we turned to go, a sound from high up in a tree stopped me. I looked and saw a cub. My mother tried to make me leave, but I would not go without knowing the cub was safe from danger. I climbed the tree and removed it. My mother allowed me to take it home. It was then that my father gave me the name Bear Cub." He again paused, and another smile came to his lips. This time he did not try to stop it. "My father said that when I become a warrior, my name will then be Angry Bear."

"That is a good, strong name for a warrior," she said. "I can see that it will happen very soon." The flattery worked as the smile grew even more genuine.

A noise from behind her drew their attention. "What have we here? Are you two old friends or something?"

Bear Cub lowered his gaze out of respect for this man. "No, my chief. We were—"

"We were trying very hard to become friends," Birdsong said and quickly added, "He was doing his job and would not let me leave."

"Did you want to?" Running Antelope asked. "Never mind. Don't answer that. I think I would rather not know."

"If it will make you feel better, I will tell you anyway. Your people are nice to strangers, your father is a wise man, your lodge is very neat and clean and I have made a new friend."

She smiled at Bear Cub, and he started to return the smile, but remembered that Chief Running Antelope was nearby and the beginnings of the smile quickly disappeared.

She turned to look again at Running Antelope. "My man has been gone for only two days." Pausing, she waited for the words to come to her. "I am in mourning, but I do not want to leave this place." She lowered her eyes to the ground, hoping he would understand that she was drawn to him but needed time to properly mourn her lost husband.

197 ➡

"Bear Cub, you may leave," he said to the young buck. "I think she will remain and no longer needs to be guarded."

Bear Cub nodded, grabbed his lance from its position against the outside of the lodge and walked away.

"Thank you, Running Antelope. You will not be sorry for believing me," she said.

Each looked into the other's eyes and it became clear that they were enticed by each other.

"What do you have that I may fix for you to eat?" she asked after finally regaining her senses.

Toward a New Beginning

֍֍֍

Mary Jane peered out through the entrance and, picking up a pebble, tossed it in front of the guard. Through the use of hand gestures she made him understand that she had a need to relieve herself.

He grunted and motioned her outside.

She got to her feet and hurriedly headed for the woods. She was thankful that he let her go into the trees by herself. She enjoyed the brief respite from the confines of the teepee, but also knew that if she dallied too long he would probably come looking for her.

She finished quickly and was making her way back toward the teepee when her attention was drawn to what appeared to be a familiar figure on the far side of the main clearing at the center of the village. She stopped and shielded her eyes against the morning glare. A smile came to her face as she realized that it was indeed Birdsong. She wanted to call out, but realized what a mistake that would be.

As she returned to the teepee where the others awaited, her heart was filled with happiness at the possibility of finally being rescued. Her chest was nearly bursting with excitement as she ducked through the opening and into the interior.

֍֍֍

Concerns for the missing children continued to grow as the small group of men discussed the situation. Although none of the returning threesome had seen the children in the Indian camp, there was a general feeling that they were indeed being held there.

"So what'dya figger, Heck? We cain't just sit here 'til we run outta water and die a thirst." Charlie said. He looked around at the faces before continuing, "Them Injuns ain't showed at all today. I figger they maybe ain't willin' ta lose no more braves fer the sparse pickings they been gettin'."

"Maybe you're onta somethin' there, Charlie, but we cain't just run off an leave them young'uns," Heck said.

"Mary Jane neither. I ain't leavin' Mary Jane," Stretch said with a not-to-be-denied fervor.

"My sentiments exactly," Sam agreed. "And the rest of those children as well. It makes sense to pack up the train and head for water, and so be it, but—"

"You sayin' that if we was ta pull out, you two wanna stay behind and go after them youngsters all by yer lonesomes?" Heck said.

199

"I don't relish the idea," Sam said, "but if that's the only way, well..." His voice trailed off as he realized the implications of what was being proposed.

"That's exactly what we're sayin'," Stretch said, settin' his jaw and propping his fists defiantly on his hips.

Heck bowed his head and looked at the grass in front of his cross-legged position on the ground. He thoughtfully pulled a blade and placed it between his teeth. He fingered the blade as he remained deep in thought. Finally, he pulled it out and raised his eyes. "I don't cotton none ta leavin' any folks behind, and that goes double for them kids."

An excited grin began to spread across Stretch's face as he figured he knew what Heck was about to say.

He listened respectfully while Heck continued, "If them riders return tonight without findin' water, and them Comanches stay off our tails, then we'll look at movin' out first thing in the mornin'. If you two have a notion ta try fer rescuin' them kids, well...God bless ya. But I hope ya come to yer senses before mornin'."

"Make that the three a ya," Kyle said. "That's my boy out there. I figger his ma'd be givin' me whatfor if I was ta just up an let them heathens have him. Sides, I'm right handy with a six-gun." He then proved it by pullin' his hog-leg with a flash of movement that surprised everyone present. "Done me a stint as a lawman back home in Tennessee. 'Bout four years ta be exact."

"I'm stayin' too," Jacob said and rose to stand beside the others.

Stretch looked at him, and the sincerity was evident as he spoke, "Mr. Greenberg, we appreciate the offer, but I ain't allowin' it."

"What'dya mean, *you* ain't allowin' it? *You* ain't got no say-so over what I do."

"No sir, I don't, but I'm askin' you ta reconsider. I'm promisin' that I'll be doin' all I can ta bring Mary Jane back safe 'n sound. The good Lord willin', I'll be havin' the pastor here," he gestured toward Pastor Jenks, "marry the two of us, just as quick as the law allows."

Pastor Jenks smiled. "I'd be honored to, Mr. Henderson."

Jacob eyed Stretch, appearing to decide if he was likin' what he was hearin' or not. "That your last name...Henderson?"

"Yessir, that's it."

"Alright, boy. If you got that much interest in her, I reckon I'd most likely just be in the way. You go on about yer business and bring her back to her ma 'n me and her brothers."

"And me," Stretch added.

"Yeah...and you."

"Glad that's all settled," Heck said. "We'll assign some a the extra fellas ta drive yer wagons. Shouldn't be much of a problem. We'll also be needin' ta get someone fer Willie's wagon as well."

Charlie pushed a hand against his knee and rose as he spoke, "Don't fergit about mine, too. If it comes down ta needin' a tracker, I figger that's where I'll be of use...not ta mention that I have a way a knowin' things about Injuns."

"OK, that's four of ya, and that's the end of it," Heck said. "I ain't allowin' no more than these here fellas." He motioned to the four standing in front of the rest of the men. "Besides, them fellas just might find that water and this'll all be fer naught."

201

CHAPTER
Twenty-one

The mood the next morning was one of relief and concern—relief that the train would be pulling out soon, and concern for those four men who would not be going with it. George and Rip had returned just after dark without so much as seeing a puddle of water, let alone enough to do the train any good.

Jay had not been at all pleased with Sam's decision to remain behind. She'd hugged young Tom to her bosom and cried nearly all the while as she tried her darndest to talk him out of his foolishness. But with Stretch's help, he was able to finally convince her that it was the right thing to do. The clincher was when he asked her if she would favor the idea if it were Tom who needed rescuing. She resigned herself, but cried softly the rest of the evening and well into the night.

Ronnie had volunteered to share the driving with Jay, while Danny would drive the Conestoga all by his lonesome. With the loss of the gray mare, Stretch rearranged the remaining horses in such a way as to compensate for the missing animal. The vacant slot was left to the right hand side, next to the wagon.

"Now remember, Danny, you ain't ta change this setup for no reason," he said as the two of them were makin' the final adjustments to the harnesses. "That blaze-faced bay is the best of the lot and will take charge when the need arises." He buckled a strap and fed the end of it through its retainer. "Keep the other bay right behind her, and—"

"Look, Stretch, I understand what cha got goin' here and I'll not change a thing. The best you can do would be ta get yer mind right with the Lord and start storin' up all the help you can get for what's facin' ya."

"What'dya mean, get my mind right?"

"If I was you, I'd be havin' me a talk with the pastor about trustin' in the Lord about knowin' for sure I was goin' ta heaven if this whole rescuin' business was ta fall through. Without acceptin' the Lord Jesus as your personal Saviour, you'll be goin' straight ta hell if them Comanches get cha. Nosir, without the Holy Spirit settin' up camp inside a yer soul, you'd not like where you'll be headin'."

Stretch hadn't suddenly become blind or deaf since they'd started the trip. He'd seen and heard things and was gettin' a pretty good handle on knowin' what it 203 meant to be saved by grace and washed in the blood of Jesus. He'd also realized that it was somethin' that was necessary if him and Mary Jane was ta ever get hitched and live a good Christian life together as married folks—and not ta mention the fact that Danny was right about havin' the Holy Spirit come inside a him before it was eternally too late.

He let fall the part of the harness he'd been fiddlin' with. "You reckon now's as good a time as any?" he asked.

The makings of a grin appeared across Danny's face. He stacked his forearms on the rump of the sorrel and looked across at Stretch. "There ain't never been a bad time to decide ta go to heaven," he said and spread the grin even wider.

"You willin' ta finish things up here?"

"I'll take care a what needs tendin' to. You go find the

pastor and take care a what needs fixin' for yer soul."

"Believe I'll do just that," he said resolutely and turned away. After taking just a few steps, he stopped and turned back to Danny. "And Danny...thanks."

"I appreciate that, but I'm thinkin' that when I see you again you'll be understandin' that I ain't the one who's deservin' of the thanks. I'm thinkin' by the time you get back you'll be knowin' that all the thanks goes ta Jesus for all the sufferin' He did fer us sinners. And Stretch, this might be a bit early, but welcome to the family...in more ways than one."

Stretch nodded his thanks, sucked in a deep breath and headed off to find the pastor.

Sam and Jay were silent during their final preparations, as was Ronnie. The silence was even to the point of being awkward, especially for Ronnie. Sam noticed Stretch as he was leaving the Conestoga and heading across the circle. He wondered what was so important that it would take him away from completing hitchin'-up the team.

He dismissed the thought as Ronnie interrupted the silence. "You folks is havin' a difficult time with this, and I can fully understand that, but—"

Jay had looked up from the packing she was doing. "I-I'm sorry, Ronnie. It's just that...well, I'm just not at all partial to having Sam put his life in jeopardy by going out to face those horrible Indians. Why, there's a good chance that—"

"Ma'am, 'scuse me fer interruptin', but there's a good chance that my sister is in need. I done me a heap a prayin' yesterday that the Lord would find a way to bring Mary Jane back to her family where she belongs."

Jay started to interrupt again, but thought better of it as he raised a hand and continued, "I'm sorry ta not let cha get a word in edgewise right this minute, but ma'am...I'm figgerin' them prayers was bein' answered when I found out last night that Mr. Bartlett and the rest a them fellas had volunteered ta stay back and see what they could do about the situation. Now I understand that ya got some concerns about yer husband as well as yerownself and little Tom there, but ma'am, the Lord has ways a makin' things work out for the better, and—"

"OK, OK, I get the picture," she said and placed a hand on his upper arm. "You ever thought about becoming a preacher?"

He grinned sheepishly. "No ma'am, I ain't."

The packing and final preparations were then resumed with a slightly more at-ease atmosphere than before. There was even some small talk, but it was still plain to tell that Jay was anxious about the safety of her man.

Once everything was in order, Sam gathered everyone together, and they headed for the Greenberg wagon. They joined with Jacob and Mabel, and Sam prayed for the safety of the train and the safe return of the captives. Just as he was finishing up, Stretch approached with a huge smile spread across his face and a bouncing lightness in his step.

"What's got into you?" Sam asked.

"You'll see. C'mon. The pastor wants everyone ta gather for a blessin'."

They all headed for the center of the circle. Word had been passed around quickly, and in short order every member of the train was present.

Toward a New Beginning

Heck stood in the middle of the assemblage with hat in hand. "Folks, as you all know, we're gonna try ta make a beeline fer the Arkansas. We're gonna be doin' some hard pushin', and I ain't about ta tell ya it'll be an easy trip, 'cause it won't. I've asked the pastor here," he wagged the hat toward Pastor Jenks who stood right behind him, "ta say a blessing on our wagon train and a prayer for the young'uns we're bein' forced ta leave behind Pastor." He motioned him forward.

Pastor Jenks moved forward slowly and stood with his hands clasping his Bible to his chest. His face was filled with a sadness that made it plain to everyone that his heart was heavy. "Folks," he finally began, "the past couple of days or so have been trying ones for all of us. We lost Bill Hawkins. We lost Jack Walker. And...and we have some folks wounded." He walked over and placed an arm around Harry Carter's shoulders. Agnes brushed at a tear as the pastor patted her husband. "And probably the most devastating thing for us to endure is the capture of our beloved children." He looked at the tear-streaked face of his wife as she pulled her remaining three sons closer to her. "As you know, I have been seriously hampered by the loss of my youngest. As for the rest of you, who also have children being held captive, I want to assure you that I share your sorrow, as I'm sure we all do. But we must keep the faith and trust in the Lord to work things out. I think that's why He's dealt with four of our men to stay back and attempt a rescue." He glanced around at the faces. "At this time, I'd like those four Christian souls to step forward."

While he waited patiently, Sam, Stretch, Kyle and Cottonwood Charlie stepped out and gathered on either side of him. The pastor placed a hand on Kyle's shoulder. "These men are what loving thy neighbor is all about. They have committed themselves to the possibility of giving up their lives in an attempt to return our children to us. They have also committed themselves to the Lord."

Sam turned a sideways glance at Stretch and was pleased to see him return a wide grin. He knew at that instant what it was that had seemed different about him.

The pastor then placed his arm around Stretch's shoulders, and for the first time since the start of the get-together, a smile appeared on his lips. "At this time I am pleased to tell you that Stretch Henderson here has just this morning accepted the Lord Jesus into his heart and is now a child of God."

The "Amens" were heartfelt with everyone genuinely praising the Lord for harvesting yet another soul into His family. That is...everyone except Noah. He stood toward the outside of the circle shaking his head. He just couldn't understand what the big hullabaloo was all about with these "Bible-thumpers."

His thoughts were interrupted as the pastor continued, "Let us pray."

Noah watched the hypocrites as they did their prayin'. He heard snatches of what the preacher was sayin', but it didn't send a blessing through him, in no way, shape or form. It was just words asking for God's protection on the wagon train and the captured children, plus some gibberish about protectin' those idiots that were stayin' behind to go out after them young'uns. When the prayin' was done, he shook his head with disgust and headed for his wagon.

Heck broke up the meeting by instructing everyone

207

to go to their respective wagons and get ready to get under way.

Sam and Jay walked with their arms around one another and Jay's head leaned over resting against his shoulder. Stretch tended to Tom, which gave him a chance to say good-bye and tell the boy to mind his ma. Across the circle, Heck was pumping Charlie's hand, while two wagons away, Kyle was havin' a tearful departure from his wife and family.

Finally, Heck mounted and shouted the order for everyone to climb up. Jay kissed her husband with a tenderness that had him wondering why he was being fool enough to stay behind. Ronnie extended a hand down and pulled her up onto the seat next to him. From somewhere off in the distance Sam heard Heck give the order to "Head 'em west!" but his attention was glued to his beautiful wife as he held her hand and gazed up into her tear-streaked face. Tom sat on her lap as she held him close. All too soon, it was their turn to head out, and Ronnie snapped the reins.

"Hee yaw! Get up there!" he said and snapped them again.

The wagon lurched forward, and Sam took a couple of steps alongside, not wanting to let go. Finally, their hands separated, and as the wagon pulled away, Tom leaned out over the side and waving, said, "Bye, Daddy."

Sam raised a hand in return, and with the tears streaming down his cheeks, said softly, "Bye, son."

Charlie sided up to him as the wagon pulled away. "Mite hard on a fella ta watch his family disappearin'," he said. "I reckon there's somethin' ta be said fer a fella bein' a loner. Never did have no family of my own ta speak of...leastways that I kin remember."

No one responded; they were content to just watch in silence as the wagons rumbled toward the horizon. None too soon, the tail end of Pastor Jenks' wagon disappeared down a small hill.

The silence continued a while longer, then Stretch put it all into perspective, "Sure is a good thing that little hill was there, otherwise we might a been standin' here most a the day watchin' them wagons 'til they pulled clean outta sight."

That brought Sam back to his senses. "Eh...yeah...eh, what do you fellas say to us maybe getting away from this spot in case the Comanches decide to come back?"

"I think that'd be a fairly sensible move," Charlie said and looped the reins over his horse's head. "Ain't no sense endin' our little adventure 'fore it even gits started real good."

❊❊❊

Mary Jane's excitement at seeing Birdsong earlier that morning was infectious to the other children, and she had her hands full trying to keep them from getting overly exuberant. "You mustn't let on that I even seen Birdsong," she said as she hugged Charlette against her chest and stroked her tangled blond hair. "If the Indians even think there's a chance that she'll be rescuing us, well...I shouldn't have to tell you that our chances would pretty much disappear right out from under our noses. Just keep on the same as you have been, but deep down inside it's OK to know that the Lord is doing what it takes to get us outta here."

"I sure do hope Him and Birdsong hurries up and gits it done," Josh said. "I've had just about all this kinda fun I can handle," he added and grinned.

"Well, you can call it fun if ya want to, but all I can say is that I never in all my borned days thought I'd be happy to see them ugly faces of my brothers again," John commented. "Shoot, if I was hard-pressed, I expect I'd even admit ta missin' 'em."

Josh pushed a hand against John's shoulder and tipped him over. "Now, that's *really* sick," he said and giggled as John snickered his giddiness.

Suddenly, the entrance flap was pulled open and the guard stooped his way into the confines of the teepee. He said something that none of them understood and gestured toward the outside.

"He wants us to go outside," Mary Jane said, wondering at this sudden development.

They rose and filed through the opening. Once outside, they shielded their eyes against the bright sunlight until eventually Mary Jane was able to make out an ugly man with a very big mustache and an oversized hat that had the brim curled up all the way around. He was walking straight toward them, accompanied by an old Indian man and Birdsong.

"Don't act friendly toward Birdsong," she said from the corner of her mouth.

"But—"

"Just do like I say. If we seem too friendly to her, she might get in trouble. Trust me," she whispered just before the ugly man came to a stop in front of them.

He spoke with a heavy accent. "Hello, little one. You are happy to see Sancho, no?" he said, resting his gaze on Charlette.

She didn't answer.

"How about you, señorita?" he asked, hooking a knuckle under Mary Jane's chin and lifting her face until their eyes met. "You are not happy to see Sancho. You do not want him to take you away from this place?"

Mary Jane, too, did not answer his questions. She instead closed her eyes as the tears welled up and spilled over.

"Do not be sad, Señorita. I will not hurt you. Sancho will be your friend. You will grow to like him very much." He emphasized the words by running his hand along the side of her face.

"Leave her alone," Josh said, taking a threatening step forward.

Without warning the Mexican lashed out with a backhand that sent the boy sprawling. "I will talk with you later, but for now, you will shut up and say nothing."

"It is not good to be mean," Birdsong said as she'd decided she'd put up with just about all she could. "These children do not threaten you. You do not need to hit them."

The fire in her eyes surprised him. He was not at all used to a woman, any woman, telling him what to do. He turned to face One Eye and spoke in Spanish, "Does this worthless squaw have the freedom to make decisions for the mighty Penateka chief?"

"She has always spoken true to me. I have no reason to distrust her," One Eye replied.

Birdsong was able to understand enough to get the gist of the conversation and smiled at the comment from One Eye.

"She tells me to not hit the boy. I do not like a squaw who tells me what to do."

"Ummm," One Eye responded, then turned to Birdsong, and, knowing the Mexican did not under-

211 →

stand Comanche, spoke freely with her. "Why do you tell this pig to not hit the boy? Did not the boy say something disrespectful to him?"

"No, he did not. This filthy animal was being suggestive with the young girl and the boy told him to leave her alone."

"And that is the only reason for hitting him?"

"Yes."

One Eye then turned toward Sancho and went back to speaking Spanish. "I have been told why you hit the boy. I do not think you deserve a good price for the white-eyes children. Now, you will pay more."

"What? You cannot do that! We have an agreement!"

"I am the one to say what the price will be. You will pay more...much more."

Sancho turned to face Birdsong. "What did you tell him?" he asked angrily.

"I only spoke true to him."

He began to get irate and started to tremble. "You have shamed me. Now, I will—" He raised a hand to strike her.

One Eye may have been old, but he retained the reflexes of a cat. He quickly grabbed Sancho's wrist and gripped it tightly.

The children drew back from the confrontation, not understanding exactly what was going on, but knowing that things were getting out of hand. Mary Jane pulled them together around her as they watched the conflict.

Holding tightly onto the man's wrist, One Eye said softly, "Now you do not have enough to trade for these captives. They are no longer for sale to you."

Sancho had never before heard of such a decision as

this. He wrenched free from the old man's grasp. "We had a deal! You will keep the agreement!" he said, glaring at the chief.

"If you value your life, Mexican pig, you will speak no more and leave my village before I feed you to the dogs."

Sancho may have been a fool, but he was not completely stupid. He knew the chief had reached the end of his rope. He glared first at the old chief, then at Birdsong. He then moved his gaze to Mary Jane and said, "I will see you again, my sweet señorita. Of this you can be sure." He pursed his lips and smooched a mock kiss to her. She felt repulsed as his face erupted in a wide grin that showed his decayed, brown-stained teeth.

"You will leave now," Birdsong said flatly.

"You too will see me again someday," he said with a vengeance that left no doubt about his dislike for her.

Miguel Sancho turned and stomped away toward his horse.

Mary Jane watched him go while she continued to hug the children to her. She breathed a deep sigh of relief and closed her eyes. *Thank You, Lord,* she said to herself.

213 ➤➤

CHAPTER
Twenty-two

Birdsong watched Sancho's every move as he mounted his horse and rode out of the camp at the head of his band of banditos.

"He is not a man to be trusted," One Eye said. "If you meet him again, do not turn your back to him."

"I think he will be trouble for me some day. He does not like for someone to speak true of him," she said.

One Eye smiled. "I think maybe you are a wise woman."

She bowed her head to him in respect. "Thank you for speaking well of me." She glanced at the children who were huddled off to the side. "May I speak with these captives?"

"Why would you speak with them?"

"Because they were afraid of the Mexican pig and did nothing to deserve this fear. I think they would be more at ease if I could tell them what has just happened. But…if you do not trust me to speak with them, I would understand this."

"You will do nothing to help them escape?"

"I will only attempt to make them feel at ease."

He nodded thoughtfully. "I believe what you say is true. I will let you speak with them." He then turned and left.

She watched him go before turning toward Mary Jane and the children. "We have little time together. Do not speak; only I will talk. Do not get excited at anything that I will say to you. You were nearly sold to that filthy pig of a man. But the chief decided not to sell you, because—"

"Never mind that," Mary Jane said. "What are you doing here? Is my pa here, too? Is Stretch here?" She glanced around.

"Please do not get excited. I will speak quickly. You must listen. Last night we came to rescue you. I was captured. The others got away. I was not killed after I was captured because I cared for the wounded leg of the chief's son after he was taken in the attack on the wagons. His name is Running Antelope, and he has been given permission to have me share his lodge with him."

Mary Jane was incredulous. "But you're *married!*"

A heavy burden appeared in Birdsong's eyes. "My man is dead," she said sadly. "He was killed during the second attack on the wagons. He died as a true warrior."

215 ➤

"I-I'm sorry, Birdsong. I liked Willie."

The sound of approaching footsteps made Birdsong realize that her time was almost up. She glanced momentarily at the approaching brave and spoke quickly, "Do nothing to upset these people and do not show them your fear. They will understand that as a sign that you are weak and may kill you."

Charlette could hold her curiosity in no longer, "Is my ma and—?"

"Your family is well. As are all of your families."

A smile came to each of the faces at this bit of good news.

The brave stopped immediately behind Birdsong and spoke, "Tell them to return to the lodge," he said.

"He wants you to return to the lodge where you

were being held," she said in response to their inquisitive looks. "Do it without question."

She watched as the children obediently returned to the nearby lodge with the brave close behind. She then returned to Running Antelope's lodge. He was lying on his sleeping mat, but was not asleep. "How is your leg?" she asked, genuinely concerned.

He grimaced as he swung it around for her to see. "It is painful. Perhaps it is not healing as well as it should."

Birdsong was apprehensive as she carefully began to unwrap the leg. "I will see why this is so," she said.

Once the final wrap was removed, her concern deepened. There was redness around the wound that did indeed indicate an infection. "I will go to make a medicine that will chase the angry redness away," she said.

He nodded slowly. "Bear Cub will go with you to carry what you need. Go quickly," he said, and squinted as a stab of pain shot through the tenderness of the infected wound.

"I will return soon," she said. She then disappeared out through the flap.

꙳꙳꙳

The hopeful rescuers had settled themselves on the crest of the hill to the north in plenty of time to witness the entire scene with the Mexicans.

Sam pulled his hat, rested it on the ground and ran a hand over his hair. "Just don't seem like she's a prisoner," he said. "Kinda looks to me like she has the run of the camp. Anyone see it any different?"

"Sure looks like maybe she went right back ta bein' a Comanche," Charlie said. "Kinda sorry ta see it though. Wish she'd a waited 'til after we had them young'uns outta there. Oh well, I reckon there ain't no use ta reminisce 'bout what mighta been. The thing we gotta do now is ta figger a way ta get 'em outta there without her help."

"Look...look at that!" Stretch said.

Birdsong had just emerged from one of the teepees. She carried a basket as she and a Comanche brave disappeared into the nearby trees.

Sam and the others watched patiently. It was a good 10 or 15 minutes before they reappeared, with the brave now totin' the basket. She took it from him, and sitting in front of the teepee, busied herself with mixin' something together, using the contents of the basket, some water from a container at her side and a handful of dirt every now and then. Presently, she rose and carried it into the teepee.

217

"What'dya figger that was all about?" Kyle asked, looking at Charlie.

"I ain't real sure, but if'n I was ta make a guess, I'd say she just mixed up a batch a medicine. I'm figgerin' that that fella what we had prisoner is havin' a peck a trouble with that leg a his. I'd say she's tendin' him."

"Maybe, just maybe, that's why she's got the run of the place," Sam said thoughtfully.

"You mean because she's been working on that fella's leg they figger she's worth keepin' around?" Stretch asked.

"That plus the fact that he's most likely told 'em that she helped him when he was in need back at the wagons," Charlie answered.

"Would that be cause to give her the run of the camp?" Sam wanted to know.

Toward a New Beginning

Charlie thought for a moment or two, rubbing his chin all the while. "I'd be inclined ta say that's exactly what's happenin'. If they figger that wounded fella is as important ta them as I think they do, that'd make her a mighty important person as well if she was keepin' him alive. Didn't she say that he was the chief's son?" he asked, looking at Sam.

"Yep. She sure did."

بۀ بۀ بۀ

Birdsong had easily found the needed plants and sat in front of Running Antelope's lodge while mixing them to a mudpack consistency. She had been taught these things by her mother's brother when she was still very young. She finished her preparation, rose and carried the medicine into the lodge. Running Antelope smiled a painful smile as she entered. She placed the remedy on the floor and began to examine the wound gingerly.

"Why do you not have your medicine man tend this wound?" she asked.

He flinched as she touched a tender spot. "Because he is very old and will soon die."

"The wound is very painful for you. This medicine I have made will very quickly bring happiness to you."

She'd no sooner said the words, while spreading a handful of the concoction on the area, then he started feeling a soothing coolness that did in fact bring a smile to his lips.

Pausing her healing hand above the wound, she looked into his face. "See, you are happy already," she said and continued with the soothing application.

He watched as she deftly applied the remainder of

the mixture and covered the area with the same bandage she had removed originally. When she had finished, she picked up the bowl and started to rise. He placed a hand on her arm and said tenderly, "Birdsong...do not go. I would speak with you."

A constricting tightness gathered in her chest as she felt certain she knew what was coming. She let the bowl rest back to the ground and lowered herself next to it. She slowly raised her gaze to meet his and let him see her tears.

"Why do you cry?" he asked as he brushed a thumb across her cheek.

"Because I know what you will say and I am still in mourning for my man."

"After you have finished your mourning, I would ask that you be my woman," he said softly.

219

Just being in the Comanche village for such a short time had brought back fond memories of her childhood. She had nothing left to make her want to return to the white man's wagon train. Her man was gone and so was her desire to be a part of the white man's world. Although she had hoped for and expected to hear those words from him, she had not expected them so soon. She was pleased that he had offered her the time to mourn her man. She smiled, closed her eyes and nodded slowly. "I will tell you when it is time," she said simply.

She kept a close watch on his wound throughout the rest of the day. Toward evening she replaced the potion with a fresh, but slightly different one that she'd collected and mixed. During those times together, he was very respectful and did not speak again of the commitment that had been suggested.

As she sat across from him, sharing his evening

meal, she wondered about the captives. "Now that the Mexican pig cannot have the captives, what will happen to them?" she asked, managing to keep the question in a matter-of-fact tone.

He was not at all fooled. "I understand your concern for the white squaw and the little ones," he replied. "I do not understand why my father refused them to the Mexican, but someday he will tell me."

Although she knew the reason, she did not offer it to him. It was not her place to get involved in such matters. "I am sure that is so," she said.

"You have great concern for the prisoners?" The inflection in his tone indicated that it could have been either a question or a statement.

Taking it as a question, she replied, "Yes. They are my friends. Just as you are my friend and this village is my friend. I have a troubled heart because they will not see their families again." She set her food aside. "I remember my own family, and often wonder if my life would have been better if I had been allowed to remain with them." She watched as his face took on a vacant look. "You are troubled?" she asked, reaching a hand to his arm.

"Yes. I am troubled because I too have felt this way. Although I have many friends in this village, and my adopted father has treated me well, I still think of what might have been if I had been allowed to remain with my people."

"But you have said that these are now your people."

"Yes. These are now my people. But things are in my head that will not go away. I sometimes wonder if my sister is pretty. I sometimes wonder if she has a good man and many children. I sometimes wonder of what could have been." He took her hands in his. "I am happy that you are here. I am pleased that we are of the same people. And I am happy that someday you will be my woman."

Their eyes met and locked in a joining of souls that both knew would be a long-lasting relationship. A soothing warmness descended from the sky and surrounded them as they enjoyed the moment.

Birdsong realized an opportunity to further touch his heart and maybe plant a seed as well. "The young captive squaw too has a man waiting for her," she said tenderly and watched his eyes. "She has been promised to a young man who is also my friend."

He squinted a sideways, questioning look her way. "Are you saying that these captives should be released to return to their people?"

"I am saying that they are people just as we are people. They have families who love them. The young maiden has a man waiting for her who would make her a good husband. She has two brothers, just as the others have brothers and sisters." She looked again into his eyes. "Just as you have a sister." She released his hands and took up her plate of food. "I am just wishing out loud. I understand that the captives will be sold to another tribe someday soon. But I have a heavy heart wondering if they too will someday sit in a lodge and speak of such things as we have done today."

"I understand what you are saying, and I too feel a hurt for them. I will speak with my father and ask if they may return to their people."

221 ━▶

CHAPTER

Twenty-three

As they continued their vigil from the crest of the hill, the men saw each of the captives at least once. The Comanches seemed gracious enough and allowed them to go off into the woods from time to time to do what needed doing. They were brought food periodically, alleviating any fears the onlookers may have had about them being starved. There was also no sign of abuse, and that served to lessen the feelings of haste and apprehension the rescuers had harbored when they'd first set out to find them.

Sam lay with one fist stacked on top of the other and his chin propped on top of that. He watched with peaceful contentment, thinking of his wife and son. He wondered if they were safe and how far they'd managed to travel before stopping for the night.

His thoughts were interrupted as Kyle spoke, "Should be 'bout anytime now," he said as he glanced skyward at the waning daylight. "By the time the two of ya get down ta the south end of the camp it'll already be dark."

They had decided earlier that once it got dark enough, Sam and Charlie would sneak into the camp and see if there was any way they could attempt a rescue.

As the pair prepared to leave, Stretch and Kyle swallowed the last of their canteens that they'd filled only partially that morning. Sam had assured them that he would be able to refill them in the brook he'd found on his previous trip to the village.

Sam slung the carrying strap of Stretch's canteen

around his neck and stuck an arm through, positioning it on the opposite side from his own. Charlie did the same with Kyle's. Once they were ready, they shook hands all around and mounted. Sam then tipped his hat, and without another word, he and Charlie reined around and coaxed their mounts into a slow canter, keeping the horizon between themselves and the Comanche village.

They rode slow and easy until Sam figured they were far enough to the southwest to safely skirt the camp. He motioned and they turned eastward. In less than half an hour, they were nearing the stand of trees where he and Birdsong had parted the night before. There was still maybe an hour or so of moonlight left when they reined up under the expansive branches of a huge cottonwood.

223

They dismounted and whispered as Sam gave Charlie the lay of the land, "Just a ways north of here is a clearing that leads to another grove of trees. Once we get across that, the teepees start pretty much right away."

"Where's that trail you was talkin' about?"

"Once we get into the second stand, there's a huge willow whose branches touch the ground. That's a good spot to settle for a while and decide what our next move should be. The trail is just to the east of there. It pretty much runs the full length of the camp. There's places where it gets mighty close to the teepees, and I'm hoping maybe it'll get near the one where the kids are."

He could just make out Charlie nodding his understanding in the shadows.

Sam pointed. "The stream is just over there. Let's fill the canteens first and leave them with the horses.

That way, if we need to get outta here in a hurry, that won't be holding us up."

"Good idea."

They made their way to the slowly running stream and patiently dipped the mouths of the four canteens under the surface of the water. After gurgling the containers full, they took the time to drink a sufficient amount of the refreshing water. Once they'd quenched their thirst, they topped off the canteens again, carried them back to the horses and draped the straps over the saddlehorns.

With the water supply safely tucked away, Charlie felt for the haft of his knife and, satisfied that it was indeed where it belonged, said, "OK, let's go see this Injun camp."

They cautiously made their way through the trees and halted once they reached the edge of the clearing Sam had remembered. Scanning the expanse, they decided it was indeed safe, and they crossed to the security of the foliage on the far side. Once there, they knelt and listened for any sound that would indicate the presence of any nearby threat. They heard nothing, so they crept their way to the protective branches of the huge willow. As soon as they were safely inside the confines of the tree, they breathed easier. A dog barked somewhere off in the distance, but not close enough to threaten discovery.

"Which way's the nearest teepee?" Charlie whispered.

"Should be right over there," Sam said equally as softly and pointed. "The trail's right over that way. Let's head for it and see what turns up."

Sam led the way as they quickly made their way to the back side of the willow. They ducked under the branches and disappeared into the blackness of the surrounding forest. After just a short distance, they came to the pathway and knelt to get their bearings.

Again Sam spoke in a soft whisper, "It'll angle off to the northeast for a ways, then it turns back toward the camp. Last time I was here they had a bonfire going up by the north edge of the camp, but that's a good ways away from where the kids are most likely being held."

They continued along the trail until it turned back toward the camp. They then hunkered down and tried to make heads or tails out of the layout. But try as they might, it was next to impossible to get their bearings. Everything seemed completely different from their new point of view.

"I just can't tell," Sam said while glancing around. "I think the problem is that we're a lot farther back in the trees then we realize. I'm thinking the camp is a whole lot bigger than we might expect."

225 ➡

Charlie too was at a loss. Nothing looked familiar as he craned his neck to see around the bush immediately in front of him. "I think yer right. Things just ain't the same from down here. We might do well ta head back and do some real close payin' attention from up on the hill after first light. Kinda looks like the part we seen from up there is just the beginnin' of what's really here."

"Let's get outta here then while the gettin's good and get on back to the horses," Sam said dejectedly.

The sound of someone approaching demanded their attention. They made themselves as small as possible, scarcely daring to breathe as a Comanche brave walked past not more than six or eight feet away.

Once the sounds of his presence had diminished

enough to ensure their safety, Sam heaved a huge sigh of relief. "That was a mite closer than I like," he whispered and took yet another deep breath. "C'mon, let's get outta here."

The trip back to the horses was cautious but uneventful. The animals appeared undisturbed, and the canteens were as they had been left. Satisfied that their visit had gone undetected, the duo mounted.

※ ※ ※

The morning erupted in a blaze of sunlight as the shadows of the night gave way to the rising orange globe. Birdsong had prepared a breakfast fit for her chief. He had devoured it hungrily and feigned disappointment when she told him there was no more. His protruding stomach attested to the fact that he had indeed ate more than his share.

"You have a good sense of what a man's needs are," he said, resting a hand on his belly. "The food was very good. You are an amazing woman, Birdsong."

She smiled at his appreciation. She had feelings for wanting to please this man, and it seemed as though she was being successful. "How does your leg feel today?"

He moved it with the assistance of a supportive hand. "It is much better. I have very little pain. It seems as though the redness will be gone if we open the cloth and look inside."

"We will wait until I make more. Then we will look for the redness, and I will again change the medicine."

She rose and disappeared outside. She found her ingredients just as she had left them and began mixing the plants with water and dirt. When she had the mixture at just the right consistency, she brought the bowl into the lodge, set it down and began to carefully unwrap the wound.

Running Antelope had been right. The redness was nearly gone. It was plain to see that the danger had passed. "You were right. The redness has almost gone. I am pleased," she said. She also noted that he was being less jumpy about her touching the area around the wound. She smiled at her success. "When will you speak to your father about the children?" she asked, not looking up.

"I will speak with him today," he said, and that ended the conversation.

She expertly repacked the wound and retied the bandage. Once she had cleaned up the mess, they talked of things such as how old each of them had been when they were taken from their parents, how he had grown into becoming a sub-chief of the Penateka Comanche and why he had never taken a wife. All these things were of interest to her as she watched his face while listening to him talk. She was pleased to see that his eyes spoke true when he said he had not found the one special person to share his life with— until she'd came to him, that is. She knew in her heart that it would not be long before they would be together.

227 ➡

༄ ༄ ༄

The area under the overhanging ledge was comfortable enough. Once daylight had spread across the land, a fire was built for cookin'. Charlie did the honors, sayin', "I been eatin' my own cookin' fer longer'n I care ta admit, and I ain't near come close ta givin' up the ghost from it yet."

He did a real good job of warming up some of the bacon they'd brought along. They made short work of it, along with some hardtack. Not wanting to use any more water than was absolutely necessary, they decided against making coffee. That decision didn't sit too well with any of them, as they all were partial to sippin' a cup first thing in the morning. But they mutually agreed that doing without the coffee was a sight better'n doing without water, if it came right down to it.

Once the breakfast was finished, they cleared up the eating utensils, and using sand to scrub the frying pan, managed to do a tolerable job of cleaning it. After wiping it out with handfuls of grass, they packed it away along with everything else they'd gotten out.

They smothered the fire with sand, saddled up and headed for the Comanche village. The trail took them through a narrow passageway between two large rocks at the bottom of a dry wash. No sooner had they entered the cut, than a sound reached their ears that right away got everyone's attention.

The arrow hit Stretch high in the left arm, but it missed the bone as it passed through, stopping with just about equal lengths sticking out either side. As they struggled to control their horses, another arrow took Sam's gelding in the neck and he reared, throwing Sam to the ground. He hit hard and rolled while pulling his pistol. He hastily threw a shot at a figure that had appeared from around the edge of one of the huge rocks. The Indian yelled, and Sam saw his bow and arrow go flying.

By then the rest of the fellas, including Stretch, had managed to pull their guns and were giving a pretty good account of themselves.

There were just three Indians that were taking part in the attack. The arrow that had found its mark in Stretch's arm was the only one that did any damage to the white men. The one that put Sam's gelding down was the only other one to stop short of buryin' itself in the dirt.

With all four of the whites throwing bullets their way, the trio of Comanches smartly broke off the attack. The fella that Sam had winged was not hurt so badly that he couldn't swing up onto the back of his pony and ride off with the others.

The aftermath was one of confusion as well as relief that no one had been killed. Sam was shaken from his fall, but unhurt.

Kyle rode to the crest of the wash to make sure the attackers had indeed left the area. "They're high-tailin' it toward the Comanche camp," he said, looking down into the wash where Sam and Charlie were helping Stretch off his sorrel. They carefully propped him against a small boulder.

229 ➤

"Looks like I picked up a souvenir," he said and grimaced as the feathered end of the arrow brushed against a portion of a small uprooted bush.

"Ain't gonna take much ta pull that little ol' stick outta there," Charlie said and reached for the shaft.

"Wait a minute! Just 'cause you say so, don't make it so. It's my arm, and I say it's gonna hurt more'n just a little bit."

"I ain't sayin' it ain't gonna hurt. I'm sayin' the point ain't stickin' inta the bone is all. It's gonna hurt like the dickens, but that stick still needs ta come out and the sooner the better."

With that, Charlie looked off to the side as if something had suddenly demanded his attention. No sooner had Stretch fallen for the ploy than Charlie drew back and delivered a Sunday punch to the point of his jaw that knocked Stretch about as unconscious as a doorknob.

"Nice punch," Sam commented. He then held Stretch steady while Charlie first snapped the arrow shaft in two, and then yanked it on through the wound. Once that was done, Sam rose and retrieved his spare shirt from the saddlebags that were still behind the saddle on his dead horse. He tore off three strips, wadded two of them up and placed them against the holes on either side of Stretch's arm. While Charlie held them in place, he used the third strip to securely bind the wound. Satisfied with the job they'd done, Sam said, "Let's bring him around and get outta here before they return with their friends. Once we get to somewhere that's safe, we might wanna think about cauterizing that with some gunpowder."

Charlie nodded and retrieved his canteen. He then poured a small amount of water into his cupped palm while letting it dribble between his fingers and into Stretch's face. The youngster jerked awake.

"What the...?" Stretch said and glanced around. "What happened? Who hit me?"

"Ain't nobody hit cha," Charlie lied. "Why, you just up and fainted dead away from the pure pain that little-bitty stick was causin' ya."

"No I didn't. Someone hit me." He looked from one to the other. "Why else would my jaw be so sore?" he asked, rubbing the spot where the punch had landed.

"Well, whatever happened," Sam said, "the arrow's gone and so are we." With that, they each got a good hold under an arm and helped Stretch to his feet and onto his horse. Not wanting to risk causing any more discomfort to Stretch's wound than was absolutely necessary, Sam got up behind Charlie, and they rode out of the wash, joining Kyle who had continued to keep watch.

They rode for a spell until they felt secure enough to stop and give Stretch a breather. His wound was serious and he was in a lot of pain. They all realized that they needed to keep a close watch on it and get him to the wagons as soon as possible. There were enough medical supplies there to allow him a good chance of keeping the arm.

After talking the situation over, they decided that their chances of sneaking up on the Comanche camp had dropped down to right around zero. The Indians would now know that some of the white-eyes had remained behind to rescue the children and would tighten their guard around them.

231 ➤

It was especially hard on Kyle to own up to abandoning the rescue attempt. Stretch also was opposed to calling it quits. But after promising that they would form another rescue attempt after getting him back to the wagons, common sense won out and they headed west-northwest in search of the train.

CHAPTER

Twenty-four

They had just completed the noonday meal, and Bear Cub patted his full stomach while belching appreciatively. Birdsong had invited him to join them, and after being assured that it was all right with Running Antelope, he had gladly accepted.

"Bear Cub, I have need to speak with my father. You will go tell him so."

"You want *me* to speak with Chief One Eye?" Bear Cub asked with a wide-eyed expression that pulled an amused smile from Birdsong.

"Yes. Tell him that I have a proposition for him and cannot yet walk well enough to come to him. Tell him that if it does not please him to come to me, then I will wait until my leg is better."

"You are sure that he will not think badly of me if I speak these words to him?"

"I am sure. Now go."

Bear Cub reluctantly headed for the exit, but before ducking through, he looked back at Running Antelope and asked, "You're sure?"

"Yes! Now go before I..." Running Antelope's meaning became clear as soon as he'd picked up a moccasin and good-naturedly threw it at the young Comanche. It missed its mark, but Bear Cub, being the type of fella that could pick up right away on a subtle hint such as that, disappeared through the opening and headed off to find the chief.

Running Antelope lay back on his mat and watched Birdsong as she gathered up the remains of the meal and straightened up the lodge. He centered his attention on her profile as she worked. He watched as she brushed an unruly lock of hair away from her face.

The effort caused her to turn her head slightly in his direction, enabling her to notice his attention on her. "I am sure there are other things for you to do instead of watching this worthless squaw while she works."

"You are probably right, but at this moment I cannot think of one. I would, however—"

The conversation ended as the entrance flap flew open and One Eye ducked inside. He stood with folded arms and looked first at Birdsong, then at his son. A concerned expression wrinkled his brow. "You are not happy with this woman?"

"Why do you ask such a question?" Running Antelope asked.

233

➡

"Because she is over there," he motioned with a tilt of his head, "and you are over there." The tilt went in the opposite direction.

Birdsong decided it was time for her to intervene, "Chief One Eye, I am very happy and honored to share this lodge with your son, but..." A tender sadness appeared in her eyes and Running Antelope quickly came to her rescue.

"Father, this woman will someday be my woman. Of this we have already spoken, but for now we will wait."

"Why do you wait?"

"Because she is mourning the loss of her man. He was killed in the final raid on the wagons."

He looked down at Birdsong. "Is this true?"

"Yes, it is so." She wiped an escaping tear from her

cheek and continued, "My husband was a brave man, but he is now gone to the place he called heaven. I have been in this village only a short while, but I am now ready to spend my life here if you will allow this. I, too, am of the northern people, just as your adopted son was from the northern people." She paused, and turning her gaze to Running Antelope, was pleased to see a smile in his eyes.

One Eye glanced at his son, then returned his attention to Birdsong. "He has told you this?"

"Yes, but—"

A wide grin had spread across his face. "This pleases me. Long ago, his adopted mother once told me that I would know when the proper woman comes into his life because he will keep no secrets from her. Maybe you are this woman."

A silence hung in the air as no one spoke. Finally, Birdsong said in a very soft voice, "Yes, I am this woman."

"Uh...this is not why I asked to see you, my father."

"Why then did you send word for me?"

"Because I ... ah ... because we have an offer to give to you."

"An offer for what?"

"For the release of the captives," Birdsong said and was immediately sorry for speaking out of place.

One Eye quickly moved his gaze from his son to her. "What is this offer?" he asked eyeing her closely.

"I am but a female. It is not my place to speak. Running Antelope will speak for us to his father," she said, and looking at Running Antelope, assumed the proper submissive posture by folding her hands and placing them in her lap while she bowed her head.

"I say again, you are a wise woman," One Eye said, smiling his satisfaction.

Running Antelope took up the cause, "As you can see, my leg is much better today. This is because I was able to have use of the healing powers possessed by this woman." He gestured toward her. "She has a gift and great knowledge of the healing plants that is better than anyone I have ever seen before. Even better than Buffalo Horn when he was young."

One Eye could not believe what he had just heard. Buffalo Horn, although very old now, was legendary among all the Comanche tribes as the best to ever understand the use of the healing plants. "Where have you learned about the healing plants?" he asked, looking at her.

"My mother's brother was our tribal medicine man. He had much patience and took the time to teach me."

235 ➡

"What has this to do with the release of the captives?"

"Birdsong has agreed to become our new healing one if you will set the captives free and allow them to return to their people."

This was indeed a bold proposition. One Eye did not indicate his pleasure or displeasure with it. Instead, he focused his attention on Birdsong. "Why do you think I would feel the need to make such a trade?" he asked and folded his arms across his chest.

She rose and walked to the front of One Eye. Fixing an unwavering gaze on his, she said, "These children were taken to sell to the Mexican pig that shows no respect to you. You wisely did not sell to him. I think that now they are either to be traded to another tribe or you will keep them to use as workers in this village.

But..." She took a deep breath that did not escape his notice.

"Continue," he said.

"I was taken from my village when I was very young, as was Running Antelope. I have brothers and sisters, just as he, too, has a sister." She looked at Running Antelope and saw a hint of sadness that quickly disappeared.

One Eye, too, looked his way and was pleased that he had told her about his long-ago sister.

"These children who have been taken from their families also have brothers and sisters. The young white squaw has a man who she would soon marry if she were allowed to." Taking a dramatic chance, she reached a hand to the side of One Eye's face. "You have a son that loves you very much, but he has never forgotten that he was taken from his sister. He will never know if she is a beautiful woman. He will never know if she has married a brave warrior. He will never know if she has many children." She removed her hand from his cheek and looked down again at Running Antelope. "He will only know that if you give these children back to their brothers and sisters, it would be the same as giving him back to his sister." She then turned to once again face the chief. "Please excuse me for speaking out of place," she said and lowered her eyes to the floor.

"Are these your feelings?" One Eye asked his son.

"Yes, my father. These are my feelings. She spoke well."

"I will think on it," One Eye said resolutely, turned and ducked his way through the exit.

A silence filled the air around them as Birdsong and

236

Running Antelope sifted through their thoughts. With a sigh that came out louder than intended, she knelt beside his wounded leg and started to unwrap the bandage.

"He is a fair and wise man. He will decide quickly," he said.

"I am afraid I have made him angry. I am but a woman and should not speak directly to him as I have. I am sure he does not like me anymore." A tear rolled down her cheek as she stopped fiddling with the bandage and looked into his eyes. She scooted closer to him, and with a tenderness that touched his heart, said, "Please hold me. For now, I am afraid."

ﺴﺴﺴ

Miguel Sancho sat on his horse and watched the approach of the small group of riders. He had split his band into two parts in an effort to cover more territory. Pickings had been slim as of late and tempers were short. The episode back at the Comanche camp the day before had left a bad taste in his mouth and he was itchin' for a fight.

"We will stop these gringos," he said. "Diego...you will take the woman into the trees and keep her away from the eyes of the gringos."

Diego nodded and motioned to her. "Come, señorita, come with Diego. We will go into the trees an have some fun, no?"

"I will go nowhere with you," she said and set her jaw in strict defiance.

"Sancho, she say she will not go."

"You will do as I say!" Sancho ordered, as he fired a stare at her that accomplished nothing in the way of its intended intimidation.

"You maybe can make others afraid of you, but I am not afraid. You have killed my family, but I will not do as you say." She returned the stare and added a hate to her glare that angered him.

"You are making a big mistake, señorita. After we rob these gringos, I will make you sorry for your insolence to me. You will say nothing, or we will kill these gringos, and you, too. You understand?"

She did not acknowledge his question. Instead, she smirked and tossed her head defiantly.

As the riders neared the group of Mexicans, it became clear to Sancho that one of the horses was carrying double and another of the riders was dangling a wounded arm. The gringos waved a greeting as they reined up.

Sam was leery of the group because of the stories he'd heard back in Independence about the banditos that had been robbing travelers along the Santa Fe Trail. Even though they were a good ways north of the usual route, it didn't pay to get careless. As soon as they'd gotten close enough to recognize the group ahead as possibly Mexican, he'd suggested that everyone be on their guard and be ready to pull down on them at the slightest indication of trouble. Sam himself had pulled his pistol and held it hid between himself and Charlie.

"Howdy, fellas," Charlie said as they reined to a halt. "Bit of a lonesome spot ta be out sightseein'. Wouldn't be that yer out lookin' fer yer lost dog, now would it?"

Sancho tipped the front of his sombrero. "Hello yourself, señor," he replied with a hint of amusement.

"The only dogs we are looking for are gringo dogs that have more food and water than they have use for. Have you seen some gringos like this?"

"Nope. Cain't say as I have."

Sam had been watching the young woman's face, as she seemed to be a bit on the nervous and apprehensive side of things. Her eyes darted around with what seemed to him to contain a plea for help. Feeling uneasy about how this conversation between Charlie and the Mexican was going, he leaned back slightly, allowing both Stretch and Kyle a look at the pistol. Once he knew he had their attention and they would back up any play he made, he leaned forward and once again hid the gun from everyone's view.

"I think maybe you are such a gringo," Sancho was saying.

"You'd be wrong about that, Mex. Fact is, I'd say it'd be a big mistake fer you ta be thinkin' that-a-way."

Sam caught a slight movement out of the corner of his eye and realized that one of the Mexicans was making a slow move toward his pistol. Deciding to keep the upper hand, he pulled the pistol from its hiding place and eared back the hammer. "Now I figure that would be a fatal mistake," he said, and leveled the barrel at the man. Kyle, Stretch and Charlie also pulled their guns, backing up his play.

"You are not being very friendly," Sancho said as anger began to shroud his face. "It is not a good thing to point a *pistola* at someone who is wanting to be your friend."

"If I thought for one measly little minute that you were of the friendly sort, why I 'spect I'd be apologizin' and askin' yer fergivness," Charlie said while keeping

239

his six-shooter leveled at the Mexican's chest. "But as you can see, I ain't neither apologizin' nor askin' fer no fergivness."

"You look like you're having a bit of a problem, young lady," Sam said.

She kicked her horse forward. "Not no more, señor."

"You will stay where you are!" Sancho ordered and reached for the passing horse's bridle. He managed to hook it with a fingertip and held on.

"You will let go of my horse!" she protested and slung the end of her rein, slapping it against the back of his hand.

"You little…" Sancho reached out for her, but he changed his mind as Sam fired off a shot that shifted his attention to a more pressing problem.

"I'd say she doesn't have much of a desire to remain with you fellas. That right, ma'am?" Sam asked.

"Yes. That is so. These men are pigs that have killed my family and have made me to be a prisoner. I will come with you now, Señor."

"Sounds good to me. Let go of that bridle, Mex." Sam raised the pistol to eye level. Miguel Sancho's eye level.

Sancho was fuming, but he released his hold on the bridle. "It is not right for you to steal my woman," he said, scowling into the end of the barrel. "She is mine, and I will find you and kill you someday because of what you are doing."

"That may or may not be true," Kyle said. "But fer now, you fellas just pull them hoglegs and let 'em settle in the dust." Noting the hesitation on the part of the Mexicans, he thumbed back the hammer and added, "I'd be advisin' ya ta do it right quick. This here trigger finger a mine is startin' ta pull tight. I'm figgerin' that the longer ya take ta git shed a that hardware, the tighter it'll git. Next thing ya know...boom! And there goes some poor fool's head...if ya git my drift."

They grudgingly lifted the pistols from their holsters, but not without more than one thought of trying for the upper hand. But the thoughts were just that and nothing more. Each of them finally unloaded his hardware into the dirt and waited for the gringo's next move.

"Now, turn them sorry excuses fer horses ya got 'tween yer legs, and don't look back 'til ya figger the rest of us has been disappeared fer quite a spell."

The band of would-be robbers reined around and kicked their horses into a slow canter, glad to be away from those crazy gringos.

The foursome replaced their guns as they watched the Mexicans ride away. Kyle dismounted and collected the pistols. He slipped them into his saddlebag and buckled it shut.

241

Sam slid off the rump of Charlie's horse and looked up at the girl. "What's your name?" he asked.

"Constance Maria Consuelo Valdez," she replied as a huge smile spread across her grateful face. "But you can call me Lucky."

"Well then, Lucky, how about you and me sharing your horse and giving Charlie's here a rest?"

She slid back onto the brown mare's rump and said, "Come, señor. You can have this horse. I will ride behind you."

Sam mounted, swinging his leg forward over the horse's neck. Once he was firmly in place, she circled her arms around his waist and wrapped her fingers around her wrist.

Toward a New Beginning

"You have saved my life, señor," she said as they started forward. "I will always be grateful and will always be your friend."

A smile graced Sam's face as he kicked the mare forward and they resumed their attempt to cross the trail of the wagon train.

CHAPTER

Twenty-five

As Bear Cub approached, Birdsong looked up from her sitting position in front of Running Antelope's lodge. There was a sense of urgency in his voice as he said, "Come. Chief One Eye would speak with you."

She hastily set aside the mending of Running Antelope's deerskin trousers and rose. A feeling of eagerness accompanied her as she followed Bear Cub to One Eye's lodge. Once they arrived, she stood before the opening and sighed heavily.

Bear Cub leaned down toward the entranceway and announced, "She is here, my chief."

"You will come inside, Birdsong," One Eye said from within.

Bear Cub motioned her into the lodge with a sweeping motion of his hand.

"Good luck," he whispered as she passed by and disappeared through the entrance.

One Eye was seated cross-legged on the far side of the enclosure. His hair was untied and hung over his shoulders. A young maiden was sorting through the tangles and rat-tails with the help of a wide-toothed comb that had no doubt come from the white men.

Birdsong stood silently before him with bowed head and downcast eyes. She clasped her hands together in front of her and waited for him to speak.

"Leave us, Spotted Fawn," he said and waved the young maiden away.

She released the comb, leaving it imbedded in his

hair, and rose. With a smile to Birdsong she obediently ducked her way out through the opening.

One Eye indicated her spot with a gesture to his
left. "You will sit."

Birdsong remained apprehensive and did as she was
told. She crossed her ankles, lowered herself to the
ground and pulled them in toward her. "You have
thought of this thing?" she asked.

"Ummm...I have thought of this thing. I have
decided that if you are as knowledgeable of the healing
plants as my son seems to think you are, then it would
be a good trade."

Her heart jumped at this good news. A pleasant
smile appeared. "You say *if*. That means you are not
convinced. What must I do to convince the wise chief
of the Penateka?"

244

"You will talk with Buffalo Horn. He alone will
decide if you are to be the healing one. Do you agree
to this? If he says no, then the agreement is off and we
will speak of it no more."

"But if he says yes?" she reminded him.

"If he says yes, then the captives will be set free and
you will return them to the white-eye's wagons."

"Where will I find Buffalo Horn?" she asked, eager
to prove herself.

"His lodge is in the trees along the side of the camp
where the water runs. You can find it by...wait." He
leaned toward the opening. "Bear Cub, come inside."

The young buck appeared almost instantly. His
nervousness was evident as he swallowed with wide-
eyed apprehension. "Yes, my chief. What is it you
wish?"

"You will take this woman to see Buffalo Horn.

When she is finished, you will return her here to me."

"Yes, my chief."

"Now go, the both of you." He dismissed them with a wave.

꼬꼬꼬

Birdsong's meeting with the medicine man had gone well. The old man was indeed good at his trade. He knew of things that she had never heard of. Their time spent together was one of respect on her part and a pleased wonderment on his. He inquired as to how she had learned of the healing plants and was pleased when he was told of her mother's brother, Crooked Foot. Buffalo Horn had remembered Crooked Foot from the days long ago, before the tribe had split into the northern people and the southern Penateka. He asked after his health and was sorry to learn that he had passed to the spirit world many years ago.

245 ➡

The meeting lasted nearly two hours, but seemed a lot shorter. She enjoyed talking with this old man who seemed to know how to heal every ailment. She asked him if he would teach her more about the healing plants, and he agreed.

"Did your time with Buffalo Horn go well?" Bear Cub asked as the two walked amongst the trees toward One Eye's lodge.

"Yes. I think it was a good meeting." Stopping, she waited for Bear Cub to also stop and return to her.

"Why do you stop here?"

"Do you understand why I have been to see Buffalo Horn?"

"I sometimes can hear parts of what is being said and think you want to remain with our people and become the healing one."

"That is true. But more importantly, if I do become the healing one, Chief One Eye will release the captives and I will return them to the wagons."

"Ummm," he said with a thoughtful nod. "Why are you telling me these things?"

"Because I would ask that you accompany me on my journey to the wagons."

"I do not think—"

"Good. Then it's settled," she said and resumed her trek to the chief's lodge with a finality that left him standing open-mouthed and scratching his head.

※※※

246

Mary Jane and the children were barely able to contain themselves. But at Birdsong's insistence, they kept the questions bottled up until they were well out of the camp.

"Now will you tell us how we were set free?" Mary Jane asked as she pulled her pony up alongside of Birdsong's.

"It is a long story and you will hear it in time. But for now you will need to understand that there are dangers for us out here. I am sure the wagons have left the place where you were captured, and we will have a long ride to find them. It will take many days. We will be hot and thirsty, but with Bear Cub's help we will find them and your families. Now, you will ride in silence. Talking will only make you thirsty. Even though our water is now plentiful, it will not be so in a few days if we are unable to find more along the way."

They rode the rest of the day with little conversation. After making camp that evening the questions and answers flew until late into the night. Once everyone understood the circumstances surrounding their release, they were at ease and slept peacefully for the first time since their abduction.

باببابب

Two days passed with the dryness of the weather taking its toll on each of the groups wandering the plains. Water had indeed become a scarcity and was forced to the front of everyone's mind. Birdsong and the children were in the best shape because they had been on the trail for the shortest period of time.

However, the rescue party was not as fortunate. Stretch's wound was painful and required constant care and attention. They had taken the needed time to cauterize it with the powder from a couple of rifle shells, and that seemed to've helped, at least it didn't appear to be dangerously infected.

247

Even though he insisted it was all right, the immediate area around the wound was dried and cracked, and it needed to be kept moist. That of course used up a good portion of the water supply. No one complained. They would have expected the same if it had been one of them that had been wounded.

Lucky did her best to keep him comfortable, and it no doubt would have been tougher on him had she not been around. A woman's touch just naturally seemed to help minimize the hurt.

Miguel Sancho and his men hooked up with the other half of their band and intensified their search for the gringos who had stolen his woman and humiliated them. There was going to be hell to pay when he caught up with them.

Toward a New Beginning

The real problems were with the wagon train. The journey had gone well enough after leaving the spot of the attacks, but the "well enough" had lasted only for a day or so.

On the second day out, Harry took a turn for the worse and died from his head wound. A hole needed to be dug so he could be put to rest. The only one who seemed to complain about it, though, was Noah. Not at all willing to jeopardize his chances of getting to the Arkansas, he'd gone to voice his displeasure to Heck.

"Ain't there no way we can just leave him? It'll take up valuable time ta plant him in the ground, and that's time we ain't got."

"Noah, I can understand yer position in this mainly because of yer beliefs, or should I say non-beliefs, but there's no way a Christian man would leave another ta be eaten by the coyotes. If ya have a problem with that, well, I'm truly sorry, but you'll just hafta deal with it."

"I'll deal with it alright. I'm takin' me 'n mine and headin' out for the Arkansas," he said with a vengeance.

"I can't let cha do that, Noah. You hired me ta bring ya out here, and I'm responsible fer you and yer wagon. I can't let cha go out on yer own."

"Well then, I'd say that's easy enough taken care of. You're fired! Now, I'll be gettin' my boys together and pullin' out." He spun angrily and headed for his wagon. "Wayman! Rip!" he hollered as he stormed away.

It was just a matter of a few minutes before Noah had pulled his wagon out of line. As folks tried their best to dissuade him, he whipped up his team, and he and his sons rolled westward and outta sight.

The buryin' took the better part of three hours, and then another 10 minutes or so for Pastor Jenks to say a farewell to the dearly departed. Once the ceremony was completed, there was still another 15 minutes or so of comforting for Mrs. Carter. She'd lost her son to the heathen Comanches, and now her husband as well. Her faith had been badly shaken and she had no desire to go on.

Pastor Jenks did his best to comfort her and give her the strength she needed, but to no avail. Finally, Mrs. Jenks was able to get through to her by having a no-holds-barred one on one with her about how she was not the only one who had lost a child on this trip. Although losing both a husband and a child in just a matter of a few days was significant, it was not the end of the world. She was finally able to reach her by saying, "The Lord never gives a person more than she can handle. You just need to keep the faith in Him."

249 ➤

Agnes reluctantly accepted her plight, and the train got under way, some three and a half hours behind the Baxters.

They had gone less than a mile when, while making its way through a skinny passageway between two closely spaced boulders, the lead wagon dropped a wheel into a deep hole and broke a couple of spokes.

Spirits were at a low point because of all the delays that seemed to be plaguing the wagons, but their faith in the Lord won out, and the men went to work to repair the damaged wheel.

They worked diligently, but were hampered by the proximity of the boulders. Unable to pull the wagon from the hole because the twisted, broken wheel was lodged against the rock, they steadfastly jacked the corner of the wagon up with a tree limb and worked their way through the difficulties.

Eventually the wheel was repaired and the wagon was pushed and pulled out of the gaping hole. It was then filled with dirt and stones well enough to allow passage of the remaining wagons, and the train was finally able to resume its journey.

❧❧❧

Sancho smiled his pleasure at the sight of the riders as they rode past his position of hiding. He could not believe his good fortune. He sat silently and watched the insolent squaw, along with the pretty young señorita as they unknowingly rode toward the trap he and his men had arranged. Although they were accompanied by the other children and a Comanche buck, Sancho paid little attention to them and focused his attention on his prey.

250

As soon as the riders drew abreast of his men, they rode out from their hiding places. A minor confusion ensued as the Indian woman's pony reared, causing a diversion that allowed the young buck to slam his heels into the sides of his pony and quickly disappear into the surrounding bushes.

"Well, well," Sancho said as he approached from behind the captives. He was barely able to control his delight. "What is this? My beloved pretty señorita is come to find her Sancho." He rode to a position alongside Mary Jane's horse and showed his brown teeth as he gave her his best smile. "I am happy you miss me so much."

Mary Jane watched the filthy man as he leered at her. The tears ran down her cheeks.

"Aww, my little señorita cries tears of joy to see her Sancho once again." He reached a hand out to touch her.

Forgetting her fright, she brushed the hand aside and glared at him through the tears. "Don't touch me!" she ordered, hardly believing the firmness of her own voice.

"Oh, I will touch you alright," he said, the smile fading. "But only when the time she is right."

"You are but a filthy pig," Birdsong said. "Why do you feel the need to frighten this girl?"

Birdsong was within Sancho's reach, and he shot out a backhand that caught her on the side of the face, sending her pitching headlong from her pony. She landed hard and glared her defiance up at him. "You are still a filthy pig," she repeated through clenched teeth as she wiped the blood onto the back of her hand.

251

Looking toward one of his men, Sancho said, "Pablo...kill her."

Birdsong quickly gathered her thoughts and sprang to her feet. She glanced at Mary Jane, then bolted for the nearby bushes. She began looking around frantically for a hiding place. As soon as she reached the brush, she heard the filthy pig say, "Go after her!"

Almost immediately she found a dense scrub oak thicket and ducked into it. She was oblivious to the pain it caused as it scratched her arms and face. Once she was safely hidden, she crouched low to the ground.

She had chosen well. The bush was very close to the clearing where the ambush had taken place. The Mexicans would not think of looking for her this close. She was right. The one called Pablo passed by without so much as glancing her way. A smile came to her face as she remained perfectly still. She listened intently to the sounds around her. The searching one was making a thorough inspection of the surrounding area, but not the bush where she lay hidden. Suddenly, a muffled cry reached her ears from the direction Pablo had taken. It was followed by silence. A smile crossed her lips as she realized that Bear Cub had found the man.

"Pablo!" The call came from the filthy one. "Pablo!" he repeated, this time with more urgency in his voice. His apprehension was met by a Comanche war cry from the victorious Bear Cub.

Birdsong smiled her pleasure as she listened to the orders being given for the Mexicans to spread out and comb the bushes for the escaped Comanches. She reached to her side and drew her knife. She remained motionless as the first of the searchers passed by. The next one, however, did not assume the bush was empty, and stopping, stuck the barrel of his firestick into it and moved the branches around. His search turned out to be haphazard, and he continued on as she loosened her white-knuckled grip on the handle of the knife.

The search continued while the sounds grew fainter. Once she felt sure that it was safe to do so, she eased her way from the hiding place and glanced around. Not seeing or hearing anything that would indicate a nearness of the searchers, she made her way quietly toward the clearing.

When she reached it, she saw what she had hoped for...the lone filthy pig was keeping guard over Mary Jane and the children. She was to the left side and slightly behind him. She eased back into the bushes and circled around until she was safely to his back.

She inhaled deeply, gathered herself and sprang from her cover.

She charged at the horse and drew the blade of the knife along its back leg, cutting it deeply.

The animal screamed its fright at the suddenness of the attack and reared, throwing the unsuspecting Miguel Sancho to the ground.

She was on him like a cat and watched as his expression turned from first surprise, then to fear as he realized he was about to die.

Without a second thought, she thrust the knife into the front of his neck with the deftness of an irate Comanche. The blood spurted out and covered her hand. She withdrew the blade and listened as the life gurgled from the lips of the soon-to-be deadman.

She was drawn back to the problems at hand as the 253 sounds of an approaching rider demanded her attention. She looked at the frightened faces of the children.

"Ride quickly! I will find you! *Go!*" The urgency in her voice, along with her pointing finger, served to answer any questions that had sprang into the minds of the children. They reined around and disappeared from the clearing just before the approaching rider entered.

Seeing the Indian woman standing over his leader, the Mexican drew his *pistola* and pointed it at Birdsong. Just when she was sure he would kill her, an anguished, pleading cry came from the edge of the clearing behind the Mexican.

As he hipped around in his saddle and fired at Bear Cub, she leaped forward and drove the knife into the man's stomach. She pulled the blade sideways, and noticing the beginning appearance of the man's entrails, did not wait for him to die. She instead ran to her pony, and grabbing a handful of mane, swung herself up. She took one last look at the motionless body of her friend lying at the edge of the clearing. She was flooded with pangs of sorrow for the loss of this brave warrior. "You will always be in my heart, Angry Bear," she said lovingly, and kicked the pony toward an opening between two bushes.

She gripped the sides of the animal with her knees as she rode hard to escape the dangers behind her. Her heart pounded with the ferocity of remembered war drums from long ago. Holding tight to the pony's mane, she twisted around to look back. She was relieved to see that as yet she was not being chased.

She continued her escape with a sense of urgency that evolved into one of relief. *Their leader is dead. They will not come after me,* she realized, and allowed the beginnings of a smile to come to her lips. *They have no more reason to risk their lives.* The smile grew even wider as she spotted the cloud of dust a good ways ahead that she knew would turn out to be the fleeing children. Encouraged at finding them so soon, she leaned forward and rubbed the pony's neck, urging her even faster.

CHAPTER

Twenty-six

Heck shaded his eyes and squinted into the setting sun. Wisps of blue smoke curled lazily into the evening sky. He twisted around in the saddle. "Circle the wagons!" he ordered.

He waited patiently as the beleaguered drivers did their best to coax the exhausted, thirsty teams into a formation that only vaguely resembled a circle. He removed his hat and hooked it on the saddlehorn. His wounded arm remained in a makeshift sling and was still pretty much next to useless. With his good one, he wiped the sweat from his brow on his sleeve and glanced longingly at the clouds that floated lazily overhead. But they weren't anywhere near being of the rain-producing variety. He replaced the hat and watched as Jacob approached, keeping his sagging bay gelding at a slow walk.

"Seen the smoke," Greenberg said as he reined up. "What'dya figger it's from?"

"I'm thinkin' it's what's left of the Baxter wagon."

"Now, that'd be a cryin' shame. I didn't much care for Baxter's outlook on most things, but—"

"Me neither," Heck said. "How about you ridin' over there with me ta make sure it's them?"

"Ain't partial ta doin' it, but I reckon it's better'n not knowin'. C'mon, let's go get it over with."

"Just a minute," Heck said. If they found what he expected to find, it'd take the rest of the day and then some to bury the Baxters.

While Jacob waited, Heck gave instructions for the

train to make camp for the night and to post a guard.

They were in no hurry and rode slowly until they arrived at what was indeed the remains of the Baxter wagon.

Although all three men were lying dead with their scalps removed, there were signs that they hadn't gone easily. The bodies of the attackers had been removed, but the bloodstains that were left behind indicated at least six Indians had been taken down. The bodies of Noah and his sons were riddled with arrows. The wagon had been ransacked, its contents thrown around haphazardly and the whole thing then set on fire. The horses were gone.

"Ain't a pretty sight," Heck said as he bent down and retrieved an arrow. He turned it over in his hands as he examined it closely. "This here's Ute. See the markings...right here?" He held it out toward Greenberg while he pointed at the cresting on the upper portion of the shaft. "Them's also Ute designs in the feathers." He tossed the arrow away in disgust. "Ain't we got us enough troubles ta deal with, what with the children bein' stolen, the Comanches killin' our folks and the water bein' gone?" He drew in a deep breath and exhaled slowly. "Now we gotta put up with the Utes out roamin' the countryside and treatin' folks like this."

Jacob had seen enough. "C'mon Heck, let's get on back to the wagons and get some fellas together to do the grave diggin'."

The general feeling back at the wagons was one of hopelessness and anger.

Folks were worn and tired. They'd been keeping the faith as well as could be expected, but the discovery of the Baxters had removed just about any lingering hope.

The lone exception was Pastor Jenks. He refused to give in to the worldly happenings and prayed all the harder. Mrs. Jenks, however, was also having her faith tested and seemed to be losing the battle right along with the others. "We must keep the faith, Maggie," he said. "The Lord will not abandon His children. You see those clouds up there?" He pointed at the soft wisps of whiteness as they floated overhead. "The Bible says that that's the dust from God's feet. It's my contention that the Lord is here with us right now and will not let us give up."

"I truly do love you, Mr. Jenks," she said and rubbed a scant tear from where it had slid to on the lower portion of her cheek. "You are a wonderful man, and the Lord has blessed you in many ways." She went to him and draped her arms loosely around his neck, clasping her wrist with the fingers of the other hand. "And you know something else, Pa? I have a feeling that He's not done with you yet." She pulled him to her and kissed him gently on the lips.

257 ➡

"Maggie, stop that," he said good-naturedly. "What will folks think?"

"I would hope they'd think that I've got one heck of a good man here. Now shut up and kiss me back."

He did.

A fire was built for enough light to see by, allowing the men of the train to work well into the night digging the three graves. Although it was generally felt that Utes wouldn't attack after dark, there was no sense in taking any unnecessary chances. A guard was posted as a precaution.

Once the graves were dug, the bodies were laid out

alongside and the men returned to the wagons. It had been decided to have the burying and the accompanying service the following morning.

❧❧❧

Mary Jane and the children had ridden hard to escape the dreadful confrontation back at the stand of scrub oak. Her thoughts had never left Birdsong as they rode without looking back. After what seemed to her to be an eternity, she thought she heard a faint voice mixed in with the drumming hoofs of the running horses. She glanced behind her and saw Birdsong riding hard and gaining quickly.

Mary Jane hollered at the children to stop and pulled hard against her pony's mane. She was relieved when the animal finally began to slow. The children were having some difficulty, but they too eventually managed to get their horses under control, and one by one they brought them to a slower pace, then finally to complete stops.

"Look! It's Birdsong!" Mary Jane said excitedly as Josh and the others joined her.

"I can see that," Josh said. "I ain't entirely blind, ya know." Even though the words indicated a bit of sarcasm on his part, the grin on his face gave him away. "Sure is a sight fer sore eyes," he finally admitted, and changed the grin into an all-encompassing smile.

Birdsong reined up and slid from her pony. "Is everyone OK?" she asked.

"I think so," Mary Jane said, looking around at the nodding heads.

"Did you kill those men back there?" Charlette asked.

"Yes. I took the life of two, but they killed my friend Bear Cub."

"I-I'm sorry, Birdsong," Mary Jane said.

"It is alright. Even though he is gone to the spirit world, he has made the journey as a warrior. That is what matters most to a Comanche. He died an honorable death."

"So what now?" Josh asked. "We just gonna sit here, or are we gonna find them wagons?"

"I am thinking it would be a good idea to go and find them wagons," Birdsong said, mocking him.

"I sure will be glad when we finally do find 'em," Mary Jane said. "I miss my family...and Stretch," she added, wondering if he missed her, too.

⋙⋙⋙

Sam and the rest of the fellas, including Lucky, had been making good progress. Fact is, unbeknownst to them, they were within a mile and a half to two miles of the train when they made camp for the night. The rolling hills that made up the distance between, not only kept the two parties hidden from one another, but neither was able to catch a glimpse of the other's fire.

The water supply was borderin' on critical as Sam unscrewed the cap from the last of the canteens and handed it to Lucky. "How's it lookin'?' he asked, watching the pain in Stretch's eyes and feeling more than just a little sorry because of the discomfort the boy was going through.

"He is doing well. I think the wound she is very painful, but it will no make him to be sick." She took the canteen and held it to Stretch's lips, keeping a cupped hand under his chin to catch any that might spill.

He took a small sip and pulled his mouth away. In doing so, a small amount leaked into her hand. She brought it to her mouth and licked the wetness from her palm.

"You must drink some more," she urged, offering the canteen to him once again.

"Naw, I figger I've had about enough. I'm plumb full, clean up ta my eyebrows."

Sam decided to try his hand at getting him to see reason. "Stretch, it might not be such a bad idea if you were to take just a little more. I reckon all the blood you've lost hasn't done your body any good. I'm sure there's a need for keeping some moisture in you."

"Thanks, Sam. I figger what yer sayin' is probably true enough, but I won't be takin' away from the rest of ya just so's I'd stand a better chance a makin' it through this mess. I'm figgerin' that right now I'm in 'bout as good a shape as any of ya. That means we're all on equal footing 'til somethin' drastic happens that says different."

Sam nodded while reluctantly accepting what Stretch had to say. He admired the boy's spunk, but truly wished he would drink a little more than the rest of them. He rose and walked away, knowing there was no way he could change the boy's way of thinking.

Lucky bathed the wound sparingly, then carefully rewrapped it with some fresh pieces of cloth she had torn from the bottom edge of her dress. "You have a pretty señorita who waits for you, no?" she asked as she gathered up the old bandage for disposal in the fire.

"Yeah, but I ain't even sure if she's alive or dead or

somewheres in between," he said as despite his efforts, he lost control of his bottom lip and felt it quiver slightly.

She noticed his show of emotion and reached out and took his hand in hers. "Your sweetheart, she is safe." His gaze met hers and she saw a glimmer of hope in his eyes. In an effort to make him feel even better, she continued, "You will see her soon. Of this, you can be sure."

بمبمبم

The following morning was not much different from the one before. A few clouds greeted the early risers as the sun peeked its brow above the eastern horizon.

Sam sat on the edge of his blanket and pulled his boots to him. After turning each upside down to dump out any varmints that mighta decided to use them for a sleeping spot during the night, he pulled them on and stood. He then stomped his feet into a proper fit and gazed out across the prairie. A movement far off to the south caught his eye and he crouched instinctively. He said a silent prayer and continued to watch as the string of figures moved slowly along the distant horizon. He figured it'd be best to wake the others just in case a hurried exit was in order. He nudged the one nearest to him. "Charlie...wake up," he said in a hoarse whisper.

Spending the majority of his life in Indian country just kinda tended Charlie toward being a light sleeper and he was instantly wide-awake. He sat up. "Yeah, what is it?"

Sam pointed. "There's a line of riders over that-a-way."

Charlie nudged both Kyle and Stretch. "Get up,

261

fellas. Sam says we got company." He then reached over and jostled Lucky awake as well.

"What kinda company?" Stretch asked as he one-handedly rubbed the sleep from his eyes.

"Don't know fer sure," Charlie said.

In no time at all, everyone was up and watching the line of figures silhouetted along the distant horizon.

"What'dya make of it, Charlie?" Stretch asked.

"Kinda hard ta say from this distance, but I'm inclined toward it bein' Injuns." He continued to squint off in the direction of the movement. "Yep. I'm pretty sure from the way they're trailin' each other that it's Injuns alright. Might not be such a bad idea if we was ta get them horses saddled and be ready ta high-tail it if we get spotted."

"Sounds like a good idea to me," Sam said. "Stretch, you 'n Lucky keep an eye on them fellas. The rest of us'll saddle up and break camp."

Stretch nodded and winced as the slight movement caused a stab of pain to shoot through his arm.

"Are you OK?" Lucky asked as her concern for him furrowed her brow.

"Yeah. Just a mite tender in spots," he said and closed his eyes momentarily as another pain hit him.

She watched him closely and thought she noticed a lessening in his pained expression as he raised his forearm up to where it was angled across his chest.

"Does that make it hurt less?"

"Yeah, seems to."

She pulled the bottom of her dress up, exposing more leg than he had ever seen in all his entire life. A hot flush of red started from somewhere down under his collar and spread upward to his cheeks and beyond. He quickly averted his gaze as she began to tear strips from the dress. Once the tearing sounds quit, his embarrassment began to ease.

The smile across her face said that she had enjoyed his mild uneasiness. "You are bashful, no?"

"Ah...yeah. Ya might say so."

"You no worry. I will no bite you." She quickly went to work and used the strips of cloth to fashion a sling that passed under his wrist and knotted together behind his neck. Once it was securely in place, she looked into his eyes. "What do you think? Does it make your wound feel better now?"

He tested the sling by first pushing against it with the injured arm, then swinging it around in an arc away from his body. After not feeling any major discomfort to speak of, he replied, "Yep. Don't seem ta hurt none atall now."

263

"Maybe it was looking at my pretty legs that make it to no hurt no more."

The flush returned as he rose and headed for the horses. "Ain't you fellas finished with them horses yet?" he asked with the sound of her soft chuckle easily reaching his ears.

"Just right this instant as a matter a fact," Kyle answered. "Somethin' ailin' ya, boy?" he asked, seeing the flushed complexion on Stretch's face. "Yer lookin' a mite reddened."

"No I ain't ailin'! So whyn't you just go on and mind yer own business?"

Kyle lifted his hat and scratched his bald spot.

Sam had been looking off to the north. "Charlie, what'dya say we walk these horses a ways off that way?" He pointed. "The prairie slopes in that direction, and if we can get just a little ways down that hill, those Indians'll never see us."

"You might have somethin' there, Sam. I reckon it's worth a try."

Without another word they led the horses down the gently sloping terrain until they felt safe enough to mount. Once the decision was made to make a break for it, they urged the badly worn horses into motion and finally into a gentle lope.

After less than a half hour, they topped a gentle rise, hauled up alongside one another and sat speechless. There on the prairie below was the lopsided circle of wagons. Off to one side were the remains of a burned-out wagon. That was also where most, if not all, of the members of the train had congregated.

"Well, well. Would ya just look at that?" Charlie said and kicked his horse forward.

As they rode slowly down the hill, it became increasingly apparent that the gathering was for the placing of more than one body into the ground.

"Looks like they been havin' a few troubles of their own," Sam said.

CHAPTER

Twenty-seven

Sam and the others dismounted and approached the beleaguered group of travelers just as Pastor Jenks was finishing up. "And so, we offer the souls of these two young men into Your kingdom, Lord. Although Noah wasn't saved and will spend the rest of eternity burning in the rages of hell-fire and damnation, I thank You for sending Wayman and Rip to me to receive You into their hearts." He looked up to see the returning rescuers. Sam and Kyle were already hugging their wives, while the rest of them looked on from a short distance away. "Amen," he said hurriedly. "Well now, looks like you boys come back at just about the right time."

"Kinda depends on what yer line a thinkin' is," Heck said. "We got Injuns killing folks, the water's gone and spirits around here are just about at rock bottom. I can also see that the children didn't return with you. Kinda makes a fella wonder what else might go wrong."

"I don't think you really wanna know," Sam said as he bent down and hoisted Tom up. "But I'll tell you anyway. Not more than a half hour ago, we spotted a good-sized band of Indians headed this way. I 'spect they could be here most any time now."

That announcement brought gasps from the women, and more than one hand found an open mouth. The men were slightly more under control, but mumbled cussing could be heard coming from a few of them.

"All ya'll listen up," Heck said. "If it's the same Utes

what done this here killin' of the Baxters, then we got us a real problem headed our way and need ta get back ta the wagons and prepare fer a fight."

The graveside service was forgotten as the members of the train hurried toward the wagons while pushing and herding their children in front of them. More than one of the youngsters suffered a swat on their backside if they failed to keep a good distance in front of their parents. *SWAT!* The sound of a hand placed strategically on a youngster's backside could be heard above the low-toned conversations of the weary travelers. "I said..." Sam heard an excited mother say, "get yourself to them wagons or I'll just leave you ta them Injuns, and you can spend the rest of your days doin' for them heathens. And I mean right now, boy!" *SWAT!*

The second one did the job, and the boy skipped ahead with both hands rubbing his rump and tears streaming down his cheeks.

Sam carried Tom and took Jay by the hand as he led her over to where Stretch and Lucky stood. "Jay, this here's Lucky. I mean...ah—"

"Hello, Señora. I am Constance. I am very happy to see you."

"Hello, Constance. I'm Judith, but please call me Jay." She extended a hand and the young Mexican woman accepted it gladly.

"And who is this?" Lucky asked, looking at Tom.

"This here's my son, Tom," Sam said with more than just a little bit of pride showing through.

Jay noticed Stretch's sling. "Stretch, you're hurt." She quickly brushed past Sam and stopped in front of him. "Is it bad?"

"Naw," he replied, trying to appear tougher than he felt. "Just a little ol' arrow hole is all."

"Oh my goodness. Sam...what happened?" she asked looking from one to the other.

"It's a long story," Sam said. "I'll tell you later, but for now, how about we get on back to the wagons with the others?"

They hastily made their way to the wagons, and Jay tended to Stretch's wound while Constance broke the ice with young Tom. She liked children, and Tom seemed to take to her as well.

While she was occupying him by taking off some of her bracelets and letting him clank them together, Jacob approached and asked the obvious, "No luck with gettin' Mary Jane and the rest a them kids outta that Injun camp, huh?"

His sorrowful expression touched Sam's heart to the point of making him feel even more guilt about not having brought them back. "No, Jacob. I'm sorry ta say the whole rescue attempt was doomed right from the start. We couldn't even get it straight in our minds where they were being held, let alone make a decent attempt at gettin' 'em outta there. But you need to know that it wasn't anyone's fault. We were doing the best we could. Then when we got ambushed and Stretch took an arrow, we figured it'd be best to get him back to the wagons, then go back for another try."

"What?" Jay said as she hooked his arm and pulled him around to face her. "You aren't thinking of going back there, are you?"

"Jay, honey, those youngsters are still in the hands of those Comanches. I just don't know how I'd ever be able to live with myself knowing that I'd given up on the lives of those children." He placed a hand on each of her upper arms. "Please try to understand that my life would be worthless knowing I hadn't given this my all."

She fell against him and rested the side of her face on his chest while his arms encircled her. "I understand what you're saying, Sam, and know that I must let you go, but why you? I just wish this was all over and done with," she said resignedly.

"Thank you for understanding," he said and kissed her on the top of her head.

"When will you be leaving?" she asked after they'd parted.

"Just as soon as we can do what we can to help get this train the rest of the way to the Arkansas."

"Who's we?"

"Me 'n Charlie 'n Kyle have decided that the three of us can pull it off...with a whole lotta God's help, that is. But we'll deal with that later. In the meantime, tell me what's been going on around here. Kinda looks like the stock is just about done-in."

She waved her hand in an exasperated arc and said, "The water's all gone, the delays have been coming faster than can reasonably be thought possible, and now the Utes have attacked and killed the Baxters. Heck seems to think it'll take a miracle to get us outta this fix. He says we're still about a day and a half from the river and...and..." She wiped her brow with the sleeve of her dress and sighed heavily. "And he doesn't see any way the horses can make it. He says the best we could hope for is that these few clouds," she glanced skyward, "will amount to something and produce some rain before it's too late." The look in her eye suggested that it was getting close to that point already.

"The Lord won't let us down," he assured her. "He knows His children are down here and in need. He'll do what needs doin'."

At that point, their conversation was interrupted as Danny hollered, "Heck wants ever'one together at the center of the circle!"

"Looks like Heck might have a plan," Sam said. "C'mon."

Heck smiled and acknowledged Sam with a nod as they arrived. "As you already know, Sam here..." he indicated him with a tilt of his head, "and Kyle and Charlie all say there's a whole passel of Injuns just southeast a here. That's more'n likely gonna mean trouble. I know that you folks have come through a lot, but there's still more that needs tendin' to." He paused as the consenting nods and gentle mutterings died down. He then continued, "You all know that the water's gone and the animals ain't got a whole lot left in 'em, but what you may or may not know is that the Lord hasn't given up on us. We just gotta hang on 'til He decides our trial is over and it's time to bestow a blessing on each and every one of us." He looked from one face to another until his gaze came to rest on Pastor Jenks. "Maybe the pastor here could say it better'n me. Pastor, would you give it a try?"

Pastor Jenks smiled and stepped forward. He remained silent to those around him while he said a brief prayer to himself. Once the Lord had given him the words he needed, he looked at the faces around him. Some showed apprehension, while most were filled with fear. "You folks have a right to believe that

269 ➤

the Lord has abandoned you, but trust me when I tell you that that is not the case."

Sam knew the importance that hinged on the words the pastor would give to these harried people. He closed his eyes and spoke silently with the Lord. *Father, please give this man of God the power and liberty to say what needs saying in such a way that'll reach 'em, amen.*

Pastor Jenks began, "Now I know that there's been more than one occasion when I've been a mite windy with both my preaching and praying."

The mumbling and chuckles attested to that statement being a true fact.

"Well, this time I'll be short and to the point. I told my missus earlier this morning that in the Book of Nahum it says that those clouds up there," he pointed, "are the dust from God's feet. That means that He's here and He's watching over us. In the book of Deuteronomy, in chapter 31, it says; *Be strong and of a good courage, fear not, nor be afraid of them: for the Lord thy God, he it is that doth go with thee; he will not fail thee, nor forsake thee.*"

Sam smiled his approval. "Amen," he said softly, and again smiled as the pastor returned to his place among the others, accompanied by a chorus of hearty "Amens."

"Sounds like some words for a fella to take ta heart," Heck said as he once again took charge of the meeting. "With Him here and on our side, how can we even think of givin' up?"

The question didn't require an answer, and it was a good thing, because no sooner had he gotten the words out than Ethelda Mae Hendricks said excitedly, "Look...over that-a-way!" She pointed to the southeast.

They all turned toward the indicated direction.

Along the crest of the nearby hill sat a line of about 25 or 30 Indian braves astride their ponies. A controlled kind of pandemonium broke out as mothers scurried off to find their young'uns and fathers brought their rifles to a more handy position, that being right about chest level.

"Don't no one make any stupid moves," Heck warned. "Keep them guns handy, but don't shoot 'til I give the word." Looking around, he spied Cottonwood Charlie. "Charlie, come on over here."

Charlie quickly moved next to Heck and rested the butt of his rifle on the ground in front of him. He then placed a forearm on top of it with his gaze never leaving the band of Indians.

"What'dya make of it, Charlie?"

"I ain't real fer sure, but..." He picked up the rifle and cradled it in the crook of his elbow. "C'mon," he said and started forward.

As they walked toward the wagons that lay between them and the Indians, Charlie told Heck his suspicions, "I'm thinkin' these redskins ain't lookin' fer no fight. They seem ta be on the friendly side. Look real close, they ain't wearin' no paint, and neither are their ponies. That's makin' me figger they's just passin' through, and they fer sure ain't Ute neither."

"So, what now? We gonna go have a parlay with 'em?" Heck asked.

"That's exactly what we're gonna do."

They climbed over the barricade and continued toward the group of Indians. As they neared, Charlie was grateful to see one of their number slide off his pony and approach on foot. Seeing this, Charlie lowered his rifle to the grass and indicated for Heck to do the same.

They continued there approach until they stood face to face with the Arapahoe they had, what seemed so long ago, given food to.

Charlie and the Indian greeted one another, and he was surprised to see that the chief knew a whole lot more English than he'd let on before.

"I am happy to see the white-eyes who gave my people food," the chief said. "I see from the fire that you have trouble. You will tell me about this trouble." He crossed his arms and waited.

Charlie filled him in. "I too am happy to once again see the mighty chief of the Arapahoe Nation. We have no more water. The wagon that was burned left us yesterday and was attacked by the Utes."

"Ummm." The chief nodded his understanding.

"We wish only to be left alone and wait for the sky to open and drop some water on us. We do not want trouble with the Utes."

"Your trouble is easy to fix. There is water very near. We will take you. The Utes will not come back. We will go with you until you reach the big river. If they return, we will kill them."

Heck spread a wide grin and slapped Charlie on the back. "Well now, don't that just beat all?" he said, barely able to control his delight. "Ain't it amazin' what kinda rewards a fella can get just from partin' with a little grub ever' now 'n then? Why the next thing ya know, he'll be tellin' us—"

His thought was cut short as he noticed movement along the crest of the hill. Looking up, he finished the sentence, in a kind of absent-minded tone, not at all believing what he was seein'. "He'll be tellin' us that they've got the children with them."

Charlie looked up the slope. Sure enough there was Birdsong leading the four youngsters down the hill toward the three of them. He pulled his coonhide hat and rubbed his bald spot. "I'd say that preacher sure does know what he's talkin' about," he said and replaced the hat. "Yessir...right down to a tee, I'd say."

The reunion with the children got everyone to rejoicing. But the news of there being water nearby, plus the escort to the Arkansas and protection offered by the Arapahoe chief, got them all to giving thanks and praising the Lord.

Stretch and Mary Jane were unashamed as they fell into each other's arms. Jay smiled at the sight and nudged Sam with an elbow. "I'd say there's most likely gonna be a wedding before we even reach the river," she said and wiped a tear of thanksgiving. She couldn't remember ever having felt a more satisfying feeling in her entire life.

273 ➤

Sam patted the back of the man standing next to him and said, "Well, Jacob...you about ready to turn loose of her?"

Jacob took note of the happiness in his little girl's face as she clung to her beau. "I don't think I'll be havin' any say-so in it."

Sam grinned. "I'd say that's a true enough fact."

♄♄♄

Sam and Jay sat atop the seat as they waited their turn to move forward. Lucky and Tom were situated on the tailgate with their feet dangling over the edge. Sam looked back through the wagon and said, "You two all set back there?"

"Yes, señor. We are all set, thank you very much. We are ready to go find a place to live."

Then turning to Jay, he smiled and asked, "How about you?"

She smiled contentedly up at him, and he knew he'd done his job.

He pecked her on the cheek.

"See, told ya I'd take care a ya out here."

There was a smile on both their faces as he snapped the reins along the backs of the team.

"Hup! Hup! Get up there!" he said and whistled through his teeth.

The End

ARKANSAS VALLEY
SERIES: BOOK TWO

UNCERTAIN TIMES

by

r. William Rogers

Uncertain Times

Sam hauled back on the reins while kicking the brake handle forward. The prairie schooner creaked and rattled to a stop. He draped a half hitch of reins around the handle and slid his arm around his wife's shoulders.

They sat in silence, taking in the characteristics of the oblong stockade below them at the base of the hill. The most obvious of which were the round bastions that sat atop the southeast and northwest corners of the thickly-walled structure.

The walls themselves appeared about 15 feet or so in height, and were lined with ominous looking cactus plants along their entire length, no doubt to ward off intruders.

The biggest portion of the interior appeared to be a courtyard and corral area of sorts that was surrounded by what looked to be general storage facilities. About midway along the eastern wall was a gateway fitted with two plank doors that appeared to be heavily plated with sheet iron. This seemed to be the only way in or out, except for a small wooden door at the base of the bastion on the southeast corner.

While Sam took in the details of the compound, he couldn't help but feel a sense of adventure. *Well, Lord,* he thought, *now that You brought us here, don't quit on us now.*

This was where he and Jay were thinking about ending their journey that had begun nearly two months prior in Independence, Missouri. Any help they could get from the Lord was...well, without Him leading the way and making the decisions, Sam figured they would be hard-pressed to get a horse-ranching endeavor off to a successful start in any reasonable length of time.

"Well, what'dya think, Jay?" Sam asked as he eyed the outpost. "At least it's a measure of civilization," he added, not sure what her reaction would be, but willing to try to entice her into a favorable one.

Judith Bartlett was not exactly taken with the dismal, drab appearance of the trading post. Neither was she anywhere near becoming ecstatic over the scattering of cone-shaped teepees situated outside the north and east walls of the mostly adobe outpost. She sighed heavily.

"That's it? That's what we came through all that bad weather and high water for?" she said, fighting valiantly to hold back the tears.

277

"I'll admit the first impression ain't much, but—"

Sam's attempt to smooth things over was mercifully interrupted as he noticed the wagon master, Heck Yeah, riding toward them. The moniker was short for Hector Yallow, but he preferred being called Heck to most anything else.

He reined to a halt, tongued the chaw over to his other cheek and gestured down the slope before saying what Jay already knew, "Ain't much, but that's it...what they is of it, anyways. We'll be makin' a circle and stayin' a spell. If you folks are of a mind, you might wanna go on down an have a parlay ta see if this is fer sure where yer gonna call it quits."

Sam pulled his arm from around Jay's shoulders. "Thanks, Heck. We'll do just that."

Uncertain Times

Heck touched a finger to the pushed-up front of his hat and nodded once. He reined around, nudging the mare's sides with the heels of his boots.

Sam began to climb down. "I'll just take a minute to let Stretch know what's going on," he said as he stepped off the hub. He headed toward the Conestoga, which was immediately behind the schooner. As Sam drew near, he cleared his throat to warn the newlyweds of his approach.

Stretch Henderson—his given name was Darrell—and Mary Jane Greenberg had been married the week before. Even though they'd been a pair of extremely bashful 17-year-olds, they'd somehow managed to put that aside and fall in love during the trip. It could've happened about the time Stretch had saved her life when her pa's wagon had been washed away during the fording of a particularly ornery river. Or it could've been shortly after he'd taken an arrow while trying to save her and those three other youngsters after the Comanches had captured them.

In any case, as nature has a way of working them things out, they'd managed to get married on a Sunday morning by Pastor Jenks, along the banks of the Arkansas.

"Howdy, Stretch...Mary Jane," Sam said and nodded his greeting. I'll be driving on down to the fort there." He waved in the general direction of the trading post, "Me 'n Jay are gonna check into the prospects offered about setting up housekeeping around this part of the country. You two go on and include the Conestoga in the circle for the night and we'll talk after we return. Save us a spot for the schooner while you're at it."

"OK, sounds good ta me," Stretch said. "You

wanna leave Lucky here with us while you're gone?"

"Yeah, believe I will...no...on the other hand I believe she might have a stake in this, too. We'll take her along with us."

"Alright then. See ya when ya git back."

Sam returned to his wagon and climbed aboard. Unwrapping the bundle of reins, he sighed noisily and said, "Well, let's go see what the Lord called us out here for." As he released the brake and pulled hard on the reins to start the lead pair in the right direction, he could've sworn he heard Jay whisper, "What'dya mean, *us?*"

Ignoring the whispered comment, he snapped the reins along the trailing pair of rumps and whistled. "Get up there!" he coaxed, and stole a sideways glance at this woman who'd been following him ever since day one. Thankfully, she was turned away from him, tending to something in the bed of the wagon. Feeling some better, he snapped the reins again.

The schooner rattled its way down the slight decline and was soon nearing the open gate of the Bent's Fort Trading Post.

The opening was generous enough, but with the hustle and bustle of all the foot-traffic heading in and out, Sam took care to keep the wagon centered. As soon as they were safely through and into the confines of the stockade, he quickly spotted a likely looking spot and pulled the team around toward it. Once there, he hauled back on the reins, while at the same time jamming a booted foot against the brake handle. The effort locked the rear wheel, causing the wagon to slide slightly. When it had safely come to a halt, he wrapped the reins in their customary place and climbed down. He looked up at Jay and was relieved to see a gentle smile on her face. Hoping against hope, he asked, "What's the grin about?"

"Let's just say that you haven't led me astray so far, and I've decided to reserve judgment on this latest whim of yours. At least until I see something that causes me significant enough concern to think differently about it."

Sam knew she was referring to their whirlwind marriage and how, barely a year later, he had managed to convince her to leave her high-society life in upstate New York to support him in his horse supply business in Independence. The hardest part for her was making the trip while pregnant with their son, Tom. Then, to top it all off, she'd later agreed to pull up stakes from Independence, and make the current journey all the way out here to the heathen-infested grasslands on the western edge of the Great Basin that folks were calling the Arkansas Valley, but because of its lack of hills or mountains, didn't resemble any kind of valley Sam had ever seen before.

He returned the smile. "I sure do love you, Mrs. Bartlett," he said and reached for her hand to help her down.

"I think that is enough of that kind of talk." The heavily-accented words had come from the interior of the wagon, just behind Jay. "If you are so much in love, then maybe you want to be alone, no?"

"Why don't you just go on and mind your own business, Lucky?" Sam said, feigning a scornful expression.

The face of the Mexican woman that had appeared from the wagon's interior was that of Constance Valdez. Sam had only recently rescued her from a band of marauding banditos led by a ruthless man, Miguel Sancho. Although her full name was Constance Maria Consuelo Valdez, she was so grateful to Sam for having rescued her that she'd informed him that he could call her Lucky. And so, the nickname had been created and was beginning to stick.

"You *are* now my business, señor," she said, with the beginnings of a mischievous smile spreading across her face. "When you save my life, you make me very happy, and so now you are my business."

Sam knew he couldn't argue with the reasoning she was dishing out to him.

The truth be known, he didn't want to neither. She seemed to be a Godsend when it came to helping out with tending to young Tom. Plus the fact, that whenever Jay would let her get close to the cooking pans, she seemed to be a right tolerable cook as well.

281

"I guess what you're saying is true enough, but that doesn't give you the right to interfere when me 'n my missus are being lovey-dovey, now does it?"

"I would think that our romantic relationship is better kept private," Jay said, with what appeared to him to be more than just a little consternation. Of course, he had no way of seeing the wink she gave Lucky as she reached for the helping hand he had offered.

Feeling chastised, he said no more as he handed her down from the wagon. Looking up at Lucky, he said, "Well, you wanna come too, or are you satisfied to stay here and mind your own business?"

"I will come with you. That way you will not have to worry how to find me when you need my help."

"Fat chance of that ever happening," he said, grabbing his son as she suspended him over the side of the wagon. He placed the boy on the ground, then helped her down, all the while secretly feeling a sense of gladness that she wanted to be a part of what was going on.

Once everyone was safely on the ground, they stood taking in the activities around them. There seemed to be busy people everywhere.

Situated around the central court were rows of low, open-fronted rooms with dirt floors. The roofs were barely 6-foot tall, made of both clay as well as gravel, and supported by pole beams about every eight feet or so. They made up what appeared to be a warehouse, a cooking area and some general living quarters. There were also some sheds that provided storage for ox yokes, harnesses and other caravan equipment. The entire setup was one of a-place-for-everything and everything-in-its-place.

Sam pulled his attention away from his assessment of the layout as he noticed a weather-beaten fella, dressed entirely in buckskins, coming their way. When the man was within arm's reach, Sam reached out and placed a hand on his arm. "Excuse me," Sam said, cordially.

"Fer what?" the man replied. He spit and a stream of brown juice splashed against the toe of Sam's left boot.

Sam was temporarily taken by surprise by the fella's unexpected response and absent-mindedly raised the boot up behind his right leg, where he slowly rubbed it against the back of the pant leg. "Well, for—"

Lucky came to his rescue. Well, kind of anyway. "For thinking you have the brains enough to answer some question…that is for what."

Sam rolled his eyes, then closed them momentarily. He was expecting Lucky's remark to start trouble and was getting prepared for it. He ventured a peek and was pleasantly surprised to see the grizzled old-timer showing the beginnings of a grin.

"Like me a señorita what's got 'er some spunk. You wanna sell 'er?" he asked, turning his full attention on Sam.

"How much you got?"

"Not much more'n a dollar 'n a half, but I got me a—"

"You will not sell me!" Lucky said, with a fire in her narrowed eyes.

Maybe it was the clenched fists perched steadfastly atop her hips that got Sam's attention, or maybe it was the fervor in her words, but in either case, he got the message and figured the fun was over even before it got started real good. He poked a fingertip into his ear and wiggled it at an imaginary itch as he pondered the situation. "Yeah, maybe you're right," he said, while looking at her. Turning to face the fella, he said, "Thanks just the same, but I think I'll keep her for awhile. I need her around so she can mind my business for me. What I do need from you, though, is some information."

As the trapper spoke, his disappointment was evident. "'Bout what?"

"About where I go to talk to whoever's in charge around here."

"Well now…" The fella interrupted his response by turning to the side and spitting again. This time it landed a safe distance away from Sam's feet—probably figuring this gent was a mite particular about the appearance of his boots. "That'd be Bent hisself," he finally said, after swapping the chaw over to his other cheek. "He's most likely over to the general store." As

283 ➤

the old-timer spoke, he also pointed a stubby, work-worn finger across the compound.

Sam's gaze found what was more than likely the intended target, as it came to rest on a slightly bigger shed that was separate from the rest. The dead-giveaway was the boldly lettered sign above the door, that read: "General Merchandise." There was also some smaller lettering along the bottom edge that Sam couldn't make out from this distance. "Much obliged," he said and touched an index finger to the brim of his hat.

The trapper gestured toward Lucky. "You sure 'bout not sellin' that Mexican? I could maybe trade my—"

"He is sure!" Lucky said and fired a squint at Sam that caused him to break out in a wide grin.

"OK, but if'n ya was ta change yer mind, anyone kin tell ya where ta find Beaver Tail Jack."

"I'll keep that in mind," Sam said, managing to keep his grin somewhat under control.

Beaver Tail Jack went on his way while Sam slipped an arm around Jay's waist and started to direct her toward the general store.

"You will wait just one minute, señor!" Lucky said angrily, the fists once again perched atop her hips.

Sam stopped, and he and Jay faced the defiance glaring at them.

"You will tell me right now that you will never sell me to these people. You will tell me right now that you will... ."

A tear had appeared. She wiped it away.

"Lucky, I have no intentions of ever selling you," Sam said. "Why, I don't think I could get more'n Beaver Tail Jack's offered dollar an a half, or maybe a couple a dead skunks for you, anyways."

The stern look slowly transformed from at first an expression of uncertainty to one of relief. "I think..." she rubbed a flat hand along the side of her face, "I think maybe you are someone that will need me to stay very close to him. I think you are someone that is no have very good stable thinking."

"What'dya mean, not very good stable thinking? Why, I'll have you know that I'm of sound mind and body."

"That's not what I say. I say you no have, how you say, good horse sense. You know...stable thinking." This time it was her turn to break into a smile. "Come. Now is time we go to the store."